Pinchgut

Phillip Strang

BOOKS BY PHILLIP STRANG

DCI Isaac Cook Series

MURDER IS A TRICKY BUSINESS
MURDER HOUSE
MURDER IS ONLY A NUMBER
MURDER IN LITTLE VENICE
MURDER IS THE ONLY OPTION
MURDER IN NOTTING HILL
MURDER IN ROOM 346
MURDER OF A SILENT MAN
MURDER HAS NO GUILT
MURDER IN HYDE PARK
SIX YEARS TOO LATE
GRAVE PASSION
THE SLAYING OF JOE FOSTER
THE HERO'S FALL
THE VICAR'S CONFESSION
GUILTY UNTIL PROVEN INNOCENT
MURDER WITHOUT REASON

DI Keith Tremayne Series

DEATH UNHOLY
DEATH AND THE ASSASSIN'S BLADE
DEATH AND THE LUCKY MAN
DEATH AT COOMBE FARM
DEATH BY A DEAD MAN'S HAND
DEATH IN THE VILLAGE
BURIAL MOUND
THE BODY IN THE DITCH
THE HORSE'S MOUTH
MONTFIELD'S MADNESS

Sergeant Natalie Campbell Series

DARK STREETS
PINCHGUT

Steve Case Series

HOSTAGE OF ISLAM
THE HABERMAN VIRUS
PRELUDE TO WAR

Standalone Books

MALIKA'S REVENGE
VERRALL'S NIGHTMARE

Dedication

For Elli and Tais, who both had the perseverance to make me sit down and write

Chapter 1

The disappearance in 2005 of Sasha Cornell, the daughter of one of Australia's richest men, was modern-day folklore in Sydney. Her father had offered a million dollars to anyone with information, and even though many had phoned the police, none would claim the money: fraudulent in most cases, idiotic in others.

Sasha's father, a rambunctious, argumentative bully, was a man who used his commanding voice to full effect, belittling those who stood up to him and bankrupting those who would not desist.

Sasha, who enjoyed the fruits of her father's wealth, was not lazy or unambitious but determined to make her mark regardless of who her father was, and ran a successful public relations company. Popular with those who knew her; to those who did not, she was the spoilt brat of a disliked man.

Josh Costello, the third generation of Italian immigrants, knew her better than most, and they shared an apartment in the Horizon building in Darlinghurst.

On a Thursday, Sasha had been at a party in The Rocks, the original settlement of the fledging colony in the eighteenth century, leaving at one in the morning. A limousine was outside to bring her home. On Friday, a book launch, a former prime minister's version of what he had achieved and what he thought of those who had dumped him. It had been a roaring success, with plenty of money for Sasha's company, a lecture tour for the former prime minister, and a hitherto unknown mistress contacting Sasha to reveal specific facts about the man who saw himself as saintly but others did not. A meeting on the following Monday to discuss what the woman intended to reveal.

It was on the Saturday, the 16th of July, 2005, that the situation changed: Sasha was missing. She had left the Horizon building at six in the morning, a jog over to Elizabeth Bay on the harbour foreshore, and a coffee and croissant in Kings Cross on the way back. She jogged daily, but this day was different. There was CCTV footage of her leaving the building where she lived, but after that, nothing.

Josh Costello had raised the alarm. Eight thirty in the morning, he phoned her father, who called the police. Their response was immediate, and the full complement of the Kings Cross Police Station was mobilised. No one, not even the police commissioner or the premier of New South Wales, failed to jump when Bernie Cornell demanded action.

The missing woman was front page news for a week, with constant speculation on the television channels. The water police had been out on the harbour, looking for a body. Divers had searched at Elizabeth Bay, near the marina. The stairwells had been checked where she lived, and the CCTV cameras double-checked. Nothing other than proof that the woman had left the building.

Josh Costello had been grilled, admitting that the relationship was rocky, and they had argued that morning.

Bernie Cornell would not accept defeat, and he was on the phone constantly, ear-bashing politicians and police alike, no inch given.

The route Sasha jogged rarely varied: up Forbes Street to the roundabout on Liverpool Street, jog up to Darlinghurst Road and then left, over William Street, through Kings Cross, cut through Fitzroy Gardens, the police station on her right, down

Elizabeth Bay Road, through the roundabout of Greenknowe Avenue, continuing down Onslow Avenue, Elizabeth Bay House on her left, colonial, restored and open to visitors. Turn right on Billyard Avenue, and at the end, turn left and down to Elizabeth Bay. A few minutes to catch her breath, and then return by the same route. She was a familiar figure in the area, acknowledging those she passed with a brief wave of the hand and a smile.

But that day, no one remembered seeing her, not even the café in Darlinghurst where she would drink a latte and eat a croissant.

Six months later, with no information about what had happened to her and no one coming forward to say they had seen her, there was a memorial service for her at St Mary's Cathedral. Sasha's father and her boyfriend were in attendance, although he had moved on and had another woman. Also present were the former prime minister, his wife, and the social set Sasha had moved in.

She would not be forgotten by Bernie Cornell, but to the others, one year, and she was barely mentioned. She had been legally declared dead seven years later, not for any other reason than that as the daughter of one of Australia's richest men, loose ends could not be left open, and there were her assets, shares in the companies her father owned. The newspapers, aware of the development, barely mentioned it. It was as if the woman had not existed.

***

The original inhabitants called it Mattewei. To Captain Phillips, who had commanded the first fleet into Sydney Harbour in 1788, with one thousand four hundred persons on board – seven hundred of them convicts, the remainder military and government officials, their wives, and children, as well as sailors, cooks, masons, and others who hoped to establish new lives in the colony – it was known as Rock Island, although it would become known as Pinchgut.

On the 11th of February 1788, three prisoners were tried in the fledging colony of New South Wales in what was then known as Sydney Cove and sentenced to a week's confinement on bread and water on that small rocky island near the entrance to the cove. It was the lack of rations and gaunt appearance on their return that led to the expressive name of Pinchgut.

In 1796, Frank Morgan was executed on a gibbet erected on the highest point of the rocky island. According to legend, his last words were to tell the hangman about the picturesque water views from where he was to die. He had time to enjoy them, as his skeleton hung in chains for four years as a deterrent.

In 1857, the construction of a fort was completed as protection from foreign powers eager to gain a foothold in Australia. And then, on the 3rd of March 2022, the remains of a woman were found in a room below the Martello Tower.

That day, there was an answer to what had happened to Sasha Cornell.

Sergeant Natalie Campbell was the first on the scene. Stationed at State Crime Command in Parramatta, west of Sydney, it had been her first day off for several weeks, the chance to be on the harbour in a sailing boat with friends.

She was dressed for sailing, not for taking the lead role in a murder investigation. She disembarked at the fort, a construction worker helping her ashore.

'Good job you're here. Gave me the creeps when I found it.'

'Sergeant Natalie Campbell. I didn't expect to be working today.'

'Unusual clothes for a police officer, I'll grant you. There's a spare set of overalls I can lend you. Not ideal, but it's dirty where the body is. Leo Hannan's the name.'

'Irish?'

'Born in Sydney, but the name's a giveaway. One of my ancestors came over in 1793, sheep rustling.'

'He might have spent time on Pinchgut.'

'He might.'

'Your reason for being here?'

'There is a team of us renovating the place, plans for a restaurant and a bar for those that can afford it. Not sure if I'm keen, prefer to be on dry land.'

'It's dry here.'

'Joking, that's all. Although when you see her, you'll not appreciate the humour.'

'You've identified her?'

'Hard not to. How she ended up there, no idea. Not much to see, but there was a handbag. It might be evidence.'

Inspector Haddock was on the way, another thirty minutes, enough time to swing by Natalie's place and pick up some clothes, a friend of hers giving him a bag to take to the fort.

Careful not to disturb the murder scene, Natalie looked through the door and saw what remained. Once, she would have been upset, but now she felt a nothingness, inured to death.

Close to the body, the muddied footprints of Leo Hannan. The crime scene investigators wouldn't be pleased with him, but Natalie understood. Underpinning had made the room safe; the plan was to convert it into a wine cellar for the restaurant and bar. Hannan had not expected a wall to collapse, revealing a body behind.

Haddock phoned. 'Ten minutes,' he said. 'Next of kin?'

'If he's still alive,' Natalie replied.

'In his eighties, in poor health, a place in Katoomba. Either we get the locals to deal with it, or you and I go up there later today.'

'Get the locals to inform the man that, subject to confirmation, it's his daughter, Sasha Cornell.'

Chapter 2

The crime scene investigators arrived fifteen minutes after Haddock. By then, Natalie had changed into more appropriate attire.

It had been many years since the magazine room had stored weapons, and the air hung heavy in a room sealed by an iron door that had been locked, bolted, and bricked over until Hannan had knocked down the bricks that barred the entrance.

Leo Hannan was only one of a team of construction workers modernising the facilities for commercial use. There was a restaurant from 2006 to 2017, but closed since then. On the water, a barge, reels of cable and piping on the deck, upgrading the electrical cables and water pipes that supplied the fort.

'It will need Forensics to prove it's Sasha Cornell,' the lead CSI said. He was a squat man, well experienced and used to the sight of death, although unprepared for a decomposed body hidden in a room for seventeen years.

'Takes your breath away,' he said. 'Not much to show, tattered clothing, mostly skeleton, a ring on one finger hanging loose, and a handbag your man picked up.'

'He's admitted to his error. Identification is not difficult, even without the DNA,' Natalie said.

'I remember when she disappeared. One moment there; the next, gone. Does her father know?'

'He's been informed of the possibility.'

'And?'

'Priority. Pathology will work overnight due to her father's importance. Forensics will confirm it's her, and you and your team are out here for the duration, no time off.'

'It could take a couple of days after being walled up here. How was it done? From what I can see, a day to seal her in, another week to ensure the artificial wall blended in.'

'Why she was killed makes no sense. There had been no ransom, and her father had offered a million dollars for information.'

After forty minutes at the fort, Inspector Haddock and Sergeant Natalie Campbell were on a boat heading over to Garden Island, the naval base in Sydney Harbour. Superintendent Payne had been on the phone. 'You're meeting with the woman's father. It's all been arranged.'

At the naval base, a helicopter waited on the pad. It was Natalie's first time in a helicopter, Haddock's second, a family treat on the Gold Coast in Queensland, fifteen minutes along the coast. He hadn't liked the first, the second, even less. To him, they were noisy and unsafe, no more right to fly than a bumblebee.

At Katoomba, forty-one minutes from lift-off to touchdown, the two officers left the helicopter, heads down low as the blades above were still rotating. A vehicle waited for them; a man dressed in a dark suit. 'Mr Cornell is waiting for you,' he said.

Overlooking the escarpment, a view to the valley below, Cornell's mansion was impressive. Inside the building, a marble floor, oil paintings on the walls, and a couple of diminutive dogs at their ankles.

'They'll not bite,' a voice hollered. 'Found my daughter, about time,' it said.

Natalie turned around to see an old man in a wheelchair. She extended her hand and felt a firm handshake.

'You're Sergeant Campbell, and you're Haddock,' Bernie Cornell said, looking over at Haddock, shaking his hand with the same strength as he had Natalie's.

'Yes, sir,' Natalie said, 'subject to DNA.'

'It's her, don't need experts, had plenty of those in my time advising me, not one of them made any sense. Tell me straight, no sugarcoating. Sergeant, you saw the body first.'

'I was on the harbour, not far to go.'

'Find out who did this, I'll give you a boat, no need to worry about cadging a ride on your friend's. Kyle Harvey, that's his name?'

'You're remarkably well-informed.'

'I make sure that I am, and it's my daughter. Josh Costello, her boyfriend at the time, is flying in from New York and will be here tomorrow. No expense spared. I don't want to hear about budget or lack of personnel, not with Sasha, the only person I cared for. Mind you, she was independent, would not use security, and jogging around where she lived was stupid. I told her enough times, but she wouldn't listen. Are you the same, Sergeant?'

'I'm answerable to Inspector Haddock and Superintendent Payne.'

'Payne's answerable to me, and so is the police commissioner. I want prompt action, no stone unturned, and no dithering. Do I make myself clear?'

'Yes, sir,' Natalie said, echoed by Haddock.

'Aren't you being presumptuous?' Haddock said.

'In what way, Inspector?'

'You've assumed that Costello concerns us. Until we have a report from the pathologist, we don't know if your daughter died in Darlinghurst.'

'Inspector, you're right, presumptuous. It's my daughter and my money. Costello is probably not involved, not that I totally approved of him at the time, not sure I do now, but he works for me.'

'We need a free hand,' Natalie said. 'If you're pulling the strings, it might complicate.'

'How? Speak up, both of you. No time for talking around it. You both know me by reputation; most see me as an ogre.'

'I've heard it mentioned.'

'I'm not an ogre or an unreasonable man. I'm driven by results, not excuses, and there are none that I will countenance. How soon before you can move forward?'

'We've just started with the investigation. Sergeant Campbell would have only been a child when your daughter disappeared,' Haddock said.

'Thirty-six hours, read all the transcripts, witness interviews, and prosecution reports, and make sure that Forensics and Pathology have completed their work.'

'And then?' Natalie asked.

'I'll have Superintendent Payne keel-hauled if the investigation is not up to speed. Any questions?'

'Just one,' Natalie said. 'You have a fearsome reputation for those who fail to maintain your standards. Are you sure we're the best people for the job?'

'I've had Haddock checked out. He's a good officer. And you, Sergeant Campbell, are still making your mark. You will not disappoint me, but I know how the police work, too much bureaucracy and politics. I'm removing any hindrance. Don't worry, I'll know what you're doing. And my daughter's death, why? Were they after me, but nothing happened, not until today? The man who found her, not involved?'

'A child when your daughter died. Do you have any suspicions?'

'None, and I should. I expect the two of you to solve this case, and if I want you here, come. Don't worry about Payne or anyone else.'

Neither was pleased with the situation that one person, due to his wealth and strength of character, intended to ride roughshod over the police. They weren't sure how it would pan out; curious on the one hand, concerned on the other.

***

Superintendent Payne was optimistic, Natalie wasn't, and meeting with Sasha Cornell's father had left her unnerved. He was a powerful man with powerful enemies. And with the discovery of his daughter's body, hitherto unknown and secret facts would be revealed.

Bernie Cornell had been the most influential and one of the wealthiest men in Australia for a long time. The daughter's best security was her father's retribution if anyone got too near. Sasha had known that, but she had died. If the father was determined, at what cost? Would he act outside the law, immune to prosecution, police and politicians in his back pocket? Policing was becoming complicated, and she didn't like it.

Haddock was blasé, having encountered the good and the bad of society for longer than her, and he regarded Cornell as an old man with a bark worse than his bite. 'He's old, decrepit, not much venom left in him,' he said on the flight back to Sydney.

The body was with Pathology, and the pathologist had been instructed to give priority. He was a man who could be difficult, not used to being pressured, but even he was subdued when the two officers arrived at his place of work.

'Not much to see,' he said. He was a man of few words, studious, exuding an odour of formaldehyde. Natalie did not like autopsies, only observing on one occasion, but the body of a dead woman, sealed in at Pinchgut for over fifteen years, didn't concern her. It looked like a desiccated prune, and even though the island fort was situated at sea level, no seepage had reached where she was found.

'Your observations?' Haddock asked. Payne was available 24/7, the conduit to the old man in Katoomba. He wanted to be updated with the slightest, most insignificant news.

'Not yet. Not much to work with. Toxicology tests might show drugs, but they can take weeks before we get the results. I should be able to tell if the death was violent or she was alive when interred.'

Natalie imagined a horror movie, The Pit and the Pendulum. She had watched it on Netflix, a sixties movie, Vincent Price, the sister locked in an iron maiden.

Had Sasha Cornell been alive at Pinchgut? Had she suffered horribly? And if she had, had others too, not as well-known as her, not with a powerful father?

They both watched as the pathologist removed the remains of the woman's clothing, speaking into a microphone attached to his lapel.

'No sign of trauma, no visible sign of either bullet wounds or a sharp blade,' the man said as he moved around what remained of a once attractive slim woman. Forensics had confirmed that it was the body of Sasha Cornell.

'Judging by the body's position at the crime scene, I believe she was dead before she was interred. With no more clues and considering the body's condition, I would say she was suffocated by a cushion over her face or a plastic bag over her head.'

'Is that it?' Haddock asked.

'I can't give you more,' the pathologist said. 'You've seen the body; what do you reckon?'

Chapter 3

Bernie Cornell had been advised against it by Superintendent Payne and the New South Wales police commissioner, but the man had made his fortune by not listening to others. A five-million-dollar reward for information leading to the arrest and conviction of his daughter's murderer.

Haddock knew those who professed to know something would be crawling out of every nook and cranny in the city. A hotline was established, and thirty people operated phones and checked emails and social media.

'Any luck with missing persons or unsolved murders?' Haddock asked his sergeant.

The two preferred to keep away from State Crime Command as much as possible, aware they would be pestered for updates every five minutes. Meanwhile, Superintendent Payne had to balance policing with public relations, a voracious media hanging on his every word and ready to criticise. Sasha Cornell was big news, and finding her body at Pinchgut brought back recollections of its turbulent history, those who had been left on the island in irons, bread and water, a starvation diet for sustenance. More than one had died on the island, yet as a fort, its cannons had never been used.

In the year Sasha Cornell disappeared, there was an ongoing debate about the future of Pinchgut and its viability as a restaurant. It needed repair, over a million dollars to replace weathered sandstone blocks and research treatments that would protect the stonework. Sea levels on the site had risen by ten centimetres in the past one hundred years, exposing more of the fort's porous sandstone to the element. It had been projected that the sea level might rise another one hundred centimetres in the next one hundred years, and large-scale work was needed.

How a body could have been hidden there, undisturbed during extensive work, baffled Haddock and Natalie.

From a Fort Denison Conservation Management Plan prepared in 2019, Natalie found out that the projected work planned in 2007 did not commence until the following year. However, a further complication in concealing the body was that a restaurant had operated on the island since 2006. With no information or evidence to the contrary, it was apparent that someone working on the island at the time, whether with the restaurant or maintenance of the fort, had to know something. Seventeen years had passed since the woman's disappearance, and the date she had been interred on the island was taken from that time. Although that could not be confirmed to the accuracy that Haddock and Natalie would have preferred. Analysis of the hastily-constructed tomb was not precise. The false wall had been completed hurriedly, rendered with cement and painted. Dating could only be accurate within five years.

The lighthouse beacon was restored in 2004, the restaurant opened in 2006, and the renovations commenced in 2008. Even without a precise date of when the body had been placed on the island, Haddock was sure the period of least activity was the most probable, and Natalie knew that Haddock's instincts invariably proved to be correct.

The reason why the woman was there, and not weighted down and in the harbour, seemed irrational. To not make a statement, to not respond to the father's offer, indicated a motive that was not based on money or love or sex or violence but something more sinister.

Haddock and Natalie had the father's confidence for now, but it was ill-founded. They were unsure how to proceed – other than to find out who had visited the island in 2005. Space was at a premium at the fort, no larger than a small football field. Why hadn't a hidden room been discovered before?

***

A team of internet-savvy personnel was established at State Crime Command in Parramatta. Whatever Haddock wanted, he got. The team's function: to find who had been at Fort Denison from mid-2004 to mid-2006, and then to correlate their movements and function at the fort, to extensively check their backgrounds, including political affiliations, criminal records, drug addiction, and, if possible, psychiatric analysis.

Based on what the team found, bring them into State Crime Command; voluntarily if possible, but not if they were recalcitrant. The resultant flak from the media and lawyers engaged by those who received the rough hand of the law would be dealt with afterwards.

Ruth Stein, the criminal psychologist, whom Haddock had reservations about, especially from a previous case when she had procrastinated, and had given a pronouncement as to who the most likely murderer was, only to be proven wrong, was to be given carte blanche access to those deemed suspect.

She was reminded that her career was on the line if she didn't comply, and her upcoming lectures at Sydney University were cancelled. She had spoken to Superintendent Payne and registered her objection, only to be told that it would be noted, but she would do her job. An arrest had to be made within the week.

Everyone was on tenterhooks, Natalie was down to four hours of sleep a night, and Haddock was lucky if he got two.

For three days, every one put in the maximum effort. At Fort Denison, the crime scene investigators continued, extending their examination, divers in the waters surrounding it, looking for anything.

After four days, Payne called Haddock and his sergeant, to his office, along with Ruth Stein.

'Nothing?' he said. Natalie could see a man under pressure. Once, he had been the senior officer at a police station a long way out of Sydney, dealing with glue-sniffing locals and drunken layabouts. But now, he was a superintendent at State Crime Command, feeling the pressure of a high-profile case.

'We have forty-four persons who visited the fort in 2005,' Haddock replied. 'Of those, eight were government surveyors, another six from the Heritage Committee, representatives from construction companies, sundry advisers, and a couple of kayakers who thought they would have a picnic out there.'

'Of the forty-four, who is a likely contender?'

'None. The usual demographic backgrounds, a couple into recreational drugs, one who has spent time in a mental hospital, another who has served two and a half years in Long Bay Prison for fraud.'

'The mental case?'

'Delusional, self-harming,' Ruth Stein said. 'Also, female, incapable of concealing the woman, insufficient strength.'

'The criminal?'

'He worked for an insurance company, embezzled close to three hundred thousand dollars. Arrested, admitted his guilt, paid back the money, served his time, and then worked for the Heritage Committee.'

'They employ criminals?'

'He had committed the crime in his twenties. He was in his fifties when he worked for the Committee. He's retired now, with no history of violence.'

'Dr Stein, you're the expert,' Payne said. 'What's your professional opinion? Aside from the obvious, Sasha Cornell appears to have been an ambitious, hardworking person with no distinguishable vices.'

'Initially, I would have said that the murderer is psychotic, but you would expect that person to want either recognition or validation for their action.'

'Validation?'

'What was the point? We are forced to conclude this is concerning her father. But that comes with complications in that nothing has changed apart from the man's grief. Bernie Cornell is not unique in that he would have adjusted to his daughter's disappearance in time, and without any information as to where she was, alive or dead, he would have continued to believe she would reappear one day.'

'Or else the murderer committed the action but never completed the plan.'

'Which means either dead or biding time,' Natalie said.

'Illogical the second part,' Ruth Stein said. 'Her body was found more by chance than anything else. She could have remained missing for another seventeen years or for eternity.'

'Dr Stein, speculate,' Haddock said. 'Possible scenarios.'

'Do we hold that her death is related to her father?'

'We must.'

'Very well. We know her father's reputation, aware he was a force of nature, unyielding, admired by those he didn't impact, loathed by others he did. More than one person had a reason to want him dead, but killing is an easy solution.'

'To make him suffer seemed a better option.'

'It did, but why Pinchgut? Why not just dispose of the body?'

'The murderer might have wanted to destroy the father at a time of his choosing, either for financial gain or personal satisfaction.'

'Even so, it remains unclear why the body has not been found before. I've been there, the restaurant when it was open, people everywhere, into every nook and cranny.'

'Including where the woman was found?' Haddock asked.

'I wasn't looking, just taking in the view and socialising.'

'There must be more.'

'Does Pinchgut have any significance to Bernie Cornell? Or to the murderer?'

'One isn't known for his sentimentality, and impossible to prove for the other.'

Changing his focus, Haddock looked over at his sergeant. 'This crack team scouring the internet, get some of them to focus on the Cornell family history, go back as far as they can, first fleet if necessary, and then correlate with any names they're checking, also other persons in Australia who have a similar history to Cornell.'

'It could take time,' Natalie replied. 'Vengeance that goes back centuries?'

'Why not? Cornell had success. Maybe the murderer believes his family had been disadvantaged because of him.'

'And festering in his mind for years,' Stein said. 'Inspector Haddock's hit on a possibility.'

Natalie agreed with Haddock and credited Dr Stein for acknowledging the inspector's sound argument. The relationship between the academic Stein and the practical Haddock had sometimes been testy, but not today, united in a common cause.

However, Natalie had no intention of pulling personnel away from their computers to focus on another avenue of enquiry. Twelve hours later, ten more persons sat in front of another bank of computers, researching early Australian history and the Cornell family and then extending it to those names the other computer researchers were putting together. Natalie realised burnout was likely due to the hours, the paperwork generated, and the cross-tabulation required due to possible errors.

***

Cornell's offer of five million dollars for information leading to the conviction of the person responsible for his daughter's death led to a massive amount of data to digest and investigate. Another team, to enhance the first, was set up in a building owned by the man, tradesmen making the building fit for purpose, cables laid in for the internet, additional telephones installed, and a central switching system that ensured no phone call was unanswered for more than ten seconds.

Natalie visited the building, spoke to those working there, and realised that some would not last: too much work and not enough breaks during the day. Although she had to admit that if you want results, a maximum of people and sufficient resources were the way forward.

State Crime Command concerned itself with crime-solving, operational efficiency, and budgetary control. The first was vital, the others were not, and she had noticed that shortcuts were being taken, reporting was not as scrupulous, and any court case against the accused would be weakened.

The answer to her concerns became evident when she, Superintendent Payne, and Inspector Haddock found themselves at Cornell's mansion in Vaucluse, east of the city. It was a Friday evening. Hopefully, the next day, a chance to unwind.

'Superintendent,' Cornell said. Instead of the wheelchair, he stood firm. The man had a focus, his daughter. Reinvigorated, he had no intention of resting while his daughter's murderer walked the street. 'What do we have?'

Payne went through the current status, persons of interest, and everyone working to the maximum. Haddock thought it was an impressive speech; Cornell did not.

Natalie could see that the superintendent was tired of being lectured by someone who thought he knew more about running a murder investigation than the police.

One hour later, after the three had been summarily dismissed, they were in the Lord Dudley Hotel in Jersey Road Woollahra. It had been her favourite when she had been at Kings Cross Police Station, a leisurely Sunday stroll to eat one of their Sunday roast dinners in front of an open fire.

'I'm not sure if the man's a hindrance or a help,' Payne said. He held a beer and paid for Haddock's and Natalie's drinks.

'He might prove to be a hindrance,' Haddock said. 'If the murderer is still alive, he might be forced to play his hand or retreat into obscurity. Low key, subtle, would have been more appropriate.'

'Your view, Sergeant?' Payne asked.

'It's too visible, too much in the news. Inspector Haddock's right.'

'Agreed, but not much I can do about it. Give it a month, and it will be old news. Why Pinchgut?'

'Illogical,' Haddock said. 'A sick mind, playing tricks, must have believed the body would never be found or thought it might soon after it was placed there.'

'No idea of the mental state of this person? This criminal psychologist? Any good?'

'Sergeant Campbell places faith in her; I don't. Too many fancy words, not enough facts. We need to know what we're dealing with here. The fort is significant, but I have no idea why. A few were hung back there in the eighteenth century. We've got our people working on it.'

'The standard reply,' Payne said. 'Usually, I would give a roasting to those who use it as an excuse, but it's a fair statement in this instance. Cornell must know more. Have you spoken to those he had dealings with? He must have cheated a few, sent them to the wall, bankrupted them, and tossed them out on the street. I can't say I like the man.'

It was an interesting statement, Natalie thought. Did she like the man? She wasn't sure but probably did not. He could be charming one minute, villainous the next, and had a formidable reputation when younger. Haddock was under no illusion; he did not like the man.

'It could be totally unrelated. Nothing to do with the father,' Natalie said.

'That's the problem; everyone's fixated on him. It could be, as you say, unrelated. What about the boyfriend? Her social set, public relations company? She would have upset a few if she was like her father.'

'The fort is still significant,' Haddock said.

'Until you make the connection, investigate all angles. The computer experts trawling ad infinitum through early and modern Australian history could take weeks.'

'Which we don't have,' Natalie said. She realised there was a decent man behind Superintendent Payne's brash exterior, but positions of authority affect a person, making them act out a part. She though Bernie Cornell might be similar but dismissed it as fanciful. If he was friendly, it served a purpose. With the superintendent, she felt it was genuine.

Chapter 4

Josh Costello, Sasha's former boyfriend, was hostile. He had driven out to Parramatta and was in the interview room at State Crime Command. He was in his mid-forties, dressed in a dark suit, his hair parted on the left, and his face clean-shaven. Natalie thought him strikingly handsome; Haddock had to admit to being impressed.

'Mr Costello, thanks for coming,' Haddock said. The man had been grilled when the woman had disappeared; his history, past and present, was known. He had met Sasha at an office function when they both worked for her father. He was in the finance department; she was in advertising. They had hit it off. Three months later, they were sharing her apartment in Darlinghurst. There had been talk of marriage, even a firm agreement approved by her father, although Costello and Sasha had argued on the day she vanished. A minor conflict, he had said, about the date of the wedding and who to invite. He felt obliged to invite an old girlfriend, a friend of his family; she did not. He was convinced it would have blown over, but she had never returned, and he had sounded the alarm, knowing the father's wrath and the daughter's importance.

'There's no more I can add that you don't know already,' Costello said.

'It wasn't us who instructed you to come to Australia,' Natalie said.

'Her father, I know that. I can't blame the man; he was devoted to her, as I was. It was a long time ago. I'm based in New York, married for fifteen years, with two children in their teens. Reflecting on a dark chapter in the lives of those who lived through it is a disservice to Sasha.'

'Yet, six months later, you had another woman,' Natalie said.

'Less than six. I was young, and pining away was not going to help. Bernie continued to believe she was coming back, or that was how he portrayed it. No one else did. Her father threw a fortune at finding her and scoured the globe, friends of hers, people she had known, and those who wished him ill, but nothing. At some stage, you accept the inevitable. I waited long enough, and then I met my wife.'

'Similar to Sasha?'

'We met five months after she disappeared and started dating one month later. I don't believe I was in error for accepting the inevitable. Even Bernie was starting to doubt that she would return.'

'Your relationship with him?'

'I had been living with his daughter. He felt a tie to her through me. He sent me to New York, and I've worked for him ever since.'

'The son he never had?' Haddock asked.

'If that means I've gained financially due to Sasha, the answer is no. He's a hard taskmaster, and I've performed well. Nobody in New York knows about Sasha and me unless they've scoured the internet.'

'Easy enough to find,' Natalie said.

'I realise that, but I've never mentioned it to anyone. Bernie would not have liked it if I had; my wife does not want to be reminded of the past. I'm sure you understand they were dark days after Sasha's disappearance.'

Both officers did.

'We believe that Fort Denison is significant, but why eludes us. Do you have an opinion?'

'We could see it from our balcony, went out there a few times, but no more than that.'

Costello planned to spend two more weeks in Sydney, but there was no reason to suspect him of involvement. He had not left the apartment when Sasha Cornell went missing; he had no reason to want her dead and, from what could be deduced, no psychological or criminal bent that would have regarded Fort Denison as a suitable place for her body.

Research would be conducted into his family history, but he was known to be third-generation Australian, and Pinchgut's early colonial history would not be important to him.

***

Natalie jogged the route from where Sasha Cornell had lived to Elizabeth Bay. She thought it might give insight into the woman, and those she had spoken to so far in the investigation had said the woman was logical, possibly OCD, in that she kept the food in her pantry and the fridge lined up, can labels to the front, and if the food was not fresh, or the date had expired, in the rubbish it went. She also spent money on clothes, a lot of money, more in a day than Natalie would have spent in a year. Her latte and croissant after a jog were a ritual rarely broken and were always ready when she arrived at the café. The same owners still ran the place when Natalie entered it, remembered the woman, and had fond words to say about her. 'All that money, and you know who her father was?' Natalie did and did not care if the woman had been the Queen of Sheba or a streetwalker – they all deserved the same respect and politeness, although social standing and wealth were all-important to some.

'Tell me about her,' Natalie said as she drank a latte and ate a croissant, emulating the dead woman's daily routine.

'Set your clock by her,' Lottie Armstrong said.

'Always friendly? Or were there days when she was distant, distracted, off colour? We all have those sorts of days.'

'Not with Sasha. We called her Sasha, she insisted. And with a father like that.'

'Like what? Have you met him?'

'No, but we used to read about him, the things he did.'

'What things?' Natalie knew but was interested to see if the woman's perception was based on fact or invention.

'A wicked man. He used to do those terrible things.'

Perception, Natalie realised. She had read up on Bernie Cornell's life and career. Corporate raider, property developer, a supporter of big business and small government, a believer in the individual defining their life, not the taxpayer to give them a leg up. Her father admired him; her mother did not.

'You've met him?' Lottie asked.

'I have, a couple of times.'

'Your opinion?'

Natalie was unsure if she should be honest or lie, but then what did she know. She hadn't yet fathomed the man; unlikely that she would.

'Tough, demanding, getting old, loved his daughter,' Natalie replied.

'Some good in him, then. We liked Sasha; remember the day she disappeared.'

'What was different? Have you seen suspicious persons in the past? I take it you have heard the news about her body.'

'We have been shocked by it. She came in regular as clockwork, sat where you are, latte and a croissant. Sometimes, she would talk; other times, she was quiet. Nobody bothered her; some knew who she was, others did not. She never spoke about business or her family, just general chit-chat, the weather, and what was happening in Sydney, where she was going for her holidays. We knew more, as she was in the magazines and social pages and living with her boyfriend.'

'Did you know him?'

'He would come in sometimes with her or others.'

'Male or female?'

'Both. Nothing strange, no holding hands. Just friends, but you don't know, do you? The women were not as attractive as Sasha.'

The woman was enamoured of celebrity and believed that Sasha Cornell could do no wrong. Lottie Armstrong was an unreliable witness.

Determined not to give up on the route Sasha Cornell used to jog, Natalie found herself outside the Horizon building again the next day. She was dressed for jogging.

As she jogged up Forbes Street, she could feel eyes burning into her from behind twitching curtains. She knew the red shorts and the white top she wore were the same as Sasha's jogging attire. It seemed hard to believe that people would remember the woman from such a long time back, but a recent campaign, seeking information and a reward offered, with a reconstruction of a woman dressed as Sasha had been that fateful day, was more likely the reason.

It had resulted in over one hundred phone calls and even more emails, but none had proven fruitful. The glances were of people remembering the campaign, not the victim.

She jogged along Darlinghurst Road, across William Street, down to the El Alamein Fountain, winding down to Elizabeth Bay. Sasha Cornell might have jogged it easily, but Natalie realised she had not. She was exhausted and catching her breath, about to take a seat alongside the water's edge, when she was approached by an elderly man.

'I remember you, Sergeant Campbell. I was hit by a car crossing the road.'

'Mr Norman, how are you? Leg better?'

'I've not seen you around here for a while.'

'Transferred to Homicide, based out of State Crime Command in Parramatta.'

'You reminded me of Sasha.'

'You knew her?'

'I often saw her in the morning, not for a long chat, but we were polite, enjoyed the view, and looked at the water. Never know what you will see early morning. Even saw a penguin once.'

It had surprised Natalie when she first came to Sydney that there was a small breeding colony of fairy penguins in the harbour, protected by the NSW National Parks and Wildlife Service.

She had seen whales, dolphins, and even a shark in the harbour but had never seen a penguin.

'We need to understand her life, who she knew, those who disliked her, and those who despised her father.'

'And would have killed her, left her to rot in an old fort in the harbour? I gave a statement when she disappeared, another

24

young woman asking me questions, not as elegantly as you, if I may say so.'

Old-style gallantry did not offend, and a compliment warmly given was always welcome.

'If you could tell me what you told her, it would be appreciated.'

'I knew her father when we were both younger. He was sharp back then, determined to get ahead in life. Not that I gave him much credence, thought him a bore.'

'Is his daughter's disappearance related to him?' Natalie asked.

'Impossible to say. When she disappeared, I thought there was more to the story, but what? She had it made, could have enjoyed her life, and done nothing. For some reason, she felt comfortable talking to me, not for long, a couple of minutes one day, five another, sometimes just a wave.'

'Any significance in Fort Denison?'

'None that I can think of. Great view from out there, but she would not have seen much. Killed over there?'

'We can't be sure; too many years since her death.'

'Similar murders over the years? Copycat killer?'

'Not that we know of.'

Chapter 5

No one could explain how Sasha Cornell had left the Horizon building and vanished into thin air. There were blind spots on the route, but she would have had to pass CCTV on the way, a shop's security system, cameras angled incorrectly, an ATM outside a bank, and the bank itself. It was a long time ago, 2005, when she had disappeared, and there were not as many cameras back then, although there should have been sufficient.

Haddock thought the woman's disappearance had occurred between the Horizon building and the roundabout at Liverpool Street or up to Darlinghurst Road. His reasoning, which Natalie thought sound, was that coffee shops were open by that time, and people were out exercising, walking a dog, or heading off to an early start at their place of employment. Sasha Cornell was too well-known not to have been seen by someone. But she had not.

At State Crime Command, the computer experts were wading through the mass of information, most spurious, some worthy of follow-up. Haddock wasn't enamoured of policing conducted in a sterile room full of computers, but Natalie could see the benefit. This was saturation policing, and even though she needed rest, she was excited. The thrill of the chase, to be there when an arrest was made.

Three days later, Natalie again jogged the route favoured by Sasha. Close to the roundabout on Liverpool Street, down ten metres on Forbes Street, outside the imposing structure that had once been the First Church of Christ, Scientist, a car was parked. A man lounged on it, his face partially obscured by a scarf. In an instant, he had hold of her. 'Got you,' he said. 'Think you're smart, just like that bitch Sasha Cornell.'

Trained in protecting herself, a black belt in karate and a gun in a small bag around her waist, Natalie reacted. She was not handling the situation well, with no time to think and no one nearby to assist. The man was stronger, with a smell of tobacco. She realised this might be the man who had killed Sasha.

She managed to free one arm, enough to reach for her gun. This was not the time to worry about the unsanctioned use of a firearm. She aimed at the man's chest. A sudden movement by him, and the bullet entered his left leg.

His grip released, and Natalie collapsed to the ground, the presence of mind to remember the car's registration number as he drove off.

Four minutes later, after she had phoned Haddock, a police car pulled up alongside her. Six minutes later, she was at St Vincent's Hospital in Darlinghurst. Despite her protestations, she was lying on a bed, a nurse checking her pulse and tending to her wounds.

For the patient, a stiff drink would have helped. A sedative was offered but declined. She needed to be cognisant of what had occurred and report it to Haddock, who would arrive within the hour.

The car's registration number was with the Homicide Squad, Superintendent Payne salivating at the thought of an early arrest. Bernie Cornell had been advised, and the team at State Crime Command were taking a breather.

'Too young,' Natalie said to Haddock when he arrived. By then, she was sitting up with a warm drink.

'Did you manage to get a look at your attacker?' Haddock asked. What had happened was more important than his sergeant's condition. Although, if asked, he would have said she was made of stern stuff, and no male, violent or on the make, would get far with her.

'Shot him in the leg, got the car registration, and saw the back end of him as he got in the car. He was limping. In his thirties, maybe younger. He isn't Sasha Cornell's killer, probably one of those nutcases on social media who revel in fame. He'll be back.'

'He could have seriously hurt you.'

'Could have made a hero of himself, a female police officer at his mercy.'

A doctor called Haddock to one side. 'Delayed shock, possible concussion. She might not be coherent.'

Haddock disregarded the doctor's last statement. He had worked with his sergeant long enough to know that if she said her assailant was young, he was.

Natalie protested and said she was fine, but she was a police officer. She did what she was told: a night in the hospital for observation and two days on sick leave.

***

For the next week, lone female joggers were fewer in Darlinghurst and the surrounding suburbs. The attack on Natalie had been planned, although not meticulously. Nine days later, a burnt-out Toyota was discovered by the side of a country road, a four-hour drive from Sydney.

Haddock and Natalie made the journey, arriving at five in the afternoon. Crime scene investigators were on the scene, checking for fingerprints and other evidence. The plates had been changed. The registered owner was on a course in Melbourne, unaware that the car he had purchased six months earlier had been involved in a crime; devastated when told it was a burnt-out wreck.

'Fingerprints where it didn't get burnt, on the driver's side rear door handle,' one of the investigators said. He took a copy, sent it from his laptop and waited. Thirty minutes later, he had a result, enough time for Haddock and Natalie to grab a bite to eat from an old-fashioned milk bar in the nearby village.

'Peter Evershed,' Haddock said as he read the message from the CSI.

'Do you know him?'

'By reputation. Anarchist, an agitator, turns up at any protest, rent-a-crowd. He's violent when riled and believes the police are corrupt and that the world's out to get him. In short, psycho.'

'Age?' Natalie asked.

'Better than that,' Haddock said as he showed an image on his phone.

'That's him. Capable of murder?'

'He's mad by our estimation, but get a psychologist and a social worker, they'll argue to the end of the day about his above-average IQ, his disadvantaged childhood, his mother on the game, and his father in prison. He's been in and out of institutions most of his life.'

'Where is he?'

'Criminally insane, he would be in Thomas Embling Hospital in Victoria, high security, serious nasties in there. But he's not insane, not by a psychologist's definition. Disturbed, troublesome, prescribed clozapine.'

'If he doesn't take the medication?'

'Attacks police officers jogging,' Haddock said.

Natalie knew it was a flippant remark, an attempt at levity when there wasn't much to be cheerful about.

Haddock made a phone call.

'I've got his last known address,' he said after he ended the phone call to Homicide, a person at the other end checking databases. 'Cautioned ten days ago, a peaceful protest turned violent. He doesn't get arrested that often now, a rap over the knuckles from a judge, more paperwork for the arresting officer. He'll be picked up today, held over for twenty-four hours, or as long as we need. Get a confession. Prove it was him who attacked you.'

'He didn't murder Sasha Cornell,' Natalie said.

'It could have been an accident waiting to happen if your gun had got into his hands. What possessed you to carry it?'

'I'm running around the area where her murderer could still be. A disturbed mind, guilt over his actions, believing I was a ghost or returned from the grave. Who knows what could have happened.'

Haddock knew what could have; he shuddered at the thought of it.

***

It was conceivable that Sasha Cornell could have been snatched off the street as Natalie almost was. A quiet area in the early morning, no more than a short walk to the hustle and bustle, but Sydney wasn't London or New York. Even at its busiest, it was relatively quiet; people minded their business and went about their daily chores. Natalie loved the city's proximity to the harbour and the endless beaches, more than enough cafes, restaurants and clubs, and a strong group of friends.

Although, maybe, Sasha Cornell hadn't been whisked off the street but had gone of her own volition. It made no sense, as the young woman had nothing of concern: a loving boyfriend, but he soon found another, a doting parent, sufficient money, and a successful business. But what if they weren't enough? What if she hankered after something else? A touch of the rough, a chance to walk on the wild side, to experience bad men. Was there a side to the woman on a pedestal that had gone unnoticed or not been told?

It was essential to know Sasha Cornell, warts and all. What was she like when the makeup was off and the public persona was not on show.

Josh Costello, soon to leave the country, met Haddock and Natalie at the Lord Nelson Hotel in The Rocks. Nowadays, the area was historical, quaint terrace houses, souvenir shops, and the Overseas Passenger Terminal, where cruise ships took on passengers for trips around Australia, up to the Pacific Islands, and worldwide.

The Lord Nelson, on the corner of Kent and Argyle Streets, the oldest continuously licensed pub in Sydney, named after the hero of Trafalgar, was an ideal locale to meet and talk.

It was six in the evening; Costello was on a flight the following day. Compared to the last time they had met him, he was relaxed and affable. Natalie, more sensitive to the signals than Haddock, knew the reason. The man was a player and hadn't spent lonely nights pining for his wife. He had another woman in Sydney to keep him company.

A player in Sydney with a wife in New York; a player in Sydney while living with Sasha Cornell. A motive to be rid of her, but not a sufficient reason for her disappearance – unless…

Natalie had seen it first and explained it to Haddock after Costello had returned to his hotel later that evening. Natalie thought the worst of the man.

Haddock nodded, aware that his sergeant's intuition was sharper than his. 'What if leaving Sasha wasn't a choice?' he said. 'What if fear of the father required drastic action? If her body had been found soon after her disappearance, Forensics and Pathology would have had a lot more to work with, and the primary suspect would have been the person closest to her, which would have been Costello.'

The man was flying back to New York in the morning. It would take more than an idea conjured up in the pub over a few drinks; it needed facts, and they had none. If they could prove he was a person of interest, that he could have killed Sasha or arranged for someone else to kill and bury her at Pinchgut, a court order could be arranged, but it was late at night, and with nothing to offer, the man's departure from Australia could not be stopped.

Even so, there was one option. Natalie made the phone call. The man was in Sydney.

Forty minutes later, after two cups of coffee apiece, and a packet of mints, they met with Bernie Cornell.

The discovery of his daughter's body had initially given him a new lease on life, but it had not lasted long. He was now back in his wheelchair with a nurse hovering nearby.

'It's late,' the nurse said. 'Mr Cornell needs to rest.'

'Not now, woman,' Cornell barked.

A sign of the aggression he was known for, Natalie observed.

'What is it, Sergeant Campbell, Inspector Haddock?'

Haddock outlined a scenario, strong on theory, weak on fact.

'Fear of me? Is that what you think? If Costello broke up with Sasha?'

'Hypothetically,' Natalie said. 'It might sound illogical, but it's an avenue of enquiry we need to investigate, but if he's not in the country, it complicates.'

'Costello would not have broken with Sasha. For two reasons: my displeasure and, if he had married her, a senior role in one of my companies.'

'Strengthens our theory,' Haddock said.

'I know what Costello is, no slouch with women. Sasha might not have known, but I recognised the signs.'

'In you?' Natalie said.

Haddock thought her presumptuous. Cornell had a fearsome reputation for those who threatened or made aspersions.

'Inspector Haddock, you have got yourself a good person there. She's got a backbone, the same as Sasha.'

'I realise that; thought she was pushing her luck,' Haddock replied.

'She was, but Costello plays the field, shacked up with a woman at his hotel now, not that his wife will ever know. I've looked after him; I owe that to Sasha. Not the senior position he wanted, but it's still good.'

'Are you able to help?'

'He'll remain in the country for another two weeks.'

Cornell picked up the phone in his lap and dialled. 'Josh, cancel your flight. Two weeks more in Australia. I've got something for you to do.'

'Thank you,' Natalie said after Cornell ended the phone call.

'I don't believe he's involved, but I need to be certain.'

Chapter 6

'Showing your hand, getting the woman's father involved,' Superintendent Payne said. 'Could backfire.'

Having involved Bernie Cornell in their further investigation of Josh Costello, both Haddock and Natalie realised that telling Payne was preferable to his hearing it through the grapevine, either from Cornell or someone else.

'We need to follow up,' Haddock said. Before the current investigation, he had been ambivalent about Payne, but with frequent interaction, he had changed his mind. Payne could be rough around the edges, but he was fair-minded, regarded the law as paramount, and appreciated proactive police officers.

'Even so, it could go against us if you end up charging Costello. Was he in their apartment when she disappeared?'

'That was proven at the time. CCTV on every floor, in the lifts, the concierge, car park. No sign of him exiting the building, and the video evidence is still available.'

'Conclusive, unless he's a wizard with technology, able to alter the times recorded.'

'Something else we need to check up on,' Natalie said.

Haddock realised there was validity in the superintendent's concern. He wasn't sure if Natalie did.

The two sat in a café not far from State Crime Command.

'We've brought Costello into the investigation,' Haddock said. 'However, there is a complication.'

'I don't see it,' Natalie said.

'What if the father is involved?'

'His daughter? Not possible.' A sharp rebuttal to a preposterous statement.

'I'm not saying that he murdered her or had anything to do with her disappearance. But we've speculated that he is the reason. What if he knows what it is? What if he's unwilling to reveal the truth, his reputation down the drain, criminal action against him, and possible financial repercussions?'

'If he knows that now, surely he knew it then.'

'Probably, or maybe not. Although why the man cares now, on death's doorstep, I can't answer.'

'Inspector, you cannot. You're honest and middle class. I don't mean that to be derogatory.'

'You're saying that men such as Cornell are driven by success at any cost?'

'How do we find out? If we ask him directly, he could tell us the truth or not, get us removed from the investigation, and out of Sydney.'

'Let us agree on one premise. He wants his daughter's killer. But no more. No enquiry into shady dealings, illegal transactions, and whatever. A business deal that went sour, a vengeful competitor, driven to the wall.'

'Costello?' Natalie asked.

'Sweat the man.'

Two days later, the previously affable Costello did not display friendliness. He knew what had transpired, a face-to-face meeting with the man who had curtailed his return to New York.

'Am I a suspect?' Costello said.

He was sitting with Haddock and Natalie in a room at the back of Kings Cross Police Station. Informed of his rights and the reason for his attendance, he sat with a sullen face, his hands crossed in a defensive mode.

'Not a suspect, a person of interest,' Haddock said. 'Subtle difference.'

'Not to me. My wife was expecting me back home. Important things to do, the children's schooling, the purchase of a new house, a medical appointment for me.'

'You were advised by Sasha's father that he had something to do for you here,' Natalie said.

'He's not a man to beat around the bush; told me why. Told me that you have both come up with a lame belief that I might have been involved in her disappearance.'

'Various ideas are formulated; most are discarded as impractical, errant nonsense, or impossible. However, one scenario my sergeant observed in the Lord Nelson. You are a player,' Haddock said.

'Whatever that means,' Costello replied.

'You know,' Natalie said. 'You have no issues with infidelity.'

'Man, the hunter, can't help myself.'

'We're not offering comment, purely stating a fact. You've found another woman in Sydney, the reason you didn't want to stay longer at the Lord Nelson. Is she still with you?' Natalie asked.

'She is, not that it's any of your business whether I'm a player or not, to use your quaint terminology. The opportunity presented itself; I took it.'

'We'll accept that for now,' Haddock said.

'I'm stuck in Sydney for now, made bearable by a friend. However, I'm uncomfortable with this aspersion that I might be involved in Sasha's death.'

'I'll elaborate, postulate if I may. You were living with Sasha, your future assured if you stayed with her and ultimately married her.'

'Our relationship was romantic, not mercenary. You've seen photos; she was a beautiful woman.'

'We have. However, soon after her disappearance, you have another woman.'

'Six months later, I did. Not while I was with Sasha.'

Natalie spoke. 'Inspector Haddock is not as perceptive in these matters as I am, as any woman would be. You're an attractive man; women come easily to you. Are you saying you were faithful to Sasha? And please don't be coy. We will find out the truth eventually, regardless.'

'A typical heterosexual male. The opportunities were there, and sometimes I took them. Suggesting I had found eternal love with another, willing to sacrifice Sasha, unable to walk out the door for fear of my career, is fanciful.

'My intent was to marry Sasha, and yes, a good position in one of her father's companies, damned if I didn't. But I didn't think like that. Agreed, another woman occasionally, but nothing more. Her father was no saint; Sasha understood the reality.'

'Did she? Women might be forced to accept, but that doesn't mean they understand or agree.'

'We have no reason to believe you killed her,' Haddock said. 'Primarily, because you were in the Horizon building at the time of her disappearance, and her incarceration at Fort Denison doesn't seem to be something you could have done, which points to another person if we follow through on the possibility.'

'What would her father have done if you had left her?' Natalie asked.

'It would have depended on Sasha's reaction, although he would have called me a bloody fool and wiped the floor with me.'

'And evicted you from your employment.'

'I wasn't working for him then, but it wouldn't have made any difference. The man gets what he wants.'

'We're aware of that. He's running us ragged.'

'Am I free to leave the country? Will you let Bernie know that you are satisfied with my innocence?' Costello said.

'The situation remains unresolved. We will further check your movements before Sasha's disappearance and in the following days. If you could assist.'

'Seventeen years ago? Are you joking? How can anyone remember that far back?'

The man was right, but he would not be leaving the country, not yet, not until his innocence was confirmed, which seemed improbable. More likely, the guilty party would be found.

***

A hitherto known fact that had not been fully investigated, although it was mentioned in Sasha's diary, was a meeting she had intended to keep but never did: a new client with evidence about a former prime minister of Australia.

The Honourable Ralph Davidson, the son of a Queen's Counsel, was educated at Sydney Grammar School, the accredited best-performing private school in Australia, the first choice for the sons of gentlemen, the elite, and those who could afford the fees, fifty thousand dollars a year.

It was way out of Haddock's pay scale, and he had only ever seen the school from the outside as he had driven up College Street in the centre of Sydney, not far from the Australian Museum and Hyde Park, with the Anzac Memorial dedicated to those fallen in battle.

He had shaken Davidson's hand once, a visit from the prime minister to open a new wing at State Crime Command, thought him to be suave and elegant, a champion of the underdog, a believer in free enterprise and the right of the individual. Even so, he was too far right of centre for Haddock.

He had heard of her, so had Natalie, but now the former mistress of a former prime minister was an Eastern Suburbs stalwart, married for fourteen years, with a real estate agency in Woollahra and a house in Vaucluse, not more than two streets from her previous lover's residence.

Natalie had proven herself more astute in reading the hidden signals. She would lead in the interview of a woman who insisted on meeting at a restaurant in Bondi, close to the beach, busy enough to guarantee a modicum of privacy. The woman's affair with a married man seventeen years previously had been conducted in secrecy. She intended to keep it that way.

'I'm here reluctantly,' Beth Madison said.

Natalie could see an elegant, fashionably-dressed, well-spoken woman in her mid-forties.

'We have complied with your wishes by meeting here,' Haddock said.

'I remember Sasha Cornell, not well though, only briefly met her that once.'

'You're not from around here?'

'North shore, went to Pymble Ladies College, not that I was much of a lady when I was Ralph's plaything.'

'Were you?' Natalie asked. 'Sasha thought you to be the disgruntled mistress of a powerful man. Was she correct?'

'I was in my late twenties; he was in his early fifties. Power is seductive. I was drawn to him, couldn't resist. My parents instilled a strong work ethic and gave me a good education. I had a bachelor's degree in economics from Macquarie University in North Ryde, ended up as an accountant for the local council: forty hours a week, superannuation, three weeks' leave a year.'

'Not good enough?'

'Not for me. I was ambitious and always interested in politics, thought I'd give it a go. I tried to get preselection for a safe right-wing seat but got the runaround. Lecherous men and stuck-up women who did not want a pretty young thing sucking up to their boring husbands.'

'You were serious?' Haddock asked.

'Deadly.'

Natalie thought it an inappropriate word to use but understood that it came from frustration. She had hit the brick wall a few times and didn't like it, but she didn't have Beth Madison's determination to fight it.

'Why were you willing to sell the man out?' Natalie asked.

'Somehow, I fell into a relationship with him, clandestine meetings in out-of-the-way locations.'

'He would have had security. Hardly clandestine with their prying eyes.'

'He said they were subject to confidentiality agreements, the Official Secrets Act, not that I believed him. And besides, I never saw them lurking in the bushes when we met. I was young, just out of a relationship, and bowled over by the man. I couldn't help myself.'

'How long for?'

'Just over a year.'

'And then?'

'He was no longer the prime minister, a book tour lined up, interviews on the television, his adoring wife at his side.'

'Did she know?'

'I'm certain she did. Not that he ever admitted to it, but a man in his position, opportunities occur. It would take a strong man to resist.'

'You weren't the only one?'

'I didn't care at the time. Trips overseas, a place to live in Darlinghurst, near Sasha Cornell, but I did not know her personally. She moved in elevated circles; I kept my head down and nose clean. Of course, I knew who she was. Who could not?'

Haddock would have said that he did not but decided not to. The woman was talking; best to give her a clear run and see where it led.

'You approached her,' Natalie said.

'I gave a statement the first time. Is this necessary?'

'It is. Back then, the police were looking for a missing woman. But now, we are looking for a murderer. What was it that you would have revealed about Davidson?'

'He acted as though he was honourable and decent, a pillar of society. But nobody knew about me, the trips at the taxpayers' expense. It would have damaged his book tour, lost book sales.'

'Or more,' Haddock said. 'If it's the truth you want, don't buy a politician's memoir.'

'Inspector Haddock's not an admirer of your former lover,' Natalie said. 'The man dumped you; no option if he intended to portray himself as the elder statesman. Did he explain it to you, ensure you were financially sound?'

'He did.'

'Then why the anger? You were in your late twenties, not an adolescent, your first crush. Or are you a social climber, thought he would leave his wife and marry you?'

'I did, but then I met another, married to him now.'

'You're successful; could you have done it without Davidson?'

'I didn't have that sort of money. My husband did.'

'And now? Is he cheating on you? You on him?'

'Never. Past the silly age.'

So was Haddock, but Natalie knew he was still meeting infrequently with Theresa de Klerk at Parramatta.

'Why did you decide to reveal what you knew? And is it damning? After all, a politician rorting his expense account, a bit of fluff on the side, is hardly earth-shattering. There must be more, enough for someone to have silenced Sasha Cornell?'

'How? She did not know the details, and I did not intend to reveal all until I had a signed contract and received an advance.'

'An inkling? You must have whetted her appetite. The woman was busy, with enough money. For her to deal with litigation from a former prime minister might have been aggravation she didn't want.'

'She would have.'

Haddock could see that silencing Sasha Cornell, who would have possibly told her father that the prime minister's indiscretion or illegal activity was of such magnitude that it would open him to a possible criminal charge, was a viable motive for murder.

But why had the relatively unknown Beth Madison not died? It made no sense to either Haddock or Natalie. They were convinced that the mistress was leading them nowhere. It was the ideal motive, and the man would have had the means to organise murder, but why Pinchgut. The reason why remained unresolvable.

Beth Madison would say no more, concerned that her perfect life might become flawed by those that had dealt with the woman.

'Why Pinchgut?' Natalie asked.

'I've no idea. I never revealed what I knew, agreed to keep quiet, and got on with my life.'

'Did you sign anything?'

'No.'

'Then why?'

'I was paid to keep silent.'

'But you've opened up with us. Doesn't that constitute a breach?'

'It will not. We are meeting to clear the air.'

'A warning?'

'No.'

Haddock knew it was. Whatever the woman had known about Ralph Davidson, it was dynamite. She had survived; Sasha Cornell had not. Was Davidson implicated in the murder? Nobody knew.

A veil of secrecy had clouded the investigation. It was important to know the truth, but it would not come from Beth Madison, who left soon after.

Chapter 7

Jimmy Rogers was scanning through video recordings from seventeen years previous. They were grainy and not easy to watch.

He had worked with Natalie before, and whereas she liked him, she did not like his appearance: straggly hair and unkempt clothes. With a photographic image, digital enhancement could be attempted. A video presented other challenges as there were days of recording, and the cameras had been for security, not identification.

Sasha Cornell could be seen leaving the building on that fateful morning and heading up Forbes Street. No suspicious persons or vehicles could be seen. Rogers worked forward from that time for one hour and then back for a similar time, unsure if those inside the building were residents or guests.

Natalie looked over his shoulder for twenty minutes of the recordings; Rogers, excited at her presence, reminded her that he was available for a date and fancied her. But then, she had known that from the first time they met, and she had made it clear she was uninterested. Although she could be interested in another. She had been too long on her own and thought it unnatural to be devoid of romance, love, and sex in her twenties, but until the right guy came along, or someone approaching optimum, it would be celibacy and extreme policing.

Haddock wrestled with his own problems: a wife he had loved but was emotionally distant from now, a daughter that continued to trouble, a diversion for him in the shape of a forty-year-old brunette in Parramatta who should know better but did not.

Natalie had warned her inspector about her, but he wasn't listening, driven by emotions other than the rational.

'There you are,' Rogers shouted. He was a man who loved technology, and the chance to wade through videos from the past on the latest equipment that money could buy excited him.

Natalie, who had drifted off, unable to squint her eyes at the screen for more than five minutes, responded. 'What have you found?'

'One day before she disappeared. I've been running a secondary program, looking for someone pressing the elevator button for Costello.'

'You've found him?'

'At 1.25 p.m. Look closely, a woman in her twenties, dressed in a blue dress.'

Natalie could see the woman; Josh Costello stood two metres from her.

'Is that it?'

'They both take the same lift. Focus as they enter, a brief touching of hands. They were heading in the same direction. Where was his girlfriend?'

Rogers was correct; Costello had another woman, not even the decency to meet at her place or a hotel, but in the apartment that Bernie Cornell had given his daughter.

It was good that Costello was still in the country. Even if the man had not been responsible for Sasha's death, he was still a rat.

'Any chance of a close-up?' Natalie asked. 'Face recognition software?'

'Not sure the cameras were up to it back then, and even if I can clean it up, the video is seventeen years old. I would need images of persons of interest back then or recent photos to age regress. Not so easy, might take time, might yield nothing worthwhile.'

Natalie's solution was quicker.

Costello felt the heat of the bright lights, no longer able to avoid a pertinent question.

It was State High Command, the Homicide Squad, a room off to one side. Costello sat on one side of the table, Haddock and Natalie on the other. This time Costello had come without complaint – a clear indication that Bernie Cornell had given the man a strong warning: cooperate or else.

A monitor was in one corner of the room. A time-stamped five-minute video was shown. People could be seen coming and going for three minutes, lift doors opening and closing, and the concierge staff picking up parcels.

At three minutes and forty-five seconds, two persons came up from the car park and past the concierge; they were separated by three metres. Closer to the lift, an acknowledgement of the other, a brief touching of hands as they entered the lift furthest from the concierge. The touch was so brief as to be unnoticeable to any other than Rogers' eagle eyes.

The video played to the end, although nothing more important was shown.

'Damning,' Natalie said.

Costello said nothing for thirty seconds. Eventually, he spoke. 'Bernie will never forgive that indiscretion.'

'Who is she?' Haddock asked. Even he could see the pain in Costello's expression. He had been found guilty of a sin that would be unforgivable in the mind of Sasha's father. His future was bleak; it was up to him to save it.

'My wife. She was in Australia, working for an American company,' Costello replied.

'You told us you met your wife after Sasha had disappeared. That was a lie,' Natalie said.

'Sasha wanted our relationship to continue; so did I, but I had also tired of it. Wrong on my part, another woman, but what was I to do? I couldn't leave her; I couldn't stay.'

'Your reasons are mercenary, not romantic.'

'In part, I would agree. And now, her father will be told, and I will be out of a job.'

Natalie could feel anger. A man who thought a murdered woman was less important than his comfortable life overseas.

'How should we reflect on your wife?' Natalie asked. 'It's one thing to have an affair. It's something else to use the conjugal bed for that purpose. It shows low morality and a disregard for another woman's feelings. Why did you marry such a person?' It was a weighted question intended to draw an emotional and, hopefully, angry response.

'My wife is not involved. You don't understand, do you?'

'We might if you explain,' Haddock said. He was conscious she was letting her feminism confuse the interrogation; to take it from interrogative to emotional, to empathise with Sasha, to dislike Costello's wife, to hate Costello. To him, emotion did not play a part. Being cold and perceptive was the way to solve crimes, not emotion, but he was an old-style police officer, believing that out on the street was where crimes were solved, not in an office. But it had been an office and technology that had Costello pinned down, struggling with what to say, aiming to protect himself, not wanting to damn his wife or Bernie Cornell to find out.

'Inspector Haddock has given you the lead. Maybe it's best to explain why you were devoid of feeling for Sasha, attempting to protect your wife, and not wanting to get on the wrong side of Sasha's father,' Natalie said.

'Sasha had me, but she had another man. Her father might not know,' Costello said.

'Her father knew everything.'

'He thought he did. Sometimes his involvement in Sasha's life annoyed her. She was capable, and apart from her father's assistance when she started, her company went from strength to strength. She wasn't as hard as her father, but she was nobody's fool. Astute, demanding, yet coupled with compassion. He treated his people with disdain. You might disagree since you've only recently met him in his dotage. We had an open relationship, founded on love and mutual respect, serious in our intent to marry, not unrealistic to the challenges ahead or the occasional distractions.'

'Do you believe what you just said?' Natalie asked.

'Her father would not have understood. I doubt you would, Sergeant Campbell, but Sasha had grown up with the elite. She had seen her father in action, the fear he engendered, and his ruthlessness. She did not have her father's determination, but she had known privilege all her life.'

'And there's no one to corroborate what you've just said.'

'No one.'

'Why wasn't this revealed when she went missing?'

'Slurring Sasha? Who would have been listening?'

'Nobody,' Haddock said. 'Why tell us now?'

'I thought that was clear, Inspector. I'm the logical suspect, especially after that video you just showed, not that I had anything to do with Sasha's disappearance, but if Bernie's convinced, then the truth is unimportant.'

'No court would convict you on hearsay,' Natalie said.

'Bernie would. His vengeance would be absolute, evicted from the company, ostracised, a leper cast out of society.'

Haddock and Natalie understood what the man was saying. It didn't excuse his behaviour, but it was plausible that Bernie Cornell would destroy the man.

'This other man?'

'Duncan Howarth.'

***

A literal cat among the pigeons. Costello's revelation that his relationship and eventual marriage to Sasha would occur, subject to an agreement between the two that both were free agents, that her father was not to know, and that occasional dalliances would be tolerated.

Natalie struggled with the concept, aware that her increasing contempt for Josh Costello should not cloud her policing. She had had a boyfriend that she had loved, the two of them cosy in a love nest in Potts Point, until he had adopted the Josh Costello approach to their relationship, cheating on her with another, returning a couple of days later, begging forgiveness, with lipstick on his collar.

Apart from his importance to the investigation, Costello was of no consequence. A capable manager, he had risen high in the hierarchy in New York mainly due to his relationship with a man's dead daughter. Duncan Howarth needed no such leg up. A supreme athlete, an Olympic gold medal in sailing, had skippered the winning boat in the gruelling Sydney to Hobart yacht race three times, and now, in his forties, the head of a merchant bank in the city.

Haddock, of a similar age, was overweight and starting to go to seed and paled in the man's presence. Although he had played rugby union for his school, was captain for a couple of seasons, and played once for the state team.

Natalie knew of Howarth, attractive, tall, and slim, of his interest in politics and republicanism. She felt a flutter in his presence.

'Yes, I knew Sasha. We were involved for a while,' Howarth said.

On the top floor of the building in the city's central business district, his office was palatial, the view of the Opera House and Sydney Harbour Bridge unimpeded.

A young woman brought in coffee. Natalie, who appreciated the finer things in life, was impressed; Haddock, with his socialist upbringing, was not.

'Why didn't you come forward when she disappeared?' Haddock asked.

'I wasn't in Sydney at the time. I returned three weeks later, and our relationship had always been casual. I hadn't anything to offer, and I hadn't seen her for several months.'

'And your social standing would have been adversely affected if you had come forward.'

'I took advice, legal and personal. The consensus was that it would serve no purpose to come forward and would not advance the search.'

'Did you care for her?' Natalie asked.

'I admired the person, the infrequent times we spent together, mostly overseas, sometimes in Sydney. She was committed to Costello but had her father's instincts. An admirable woman worthy of praise.'

'Josh Costello?'

'Steady hand. A tendency to fool around, but solid marriage material. Sasha preferred him to me. I was the illusion, the all-conquering sportsman, but I wasn't about to be pinned down, and I certainly didn't want to be at Bernie Cornell's beck and call.'

'You didn't like him?'

'Not particularly. Difficult to deal with, ruthless if crossed, determined never to lose. He has few redeeming features; his only weakness is his daughter. Costello would have behaved within certain restraints; I would not have.'

'And now, sitting in an ivory tower,' Natalie said. 'Due to your own efforts?'

'Nobody makes it to the top of the totem pole without a certain amount of luck and influence. Due to my sporting prowess, a position in the company, and the advertising face of the bank. But I worked hard, forced my way up the corporate ladder, shafted a few, and helped others if they helped me. Don't be fooled by the public persona. I can be as much a bastard as Sasha's father; why I hadn't seen her for some time before she disappeared.'

'Did her father know of you?'

'She said he didn't, but I couldn't be sure. Why else pull back from her? He could have destroyed me, let it be known that I was not what people perceived. I can accept criticism but react when it's vindictive and prejudiced.'

'But not against her father. Her disappearance, any thoughts?'

'Mysterious. I thought she had come to harm, but what do you do? What would anyone do? Come to the police, and say that her disappearance was criminal or malevolent? What would you have said?'

'Why did you think it?' Natalie asked.

'For the same reason that I wouldn't disappear without a trace. Sasha was resolute, able to take the accolades along with the brickbats. Nothing would get her down for long, not enough to contemplate suicide, to jump off the rocks at the Gap, or to swim out to sea, unable to return. It wasn't in her psyche, nor mine. But what could anyone do? I had no idea what had happened, only a gut feeling that something wasn't right. And then, time moved on, and I suppose we all adjusted to it, put it down as a mystery that would never be solved, and then, she reappears out on Pinchgut.'

'Any significance to you?' Haddock asked.

'Sailed past it many times, but apart from that, no.'

Chapter 8

The reason for the woman's death was clearly significant but unknown; the choice of location where her body was found remained unfathomable. It had the markings of a high-functioning psychotic who reasoned that Pinchgut was important.

Howarth had sailed by it; Costello had dined there, as had countless others. Any trip up the harbour, whether on a luxury cruiser or a sailing boat, could not miss it. And the countless numbers who had taken a ferry to Manly or other places on the harbour, if they thought about it, regarded it as a local point of interest, a building on a rocky island. Few knew of its early history, its significance to the indigenous people, nor why it had become a fort, never to be used in military action. It was an oddity to many but added to Sydney's beauty and allure and its early colonial history.

Not even those who looked for reparations to the country's original inhabitants had mentioned it, yet someone thought it important. It was the one factor that remained indecipherable. They needed to understand why someone would go through so much trouble to be rid of a woman and, if not for Leo Hannan, for her to remain undiscovered.

Bernie Cornell thought it might be to do with an ancestor who had arrived in Australia with the third fleet. Josiah Hapworth, a cobbler's son, was transported for stealing a pig from a corrupt landowner, a chief magistrate in northern England who viewed the illiterate serfs as his chattels.

On one occasion, Hapworth caused trouble in the colony and spent a month on Pinchgut as punishment. He married a young woman who had been transported for stealing warm clothing. Within five years of the marriage: three children, two female and one male. At sixty-eight, Hapworth had died; his wife, eight years earlier. By that time, a substantial pastoral holding not far from where State Crime Command's edifice stood now.

Cornell laid the family tree on a table for Haddock and Natalie to see. Of Hapworth's three children, one son and the daughter had married. The youngest son had died at eight from one of the diseases that waylaid the early settlers, whether military overseers, convicts, or free settlers.

The two children's offspring had multiplied in the hundreds over the intervening two hundred years. Of those alive, Cornell had no contact with any other than a cousin in Queensland and a sister over the other side of Australia.

'There's more, but I don't know them, nor do I intend to,' Cornell said.

'Why?' Natalie asked.

'The pleading letters. I keep in contact with my sister, but she married a loser, gave her five kids, and took off with her best friend. My cousin worked for me in the early days. He's capable, lives a good life, and prefers peace and quiet. The family tree was Sasha's idea. She thought there might be a book in it.'

'Did you?'

'Of interest to some, but not me. I don't like people much; I prefer they mind their own business, and why would they want to read about my life? Why not do what I did and get off their backsides?'

'Not everyone has your acumen or drive,' Natalie said.

'You're right, but you and Haddock aren't getting far. I could bring in heavy hitters from the states, get them to sniff around.'

'I would advise against that,' Haddock said. 'You're suggesting possible criminals, not adverse to rough-hand treatment.'

'Exactly. You're restrained by rules and regulations; I'm not.'

'You are,' Natalie insisted.

'At my age? With my wealth? Not a chance, could do anything I wanted.'

Even murder, Haddock thought but did not say it. That was not a road he wanted to go down; a father responsible for his daughter's death. It didn't bear thinking about, although his last fracas with his daughter had left him ragged. A trip away with a group of friends, male and female. 'Don't worry, Dad,' she had said. 'I'm old enough, know what I'm doing, and besides, we're all friends, nothing of what you're thinking.'

Haddock didn't need to think. He had seen the condom hidden in her room and smelt the lingering aroma of marijuana. He had gone through a difficult phase in his youth, but she was female, and females get pregnant and hit on by lecherous males. With alcohol and drugs, her resolve would weaken, even if it was there in the first place.

Personal issues were affecting the inspector's perspective, his ability to focus, to take in all Cornell was saying: the innuendos, the false accusations, if any. It was up to his sergeant to lead. She could sense the difficulties with her inspector as she had experienced troublesome times with a boyfriend who had cheated on her, the same as Josh Costello had done to Sasha.

They hadn't been together long, the inspector and his sergeant, but she had grown fond of the bear of a man. A flawed individual, not always the most astute or diplomatic, but determined not to give in, even when the going was tough. People were lying or distorting the truth, more focused on the present than the past.

Someone had to break soon. Cornell's determination had started to wither, the realisation that his time was finite and his daughter had disappeared long ago.

He had searched for her for seventeen years. The fact that she had died at the hand of another was shocking, but she wouldn't be coming back. The change in the father had become apparent, but he had mentioned bringing others from the United States to find out who had killed her, and they would not be friendly. Into the country, wreak their worst, and out soon after, no one willing to lodge a complaint, no chance of extradition back to Australia to answer for any crimes they might have committed.

The situation was becoming difficult, and the police would be circumvented.

Neither Haddock nor Natalie was any closer to solving the case, and the teams at State Crime Command had exhausted themselves searching databases, trying to find persons who had been out at Pinchgut when Sasha Cornell had disappeared and in the weeks after. And so far, it seemed she had died on the day she disappeared, although it could have been weeks or months afterwards. It was critical to see if that could be pinned down.

Eventually, Cornell had tired, the blustering rhetoric muted, the ancestor regarded as a weak possibility in the significance of Pinchgut.

The inspector and his sergeant set foot on Pinchgut three hours later, courtesy of the Water Police. Leo Hannan, who had discovered the body and the woman's handbag, was with them, as was a crime scene investigator. Josh Costello was present, angry that he had been required to visit the site where Sasha had been found.

Costello's presence was important, not that there was any proof or reason to believe he was involved in Sasha Cornell's disappearance and subsequent death.

Howarth had admitted to a casual relationship with Sasha, but his statement that it would not have necessarily reflected on her fondness, even love, for Costello was insincere.

Haddock would have chosen to have the Olympian hero present, but a phone call to his office resulted in a firm rebuttal.

'Why am I here?' Costello asked. He was dressed casually in shorts, a tee shirt, and trainers on his feet.

'We know when Sasha disappeared; we don't know when she was brought to Pinchgut. It could be months,' Natalie said.

'She carried credit cards.'

'There are no records of them being used after her disappearance.'

'Leo,' Haddock asked, 'you found the body, knew it was her by the handbag. Anything else?'

'Nothing. Gave me nightmares for a couple of weeks.'

'And brief fame,' Natalie said.

'Interviewed on the television a few times, hardly fame and fortune, not that I'd mind,' Hannan replied. He was smartly dressed. Natalie was impressed with his appearance.

'We don't understand the significance of Pinchgut,' Haddock said. 'Quite frankly, we can bang our heads against a wall trying to find a motive other than Sasha Cornell was Bernie's daughter. Burying a body out here was not a random act. There is the historical significance of this place, both native and convict, a few hangings in the late eighteenth and early nineteenth centuries. We know that Bernie and Sasha Cornell can trace their family history back to that time, but so can other people. Leo, any thoughts?'

'None in particular. I was out here to work and found the woman and the handbag. It's opening as a restaurant in a few months. Any likelihood it won't happen?'

'Why the interest?' Natalie asked.

'Selfish, to be honest. If the heat's on to complete the renovations, there's the overtime. I could do with the money, not that I was pleased to find the body. Why am I here? What can you hope to gain from me?'

'Clarity,' Haddock said.

'With what? I found her, nothing more. Not much fun out here working, just a few of us; downright miserable, to be honest.'

'Not much fun for those in irons on short rations or Sasha Cornell,' Haddock said. 'Was she dead when she arrived here?'

'How would I know?'

'You wouldn't. Josh Costello, anything to add?'

'Why me? I'm stuck in Sydney, a wife in New York, and two children missing their father.'

'You're shacked up in a good hotel, playing footsy with your bedtime companion,' Natalie reminded him. 'You've nothing to complain about except for us asking awkward questions.'

'Am I still a suspect? Bernie's riding me hard, believes I know more than I've told you.'

'You do,' Haddock said.

The four stood close to the tower and the room where Sasha had been found.

The crime scene investigator investigated every nook and cranny of the tower.

'I thought you and your people had been thorough the first time,' Haddock said.

'We were.'

'Leo, this handbag, with the body?' Natalie asked. The handbag was inconsistent with the clothes she had worn on the day she had disappeared. That day, she had dressed for jogging and had not carried a handbag.

'It was. I checked, saw her name, and phoned emergency services. Thirty minutes later, everyone is out here.'

'In the handbag? What was there?'

'A driving licence, a credit card, some cash, not much more.'

'Is that what she left your apartment with?' Natalie asked Costello.

'She would have had a phone strapped to her arm, ten dollars for coffee and croissant, and would leave her keys with the concierge.'

'But not a handbag?'

'Not for jogging. Plenty in the apartment, bought them all the time, not much use for jogging.'

'Which means she had a detour from the Horizon to Pinchgut. Which infers her disappearance was arranged.'

'Her death wasn't,' Haddock added. 'And she was playing footsy, to use Sergeant Campbell's analogy, with the great sportsman.'

Natalie registered her inspector's sneering referral to Howarth. Haddock had not liked the man, no doubt mutual from Howarth.

'Leo, what else?' Natalie asked. 'You are obviously keen for money, and Sasha Cornell wasn't short of money. Was there more, a few hundred dollars?'

'No. Only what I gave you.'

'Taking money is a crime, but concealing evidence could end up in a prison cell. If you took the money, there might have been a slip of paper, a business card, something that could give us a date, possibly a name of who she met.'

'Nothing.' Hannan looked flustered; Natalie recognised the signs, the shifting on his feet, the beads of sweat on his forehead. She was sure his hands would be clammy. She also knew he wouldn't speak the truth at Pinchgut.

The visit to Pinchgut had been fruitful in that Hannan was hiding something, and Costello was insistent about the handbag. It did not clear him of involvement, but it lent weight to his innocence.

Chapter 9

Approaching Duncan Howarth without evidence, when he had claimed to have been out of the country when Sasha had died, would have been pointless. The man was well-protected by legal advisers, and any mention publicly that he might have been involved with Sasha Cornell, either by an illicit affair or being implicated in her death, would open the police, namely Inspector Gary Haddock and Sergeant Natalie Campbell, to censure and would hamper the investigation.

Superintendent Payne had been informed and advised by Haddock to keep the information confidential until his sergeant could grill Leo Hannan, who was making himself scarce.

Eventually, Natalie found the man licking his wounds at a pub around the corner from where he lived. 'I was desperate,' he said. 'More than five hundred dollars, and a child on the way, schooling to pay for, and my wife, God bless her, she tries her best and doesn't complain, but it's up to me to do better, to get another job.'

'Why don't you?' Natalie asked.

'Construction is what I'm good at. No point putting me in an office, dyslexic, mild dyscalculia. I can't help it, can't do much about it. Good with my hands but hopeless with money. I give my salary to my wife and let her deal with it. She was a schoolteacher before the children and would rather stay home with them. She's Lebanese by birth and sees it as her duty to protect our children from what's happening in society, but she has to get a part-time job.'

Natalie could sympathise. Life was tough and not getting any easier, but interfering with a crime scene was an offence, and he was guilty. Initially seen in a good light by Haddock and Natalie, his crown had slipped. She should charge him but did not intend to. The money was important, and whatever else had been in the handbag.

'The money?' Have you got it?'

'In a drawer at home, untouched. My wife doesn't know. I knew I was wrong taking it, unsure what to do afterwards.'

'Anything else?'

'I put it in my pocket and then in the drawer. I didn't look too closely, only that there were five hundred dollars and some cards.'

'I need them,' Natalie said.

A visit to Hannan's home, a shouting match between husband and wife, the money and whatever else in an evidence bag on the way to Forensics with Natalie.

***

Natalie realised that the happy house that Hannan had said there was, apart from his concerns about money, was invalid. It wasn't her concern; what he had given her was.

The evidence bag was checked in at Forensics, coded, and a label was attached. Due to the urgency, Natalie intended to stay with it as one of the forensic scientists opened the bag and went through the contents.

Natalie had phoned Haddock, who informed him that Payne had updated the father with the privileged information, even though the superintendent had been told that Cornell had inferred that he had heavies in the USA, suitcases packed, ready to fly out at the first instance and pressure those regarded as suspicious.

Natalie realised that if Bernie Cornell put two and two together and did not come up with four, but with Duncan Howarth, it did not bode well for the sporting hero. He might have the protection of the law in Australia, but heavies, a euphemism for criminals who hit first and ask questions later, would not be deterred by the law, not if Cornell was willing to whisk them into the country and out again.

The realisation that Cornell saw himself above the law wasn't the shock that it should have been, as the man had a history of pushing the envelope, the reason for his success.

'Four hundred and twenty-seven dollars in notes, a couple of business cards,' the forensic scientist said.

'Fingerprints?' Natalie asked, although she knew the answer.

'Unlikely, not after so many years. We'll conduct further tests and see what we come up with, but don't believe there's much more we'll be able to give you.'

'The notes? New or used?'

'I can run the numbers through a database, see where they were first issued from, might help.'

Natalie rarely used cash; a debit card scanned on a machine sufficed most times, and cash was on the way out, another five years, so she had read. But in the past, freshly printed notes were dispatched to banks for use, which would give a location, not necessarily the person who received them. A long shot, hardly worth bothering, but she would let Forensics try.

As for her, she had two business cards; the name on one she knew, the other she didn't, but she would find out.

At Rose Bay Marina, a light lunch for both at the Boathouse restaurant, Natalie met for the second time with Beth Madison.

'I knew too much, spent time with the man, knew he wasn't above board, mining licences granted, a hefty donation to his political cause or his back pocket,' Beth Madison said.

'Anyone with half a brain realises that politics is about ego, self-aggrandisement, and wealth creation,' Natalie replied.

'He took it to an art form.'

Natalie could see the woman wasn't a drinker, and two glasses of wine had loosened her tongue. What three would do, was anyone's guess, but Natalie was determined to find out.

Clearly, Ralph Davidson had been involved in activities not included in the politicians' code of ethics. Natalie was unsure if a code was defined but thought there would be one. She knew what a politician should do, elected by his constituents for the good of the electorate and country. Although, once they had their snout in the trough, most forgot. In the small town where her parents still lived, their local member of parliament had forgotten. He rarely visited the electorate he had sworn to represent, but ensuring he'd be there at re-election with a new school, an additional wing to the hospital, a new bypass, special treatment for the elderly, the disadvantaged, the forestry industry, mining, whatever. Once re-elected, some promises were met, some diluted, and others were forgotten.

'How?' Natalie asked after she had topped up the other woman's glass.

'He did his job, can't blame him for that, nor dumping me.'

'Were you in love?'

'With the man, no. But, prime minister, powerful; a great orator, able to convince those he met that he was competent and cared for them and their needs.'

'Did he?'

'Good enough to get me into his bed.'

'And keep you there.'

'Strange, brought up strait-laced, clung to my virginity until I was twenty-four, and there I am, doing my bit for Australia by keeping their leader satisfied. He was and still is a good person. He did a lot for Australia, a lot for himself. A mining lease in Queensland, he ensured the environmental issues went away. Not that I criticised him. Protecting an endangered butterfly or small rodent or marsupial, holding back because of the risk of destruction of a historically significant part of Australia, was overdone back then and worse now.

'It's an issue around here when selling real estate. I know of a couple of properties – an aboriginal carving on a rock in the back garden. Nobody talks about it, death knell if the heritage society gets to know; any extensions to the building, renovations, doubly difficult to get through.'

'I assume you don't tell; if there's an issue, money makes it disappear.'

'Not bribes, too obvious, but sharp legal minds. Costly, though; better not to run into the problem.'

'The mining lease?' Natalie reminded Beth.

'A lot of employment and money into the local community. Ralph received a donation for services rendered.'

'A bribe?'

'Donation to his political party, financial assistance at the next election.'

'Nothing strictly illegal.'

'Ralph bought another house, much bigger than the previous, got it cheap from the owners, offshore, hiding out in the Cayman Islands.'

'The mining entrepreneur?'

'Unprovable, but yes. He admitted that to me one night over the pillow.'

'Even so, unprovable. You were not a threat, purely innuendo if it was used by you or Sasha Cornell.'

'Damning. Gain points for a mistress, but corruption is different and mud sticks. Soon enough, the opposition would be looking hard and finding.'

'And you were willing to tell Sasha Cornell this and to let her run with it?'

'I had proof, something I found the last time I was with him. Enough for her to run with, although I don't know why. She was part of the elite, and her father would have known Ralph.'

'Even so, he might use it to his advantage, leverage over Ralph. You realise this could be a motive for her disappearance?'

'I did at the time.'

'Why not now?'

'Back then, young, impressionable, a foolish notion that he cared for me above all others.'

'And now you know differently?'

'Not totally. You need to hold on to idealism, but I would not allow it to cloud my reasoning or impact my family. You can report what I've said here today but don't believe I will corroborate. This is off the record.'

'Nothing is off the record, not when there's a murder,' Natalie said.

***

The probability that Beth Madison had revealed a solid motive for Sasha Cornell's disappearance and subsequent murder brought new focus to the investigation.

The problem with talking to Bernie Cornell about Ralph Davidson was that the two men would have known each other and possibly done deals, some above board, others of a dubious nature.

Duncan Howarth was in Cornell's firing line, and Beth Madison could be soon, as could Ralph Davidson. Beth was protected due to being female and Bernie's old-fashioned chivalry. Davidson had influence; any action against him would generate a probable negative response, and as a former prime minister of Australia, he had security, both visible and hidden. ASIO, the Australian Security Intelligence Organisation, would rally to his side if needed.

Davidson was a popular figure, and if Beth Madison had continued with her testimony, assisted by the capable Sasha Cornell, and had brought disrepute to the man, then cronyism and corruption could have led to a media enquiry. It was the most significant reason to silence Sasha. And Beth, with no support mechanism, had accepted the status quo and, in time, faded into the scenery, then been resurrected as a successful woman, the wife of a successful man. Whether he knew of his wife's earlier clandestine relationship was unknown.

Haddock's take on it was to continue investigating Davidson; to see if there was truth in a mining lease being given preferential treatment. Superintendent Payne's advice was cautionary. 'Kid gloves on this one. Do not contact Davidson until you have got something tangible. Politicians always play the long game, look after each other.'

Haddock knew what he meant. Feathering the nest went across the political divide, the reason some politicians lived high on the hog, way above their salary, more than happy to state in public that if they were not a politician, they would have been a senior executive in private enterprise, earning a substantially higher salary.

Haddock, who considered himself a reasonable man, realised that some might have done well outside of politics, but others would have barely made a minimum salary.

However, Davidson was astute and competent as prime minister, even if Haddock had not voted for him.

'Still doesn't explain Pinchgut,' Superintendent Payne said.

It was his office, seven in the evening. Haddock sat on a hard chair; Natalie's was more comfortable. Off the record, a run through the case so far. The superintendent was a sociable man. 'Help yourself to coffee or tea,' he said, pointing to a coffee machine and a kettle on the other side of the room. 'Or would you prefer something else?'

Haddock knew the man liked a drink. 'A beer if you've got it,' he said.

'I have. Sergeant Campbell?'

'A beer would be fine,' Natalie said.

'Very well, what do we have?' Payne said after the three had settled down, each with a can in their hand.

'A motive,' Natalie said.

'Unprovable,' Payne replied, 'and likely to stay so until you make the connection to an old fort in the middle of Sydney Harbour. Any of those you suspect might have a connection to the place? A relative who spent time there, and remember there were military personnel there at various times in its history.'

'So far, nothing,' Haddock replied. 'Although we're not keen on Bernie Cornell's involvement, and Howarth hides behind his lawyers.'

'And Cornell's threatening to take direct action.'

'Do we let it happen? Turn a blind eye?'

'No, we can't let that happen. What else? What about Costello? The man was playing around with another woman. He could have been tired of Sasha, seen a way to be rid of her, and still maintain a relationship with her father.'

'It's an angle, but we can't prove it.'

'The idiot that tried to kidnap Sergeant Campbell?'

'Too young, local idiot, known to the police as a troublemaker. In custody now, pending trial. No doubt claim he's intellectually challenged or mentally disturbed, one year somewhere with psychiatric counselling and then on the street,' Natalie said.

'Probably. Howarth confirmed he was having an affair with Sasha Cornell?'

'Infrequent, according to him, and they weren't seeing each other when she was murdered. He was overseas at the time of her death.'

'Which hasn't been confirmed. I thought there were two business cards in the handbag. What about the other?'

'Terrence Underwood. A photographer she used. So far, we've not been able to find him.'

'Where is he?'

'Overseas. We found proof he had flown to Europe but never returned. His boyfriend said he emptied their bank accounts, never seen to this day.'

'Suspicious?' Payne asked.

'It's an angle, but the two were filming gay porn, selling it on the black market.'

'They could have set up a website and put it on the internet.'

'Not their movies, too many young faces. The usual disclaimer that all models were over eighteen and consenting adults.'

'But you don't believe they were.'

'The boyfriend, Gustav Ingesson, was arrested with Underwood. They served five years for their crimes, the depraved nature of the movies, not underage actors. Subsequently, Ingesson set up a gym in Brisbane,' Haddock said.

'No contact with Underwood?'

'Bitchy on the phone, when I spoke to him, said there hadn't been,' Natalie said.

'I watched one of their earlier productions,' Natalie said. 'This was not your usual boy meets boy. Felt like throwing up.'

'Are you convinced he left the country due to their film career?' Payne asked.

'He left Australia and returned to the UK after serving time. If Underwood could make those movies, it would prove he had few scruples. We're looking for him; he could be anywhere.'

'You've questioned Ingesson?'

'On the phone; flight to Brisbane, once approved,' Natalie said.

'It's approved,' Payne replied. 'Get up there, give him the heavy treatment, scare him if you must. Psychopath? This guy or Underwood?'

'Not possible for us to know. It would need Ruth Stein to spend time with Ingesson. She's available,' Natalie said.

'Take her. She stays there until she's got an answer for us. Any possibility this pervert is breaking the law?'

'Under suspicion for selling under-the-counter steroids.'

'A good enough reason to pull him in, forty-eight hours for you and Stein to get answers. We need Underwood, and we need him now. Another beer?'

'I wouldn't say no,' Haddock said.

Natalie held up her can, another beer for her.

Chapter 10

On Bronte Road, Waverley, a fifteen-minute drive from Kings Cross Police Station, a twelve-minute drive from Bondi Beach, Peter Evershed, agitator, rent-a-crowd, professional idiot, stood before the magistrate at Waverley Court House to answer the charge of attempted kidnapping.

The flight to Brisbane had left without Natalie. A court case where she would give evidence took precedence. Inspector Haddock and Ruth Stein had caught the 8 a.m. flight, the woman complaining as she boarded.

Natalie knew the woman was one of those apparently perpetually busy, always rushing here and there, pretending to be occupied when she was not. Natalie had checked, not that it altered the fact that a directive from Superintendent Payne was not a request but an order. Ruth Stein had four days free of lectures, no appointments slated for her private practice, and a trip to Brisbane, all expenses paid, was something that most people would have accepted graciously. However, the woman was experienced, and time was to be spent with Gustav Ingesson, who had been informed that he was to report to Brisbane City Police Station at 10.30 a.m. to assist in the ongoing investigation into the disappearance and subsequent murder of Sasha Cornell.

At Waverley Court House, Natalie realised she was in for a long day. She had bought herself a coffee outside the courthouse and sat on a hard bench, waiting to be called. She arrived at eight-forty in the morning, hopeful the trial would conclude within the day. After all, Evershed was clearly bizarre, if not certifiable. However, she did not know that Steven Pickett, the formidable advocate of civil liberties and a first-class lawyer, would defend until five minutes later when the man walked past her.

Evershed, misunderstood, destroyed by a dysfunctional childhood, on the autism spectrum, with an above-average IQ, was not responsible for his actions, and the bruising he received from Sergeant Natalie Campbell must be considered a clear sign of police brutality.

Natalie knew she didn't have a chance in the witness box with Pickett defending and Gallagher, the state prosecutor, arguing the case for the man's guilt.

'As wet as water,' Haddock had said about Gallagher once when he and Natalie had sat down in State Crime Command, chewing the fat, talking about this and that; crimes they had known, criminals they should have arrested, lawyers who believe they are smart but aren't, and lawyers who are. And two of those mentioned were in the court, standing before Judge Amanda Jeffreys, in her fifties, shrewd and severe. A woman to admire if you were proven innocent, to fear if found guilty. Out at Long Bay Prison, one of the prisoners had termed her 'the hanging judge', after a notorious judge with the same name in seventeenth-century England, known for his predilection for the convicted felon hanging from a rope instead of rotting in a prison cell.

Inside the court, the prosecution put forward the case that Evershed was a habitual troublemaker, had issues with authority and had known that the woman jogging was a police officer.

If Natalie had been in the court instead of going stir-crazy outside, surfing the internet on her phone and attempting to write a report on her laptop, she would have wanted to know how Evershed knew who she was. Her jogs had been spontaneous, an attempt to understand how Sasha Cornell could have disappeared and why hadn't anyone seen her. After all, it was daylight when she had left the Horizon building, and there were people on the street, cars driving up and down. Yet no one had seen her grabbed and thrown into the back of a car, the vehicle hurtling down the road, screeching around a corner, running a traffic light, typical when a crime had been committed.

Gallagher's opening speech lasted for twenty-five minutes. Pickett spoke for thirty-six, the jury stunned by his eloquence. He wove a tale that the man's actions had been misunderstood, and his bluntness in approaching the woman jogging resulted from a hangover compounded by frequent drug abuse, a confusion of reality with fiction.

Judging by the number of character witnesses called, Natalie correctly assumed it would be two or three days before the trial concluded. Although how Evershed had an expensive lawyer who charged upwards of two hundred dollars an hour, and Natalie assumed Pickett was closer to five hundred dollars, confused her. That question was answered that night when she researched Evershed's family and discovered they were wealthy and living in the country. They had no association with the son but ensured he had a place to live, the best medical care if he took it, and the best lawyer to defend him. To Natalie, tough love would have helped the man more. Still, it wasn't her concern, and on the second day at the courthouse, she was in the witness box.

The defence asked her to explain why she was jogging at an early hour. The investigation into Sasha Cornell's death was still in the public arena. She would say as much as she could, careful not to hamper that case while addressing Evershed's.

'I was trying to understand Sasha Cornell's movements on the day she disappeared,' Natalie said when questioned by Pickett.

'Is that customary?' he asked.

Natalie felt like saying, it's a murder investigation, and that's a dumb question, but instead, she said, 'Retracing a person's movements on the day they disappeared and were subsequently murdered is standard police practice.'

'And you're no closer to solving that case?'

Gallagher was on his feet. 'The defence is leading the witness. We do not expect Sergeant Campbell to discuss a current investigation.'

'Defence will keep their questions relevant to this trial,' Judge Jeffreys said.

Rephrasing his question, Pickett spoke again. 'There has been a lot of media coverage over the discovery of a woman's body on Pinchgut.'

'That is correct,' Natalie replied.

'And it was known that the woman was an avid jogger, that most days she would go for an early morning jog, up from the Horizon building, around the area, down to Elizabeth Bay, and on her return, she would stop at a coffee shop near to where she lived.'

'Those who lived in the area and knew the woman would be aware of that.'

'As my client does not live nearby, it is mere speculation that he was re-enacting an earlier crime.'

'He referred to Sasha Cornell. Someone must have put him up to it if he did not live locally.'

'My client may have marks against him, but he is neither a kidnapper nor a murderer. Also, he would have been too young to have committed the crime. And why do you believe, as he did, and others in the area, that she was kidnapped on Forbes Street in Darlinghurst?'

'By others, I assume you're referring to local residents, business owners, and their staff.'

'I am,' Pickett said.

'From the Horizon building, up to the roundabout on the intersection of Liverpool Street, and then up to Darlinghurst Road, were possibilities speculated about by Inspector Haddock and myself. We have not, to my recollection, told others of this. It was just that the streets I mentioned represent the best places for an abduction.

'We regarded Mr Evershed as an opportunist, deluded by the possibility of fame and notoriety. Kidnapping a female police officer would give him credibility on social media and with anarchists.'

'Objection,' Pickett said. 'It is not for the witness to disparage my client.'

'Strike Sergeant Campbell's last two sentences,' the judge said.

Natalie could see the case dragging, and she was anxious to get up to Brisbane, where Haddock and Ruth Stein were spending time with Gustav Ingesson, former lover of Terrence Underwood, camera operator on the gay porn they had been producing, and, subsequently discovered after Natalie and Haddock had watched one of the movies, one of the lead actors.

Natalie was frustrated with the procrastination, annoyed that a nonentity with psychological issues was interfering with the investigation into the murder of Sasha Cornell.

That night, she phoned Haddock and got an update on what they had gained from Ingesson, a man who acted cool under questioning and apparently regarded producing porn as a fundamental right, and if idiots wanted to take steroids, it wasn't his concern.

Haddock knew there were enough idiots, and policing took time and resources and irritated everyone who had to deal with the aftermath.

One of the detectives in Brisbane admitted the case against Ingesson was weak and that under-the-counter steroids did not figure high on their list of crimes. There was, he said, an outbreak of lawlessness fuelled by social media, everyone an expert on crime, and a view that the police were wasters, out to impose their brutal force on a benign population.

Haddock had to agree, as in Sydney, especially out west, the respect that the police once had had diminished, and in certain suburbs, the police moved in groups. Although the excesses prevalent overseas had not reached Australia yet, it remained one of the safest countries in the world.

Natalie sat in her apartment that night with a glass of wine at her side, which she realised was a substitute for a man in her life. Too much work, disappointment in her choice of mate, and inability to compromise.

On the phone, Haddock stated that Terrence Underwood was important in that he had known the dead woman. He had been Ingesson's lover, and they had shared an apartment and a thriving gay porn production facility, albeit it was their apartment and an occasional hotel room if they could, or a location close to the beach or in one of the national parks. Haddock admitted that he was sickened by the two men and that Ingesson was a leech who should be squashed underfoot. Also, twenty-three more movies from a collection had been found at Ingesson's apartment in Brisbane.

Natalie knew she should watch some of them, not out of voyeuristic intent, but to gain an insight into Ingesson's and Underwood's depravity. 'Send me five,' she said.

'If you're up to it,' Haddock said.

'I'm not, but Stein's not a trained police officer. She will focus on the participants' mental state, whether it is depraved or an expression of love.'

'Hardly love.'

'Who knows,' Natalie said. 'Whatever rocks your boat. But if some had been coerced, they might have insights into the two men, whether they are capable of murder and involved with Sasha Cornell. Bisexual, who knows, could they have slept with her? We know she was living with one man, having an on-again, off-again affair with another.'

Frustrated that she was in Sydney and the action was a one-hour flight to the north in Brisbane, Queensland's capital city. For her, Evershed was a nonentity, harmful if psychotic or radicalised by a fringe group on the internet. Her time wasted at the Waverley Court House, she was unsure how she could get out of her attendance every day.

Superintendent Payne was sympathetic when she phoned, regardless of her concern. Despite Victoria Adderley's warning, he hadn't put the hard word on her. In fact, nobody had, apart from Jimmy Rogers, who she had forgiven for the red herring in the murder case of Mary Otway, stating that he had proof positive that the homeless Joe Coster had been Mary's former lover, then admitting that the match was almost certain, but not good enough for a trial.

He had apologised profusely, admitted his admiration for her, and could they be more than friends. Although, compared to others, he had remained polite and taken no for an answer. She could see that he was in love with her, but she was not with him.

***

'Inspector Haddock, I can't help you more. It was a long time ago, an eternity,' Ingesson said.

It was the second day of questioning, and Ingesson had returned to the police station with no court order or handcuffs. Ruth Stein was inclined to give the man the benefit of the doubt, but Haddock, cynical and jaundiced, could not.

'Seventeen years,' Haddock reminded the man. 'You are in your apartment with Underwood, a camera in hand, producing sick movies, and you say you can't remember back to that period.'

'I spent five years in prison.'

'Must have been a breeze for you, all those men.'

'When you have a choice, but not in Long Bay. Men deprived of women hate you for what they do to you. Beaten up more than once for their sins.'

'You could have reported it.'

'Could I? You've put more than a few in prison. Any idea of what goes on in there?'

Haddock had to admit he hadn't, not fully, not sure that he cared. He had an inkling of it and had heard enough stories, but what happened in prison wasn't his concern. Even so, Ingesson had to give more than platitudes.

'Judging by the videos, you're a man of few morals.'

'And you don't have an issue watching porn?'

Answers were what Haddock wanted, not a discussion. One of the local officers called Haddock out of the room. 'Steroids, can't charge him, no witnesses to testify that he was selling them. No crime against Ingesson, not in Brisbane.'

It made little difference to Haddock, who was focused on a woman's death seventeen years before.

Ruth Stein felt her time was wasted in Brisbane and that Gustav Ingesson was mentally balanced, apart from his former acting career and movie making. Haddock disputed, but she made it clear. 'Homosexual, promiscuous, doesn't believe he did anything wrong in producing movies, but understood that it was criminal if caught.'

'Coercing young men to appear?'

'It depends on your definition. He moved freely within the gay community on Oxford Street, where excess was expected. The young men, upset by what had happened? Did they suffer mental trauma?'

'Not my case, before my time, and I was out in the Western Suburbs.'

'You read the case reports.'

'I did. The young men gave their evidence, said they had no issue with the videos and had received payment.'

'But Ingesson was found guilty, served his time, abused in prison, released, and got on with his life. Regardless, I believe Ingesson, although reprehensible, does not show any signs I would regard as deviant or malicious, and he has no anger issues.'

'Your movies were sick,' Haddock said when the interview recommenced.

'To you. Rose-coloured glasses will not do you any good. I've no guilt with what we did. Saw it as art, gay art if you like, but still art.'

'You were sentenced to prison.'

'Subjective. To us, it was a profitable business, risqué, illegal in part.'

'Is that what goes on? In those clubs of yours?'

'Sometimes, social. Other times, there are shows, and those performing don't hold back. We were sentenced on a technicality.'

It was not a technicality but a crime. And in the intervening years, society had become more liberal, awash with pornography.

Ruth Stein found an innate charm in Ingesson; Haddock did not. To him, he represented the worst of society, although he had to recognise that as the father of an impressionable teenage daughter, he would consider that too much permissiveness was unhealthy.

Following Superintendent Payne's intervention, a higher pay scale for Haddock had allowed him and his wife to keep the family home, his daughter was at the school her mother thought important, and the anger between her and the mother had abated.

Haddock suspected his wife might have a casual lover, which disturbed him more than he thought it should. As for his infidelity, it was a relationship in decline, and he had not seen the woman for some time. Once or twice a week, he spent the night at the family home, a room at the back of the garage, once a tool shed, now painted and habitable with a single bed.

He had considered moving back full-time, but not yet, wait and see if it was a workable solution.

Haddock was surprised he was repulsed by Ingesson and the movies he and Underwood produced. They upset him more than he thought they should. He realised that Ruth Stein could explain why, but he had confidence in her education and expertise, not in the results she put forward. In a previous case, she had identified anger issues with a young woman but missed the clues with a young man who had killed another. He knew that, if asked, Ruth Stein could give an answer long on technical, short on factual.

He would have preferred his sergeant, Natalie Campbell, with him. He knew he had taken her under his wing and that her star ascended while his stagnated.

How long before she became an inspector, possibly a chief inspector? Even though he greatly admired her, he had never felt a physical attraction, although not uncommon when two people worked together, experienced traumatic situations, saw violated bodies, and dealt with malevolent psychopathic individuals.

But with the two of them, a professional relationship. Symbiotic, Natalie would have said, but Haddock, not as sophisticated, would have disparaged that analogy.

Even so, one more time with Ingesson would not be time wasted. Hit the man hard, attempt to break through. He looked at the clock by the side of the bed; it was two thirty in the morning. His occasional lover would be asleep, but it wasn't her that he wanted to phone.

'Yes, who is it?' a half-asleep woman said.

'Just checking. In Brisbane, not going well. Thought I'd like to hear a cheery voice,' Haddock replied. He felt composed and relaxed, as though he was talking to the one person who gave him sanity, if not love. That emotion eluded them both now, too much water under the bridge, too many harsh words spoken.

'Come around when you're back. Too late to talk now. Our daughter is fine, thinks she's in love; too young, but what can I say, sixteen in a week, her friends coming over for a party.'

Haddock knew what parties were at sixteen, as he had been there, done that, and then there had been a previous case, the death of Maria Sidorov, fifteen years of age and sexually active. He hoped his daughter would not need to give herself to a spotty individual from a school in the area, but he knew the odds were against him.

'I'd like that, maybe make a night of it, go out for a meal.'

'If you like. Stay the night in the spare room. Since we're separated, we don't want to give our daughter the wrong impression. I withdrew the papers yesterday; no longer necessary to divide the assets. Better for all of us.'

The phone went dead, and his wife went back to sleep. He knew he would sleep easy even though he had to be out of bed by seven that morning.

Chapter 11

Another day at Waverley Court, a disinterested Peter Evershed in the dock, unconcerned about his guilt or otherwise. Natalie could see his glazed eyes, the gentle shaking of his hands, and signs of sweating – the man was high on a recreational drug. No mention was made of it by either the two barristers or the judge, oblivious to the fact, disinterested as she was, or because his fate had already been predetermined, a penalty agreed in the judge's room.

If that was the case, there was still time for her to fly up to Brisbane to give Haddock the support he needed.

Two hours later, at ten minutes after eleven in the morning, a judgement that Peter Evershed was to be confined to a psychiatric facility where more tests would be conducted, a determination to be made as to treatment, medication, an evaluation of his drug addiction and what troubled him. Release to be determined at a time in the future.

Suitably worded, with windbag excess, Natalie knew that bureaucracy had interfered yet again. She had observed the man and seen that behind the charade of the hopeless and addicted, there was a shrewd mind. It was addled at times by drugs and mental psychosis, but nonetheless, a person in more control of his faculties than the prosecution mentioned or the defence needed to debate.

Natalie thought the man needed a swift kick up the rear end and twelve months in prison. He was to receive neither.

It was just after midday when the flight lifted off from Kingsford Smith Airport, another ninety minutes before she was at the police station in Brisbane.

After Evershed, she found Ingesson refreshing. The man was polite, attentive, and attractive, even if he did sell steroids from under the counter and had produced and starred in adult movies.

'Pleased to meet you, Sergeant,' Ingesson said.

In the interview room, three people sat. Ruth Stein was returning to Sydney, another conference to attend, or was it lecturing. Natalie could not keep up with the woman's hectic schedule and didn't care much either. As for Haddock, his mood improved immeasurably on his sergeant's arrival, and he had told her about going to the family home on his return, and the divorce was not proceeding.

Natalie was sure it was a temporary lull as a leopard can no more change its spots than Inspector Haddock could his.

'Likewise,' Natalie replied. 'Inspector Haddock kept you busy?'

'Too much.'

Haddock sat back, appreciative of fresh blood and a fresh mind to question Ingesson.

'Terrence Underwood?' Natalie asked.

'England, the last I heard, although that was more than a few years ago, no idea what he's doing now.'

Neither officer believed him, but Natalie let it pass.

'Sasha Cornell? What do you remember of her?'

'We were friendly with her, enjoyed her company, sometimes met at a pub in Kings Cross for a few drinks, nothing more.'

'Josh Costello?'

'We used to speak to him, but it wasn't the same as with Sasha; standoffish, he looked down his nose at us.'

'Because of the movies you were making? Did he know? Did Sasha?'

'Sasha did. And yes, before you ask, as Inspector Haddock has, we knew about her and Howarth.'

'How?'

'We saw him once with her, somewhere in town, discreet, hiding out in the corner of a restaurant. No idea if Costello knew, and we were not about to spill the beans. She knew about us; we knew about her.'

'Blackmail if you had a hold over her,' Haddock said. He had enjoyed the verbal sparring, his sergeant freed of the restraint of Evershed's trial, speaking plenty and fast, hoping to get Ingesson to contradict himself.

'Not blackmail, mutual confidence. We knew about her and Howarth, kept it to ourselves; she knew about our small business.'

'No concerns from her? Criminal back then, still is, unless they are consenting adults. What would the body corporate have done if they had found out?'

'Issued a stern warning, desist or else. Sasha reckoned they were paper tigers, more noise than action. We found a place not far away, more of a garage than a studio, but deck it out with lights and furnishings, and nobody would realise the difference. Anyway, who was looking at the scenery?'

'I would have been,' Haddock said.

'Not for you?'

'Not for my sergeant or me, but you've served your time, no reason to mention it further, only it was around the time Sasha died, and she's what concerns us, and I don't believe you're telling us the whole truth.'

'I'm not,' Ingesson admitted.

'What is the truth?' Natalie asked.

'Ten minutes, take a breather,' Ingesson said. 'Okay, by you?'

'It is,' Haddock replied.

For a man who had served time in prison for producing and distributing extreme pornographic movies, his relationship with Natalie and Haddock was remarkably cordial. Haddock had even warmed to the man, but not the videos he had produced. Haddock knew why – the chance to spend time with his wife and their daughter. His marriage had been torn asunder by his infidelity with Theresa de Klerk, one floor down in Fraud Squad. Steely glances when they passed each other in the building. Natalie knew that Haddock was hopeful of reconciliation with his wife, but she knew that would not happen other than for a short period. Her inspector was a man dedicated to his craft, at his happiest with a juicy murder to solve, and Sasha Cornell's, if not juicy, considering the time since the woman had died, intrigued him more than most.

In the interview room, Ingesson leant forward and laid out further details of his and Underwood's relationship with the dead woman.

'Sasha knew what we were up to, remarkably liberal in her outlook. The business expanded with a website and online sales; we needed a cash injection. We hadn't asked her for money, but we were chatting to her, telling her what we were planning.'

'She helped you financially?' Natalie asked.

'Not with the movies, but the setup costs of another location.'

'Even though it was illegal?'

'It's a grey area, classifying what is restricted and what isn't. We were convicted on a technicality, and we were pushing the envelope, more risqué, and those acting in the movies were over the age of eighteen, mentally astute enough to know what they were consenting to, and we did not coerce, get them drunk or drugged.'

'The prosecution alleged that you did,' Haddock asked.

'Society was prejudiced, especially towards the more extreme, and we were. The judge was a lay preacher, the prosecuting barrister was a devout Christian, and the defence was hopeless. In the end, a plea deal from both of us, serve our time, Terrence deported at the end of his sentence, and, as for me, I would refrain from movie making.'

'You agreed?'

'No option but to.'

'Sasha?'

'She had gone missing before then. We didn't pay her back, could have if we had known where she was.'

'You could have contacted her father, explained that she had lent money and you wanted to honour the debt.'

'Sasha told us about her father. That was enough for us. Who knows what his reaction would have been if he had known that Sasha had given us money. A man that powerful, we could have been charged with additional crimes, and what do you expect he would have thought? His daughter was missing, lending money to queers, making the vilest videos imaginable. Our business might be construed as a motive for murder. Our lives were more precious than that, a risk we could not take.'

'Even so, he probably knew, eyes and ears in every corner. What protected you?' Natalie said.

Both officers realised Ingesson had made a succinct statement. The production of gay porn, even if Ingesson and Underwood appeared benign, must, in Australia and overseas, attract nefarious persons, the most criminal, the cruellest, the most callous. In short, people who would kill to protect their lifestyle, money, and, more importantly, their freedom.

Another thing was to find Ingesson's former lover and movie maker, Terrence Underwood. Corroboration, additional evidence, and was either of the two men implicated in the woman's death? The third that they postulated was the most concerning but would not be resolved in Brisbane, in a police station with an agreeable man who was a convicted criminal. Still was, but it could not be proved. They needed a third party to confirm if the production of gay pornography could result in a woman's death. They knew the answer; it was highly probable, but the leads would have dried up after so many years, and those guilty could also be dead.

In Sydney, a belligerent man, even though old and infirm, sat in his wheelchair. Standing up and taking the tirade was Superintendent Payne, attempting to defuse the man's wrath, informing him of developments, and giving a progress report.

When he was younger, Cornell's response would have been to march the offending person out of the building, two security guards, one to each side. But now, the man looked as though he was death warmed up.

Payne could see that the man was weakening, even in the weeks since his daughter had been found. Payne thought two months, possibly three, but no more before his death.

'I want to go where she was found,' Cornell said.

'We've been thorough out there, combed the place with extra diligence, and our best two police officers up in Brisbane at this time,' Payne said.

'Talking to that little queer, Ingesson.'

'You knew?'

'Knew what? Five years in prison, my daughter staking him and Underwood money. Always a sucker for a hard-luck case.'

'Hardly hard luck,' Payne counteracted. 'The men were making six figures a month.'

'What about the overheads? Who was dealing with the distribution? Sure, they were online or selling through the gay network but what about the backhanders, politicians, and every other low-life. Everyone is after a handout when dealing with the grubby side of life.'

Payne thought to say, as you well know, but desisted. Cornell had skirted legality on many occasions and avoided tax on others, but he had power and influence, whereas Ingesson and Underwood did not. Could it be, Payne thought, that Sasha Cornell was interacting with the two men behind the scenes while, in the shadows, the father creamed money off the top? To Cornell, making money, no matter how paltry, was a game he enjoyed, and if on the shady side, so much the better.

***

Gustav Ingesson's clarification that Sasha Cornell not only knew of their artistic venture but financed it gave concern. Dealing in the murky world of pornography was one thing, but Ingesson and Terrence Underwood had filmed, starred, and committed increasingly debased acts with others for the enjoyment or disgust of others. They had the trifecta, and then there was the criminal element overseas or even in Australia. Whenever a lot of money could be made easily, there would be the devious, the criminal, the obnoxious, and those willing to steal, maim, and kill. Sasha Cornell had died but had others?

It was necessary to investigate, but Haddock was not the person to do it. On their return from Brisbane, Natalie sat down with one officer from the Child Abuse and Sex Crimes Squad and one from the Organised Crime Squad.

Ingesson and Underwood had been convicted due to their videos, but no one had investigated the possibility of organised crime, which to Natalie seemed a serious oversight. More likely an easy conviction, as no police officer wanted to spend more time than necessary watching gay pornography or considering other angles that might be important. To her, the investigation and conviction of the two men had been shabby. She had read the case files and extracts from their trials and sentencing.

'It was a lax period in criminal law,' Judy Dowden, from the Child Abuse and Sex Crime Squad, said. She was a tall, slender woman in her fifties, her hair cut short. Not an unattractive woman, Natalie thought.

'In what way?' Natalie asked.

'In theory, any film, game, or publication is subject to classification by the Australian Classification Board.'

'In theory? That indicates that it is not as rigorous as it should be.'

'Not necessarily the Board's fault, but the internet was taking off, and it was easy to transmit videos online or to send a file. Impossible to police, and those involved in pornography are not looking for the stamp of approval, only how fast they could churn it out. Ingesson and Underwood came to our notice when we were sent some of their videos. Concerns about underage, coerced, but they could not be proved. Eventually charged and convicted due to their distribution at clubs in Sydney. A new government aiming to deal with the upsurge in violent and debased movies produced in Australia. It did not last long. I wouldn't be able to charge them today.'

'Any more against Ingesson and Underwood?'

'I would have thought that was enough,' a shortish man in his late thirties said. He was dressed in a dark suit and a tie with an emblem that showed club membership or his old school. He spoke with a slight lisp, his head to one side. Natalie realised she should not be prejudiced against the man because of his minor infirmities, but instinctively she knew she could not trust him. His name was Bryan Beck, one of the junior members of the Organised Crime Squad, Natalie assumed and later found to be correct.

'Any links to organised crime?' Natalie asked.

'Organised crime and pornography, linked probably, hard to prove.'

'Why?'

'Online, very little is a hard copy. Apart from the location for the shoot, the editing, distribution, and packaging, if there is any, can be done anywhere in the world.'

'Seventeen years ago?'

'Not as sophisticated, slower, more labour intensive, but it was mostly online, not streaming live, and the video quality wasn't as good.'

'Any records linking back to that period?'

'Records, yes, but not against the two people you are interested in. In the scheme of things, they were minor players. The consent forms had been correctly filled out and signed, proof that the participants were there of their free will and were over the age of consent. Their conviction was a farce and should have been thrown out. Prejudiced judge, prejudiced barristers, and society was looking for scapegoats.'

Chapter 12

Terrence Underwood was found with the assistance of the London Metropolitan Police. No longer using the name of Underwood, he had spent time in prison in England, three years and three months, for fraud. Haddock and Natalie had spoken to him on video conference.

'Got caught, not that they couldn't afford it,' Underwood said. The two officers saw him as attractive as Ingesson but not as charming.

'Your crimes in England aren't our concern, can't help you there,' Haddock said.

'We met with Gustav Ingesson,' Natalie said.

'I've had no contact with him for a long time. Is this about Sasha?' Underwood asked.

He appeared nervous.

'It is. What do you know about her body being found?'

'Not a lot. Fill me in. I liked her, helped us out, and then she disappeared. Even if I wanted to help you, which I don't, there's not much I can tell you.'

'Why are you talking to us if you're that hostile?'

'For Sasha, nobody else. She did not criticise us and helped financially. She deserves better than being buried at Pinchgut. Any idea why they chose a fort on an island in Sydney Harbour?'

'That's the dilemma. It must be important, easier to have tied concrete blocks to her and over the side of a boat, never found.'

'Pure chance she was found at Pinchgut, from what little I know of the case,' Underwood said.

'We've seen the videos you made, not impressed,' Haddock said. He judged Underwood not to be a man to appreciate platitudes. An interview conducted honestly by both sides was preferable to skirting the issues.

'The audience was highly focused. We might have been guilty of bad taste, depraved, depending on your moral standpoint, not for what we were convicted of.'

'You made a lot of money,' Natalie reminded Underwood. She was tired of the hypocrisy, aiming to portray himself and Ingesson as humble independent filmmakers, catering to a select audience, fully aware that they were making a lot of money, each subsequent movie more extreme than the previous.

'That wasn't the original intention, more fun at first. But, yes, we made money, which is why Sasha was a godsend.'

'Pinchgut, any thoughts?'

'Visible from where we lived. Sasha knew the history of the place. Her father pressured the government to renovate and open it up again, or maybe it was the midday cannon he was interested in. A long time ago, I couldn't be sure of the details. Her father might know.'

'It's important; think hard,' Natalie said. 'Seventeen years ago, her father is involved with the place. Why might it be important?'

'Can't help you. Sasha was a good person; that's all I know. Ingesson would have told you the same.'

'He did,' Natalie said.

Little had been gained from the interview, and the effort in finding Underwood proved to be wasted.

***

Ingesson and Underwood had been arrested eight months after Sasha Cornell's disappearance, and Haddock and Natalie felt a connection would not be made.

Davidson had a motive if Beth Madison had revealed details to Sasha. Although a more likely target would have been the man's former mistress.

Beth Madison, now respected and living the good life in the Eastern Suburbs, had cooperated with the police and was adamant she would continue to do so. However, she had made the trip to Parramatta instead of meeting with Haddock and Natalie closer to where she lived. Natalie sensed reticence in the woman compared to the last time they had met. The heat of the investigation was starting to get to her, and she did not like it; the veneer she had crafted was threatened by a period of foolishness and easy virtue with a charismatic older man who happened to be the prime minister of Australia at the time.

Beth Madison confirmed it. 'For nearly two decades, he's kept his distance, pretended to be Mr Clean, sat on the boards of a couple of banks, hit the speech-making circuit, done well for himself, but now he's contacted me, asked if I was willing to go along with him, and that he would make it worth my while.'

'Your response?' Haddock asked. The woman was not someone he warmed to. He sensed that behind the exterior was a shallow person, concerned with what others thought of her, not what she had done.

Natalie wasn't fooled either,

'If you're asking, would I be willing to destroy my hard-fought reputation? The answer's not that easy to give.'

'Money a motivator?'

'Not money, malice.'

'Malice?'

'I might have been a silly impressionable woman then, but I thought it would last. Of course, he played me along, told me he would divorce, marry me, a couple of children, a life full of love, where the sun shone day and night.'

'You believed this?' Natalie asked.

'It was good to dream, but he was good at spinning the illusion, the reason he was prime minister for so long. But I soon wised up, went along with it, and enjoyed the ride. And then, one day, he doesn't answer the phone, the next day, an official-looking car outside my house, a man in a black suit, sign for the letter, marked secret on the front.'

'Inside?'

'Ten pages on A4 paper, no name of who sent it or who it was intended for. Not that I needed names. It was him, gently at first, then more insistent that the relationship was over and subject to certain provisos, I would be financially compensated.'

'Did he apologise?'

'I was of use to him once, but then, I wasn't. If not couched in those words, my employment was terminated, but read between the lines; it was clear enough.'

Natalie thought back to her live-in lover. The man's indiscretion was to sleep with another woman. But Davidson had been much worse. A letter terminating the relationship inferred that sexual favours given by the woman were on account for what he had done for her, taken her around the world, ensured she had a good place to live, at his beck and call. Natalie couldn't be sure if she was in love or if it was the good life in exchange for sexual favours.

Haddock, more cynical, knew the truth. Ralph Davidson had seen a vulnerable woman and taken advantage; Beth Madison had seen a mature man, prime minister of Australia, convinced herself that it was love, a means to obviate the obvious, in that she was a bought woman. It had served her well, given her a focus in life, which had driven her to secure a good future for herself and damn the police, Sasha Cornell, Ralph Davidson, and anyone else who got in her way. He saw a person he did not like. He sensed that Natalie saw through the woman, as well.

Beth Madison was a hater, and she had the motive to wish ill of Ralph Davidson, but did that also apply to Sasha Cornell, who, socially, politically, and possibly financially through her father, had a reason to wish ill of the man?

An interesting question arose. Was Sasha Cornell too good to be true? Was there a side to her, conditioned by her father, the pretence of being a good person when she was not? Only one person in Australia could give an unequivocal answer to the question, her father. Neither Natalie nor Haddock had much confidence in an honest reply from the man if the question was posed, but posed it had to be.

Three hours later, after driving from Sydney up to the Blue Mountains, not the luxury of a helicopter this time, the two were ushered into the mansion and taken to a reception room to the left of the main entrance, not the palatial living room they had sat in that first time after the man's daughter had been found at Pinchgut.

'You've spoken to Beth Madison,' Bernie Cornell said. There was a sling around his neck to hold a bandaged arm. He had walked uneasily into the room, supported by two aides. They sat him in a comfy chair close to the open log fire before retreating from the room, almost bowing as they went. To some, the man's influence and wealth marked him above mere mortals.

Not to Haddock, who had little time for bowing and scraping, although Natalie felt intimidated and sensed hostility in the room.

'We have,' Natalie said, hopeful that her dulcet tones would be more palatable to Bernie Cornell's ears than Haddock's laconic Australian drawl. They were not.

'Beth Madison was sleeping with Ralph Davidson. The man pretends to be holier than thou at his book launch, and not far away, a woman cast off for expediency,' Cornell said with fire in his belly, which, according to reports, was his demeanour in his prime. Natalie could have said that she worried for the old man, who was more than likely to have a heart attack, but perceptively she realised he was not a man to have sympathy for, nor would he want it. If Sasha was tarred with the same brush, Beth Madison may have bitten off more than she could chew, and Ralph Davidson, after a tip-off from Beth or a warning from Sasha, could have reacted in any way possible to preserve his dignity, reputation, and freedom.

'It's motive,' Haddock said, realising that the man's temperament would not be calmed by soft voices but might react to the strength of argument.

'What is? Speak up, man. Don't vacillate. If you think Sasha got herself killed because of a supposed exposé on Davidson, say it.'

Natalie was conscious her approach might have been conciliatory, soothing the savage beast before putting forward a hypothesis. She decided to let her inspector run with Cornell.

'Okay, here's a scenario. Davidson's got a few skeletons hidden in the cupboard.'

'More than a few, but carry on. I appreciate a frank and open discussion. If that means criticising my daughter, do it, but keep it factual, no gilding the lily, no understating the obvious.'

Emboldened, Haddock continued. 'Beth Madison is in a mood to dish the dirt on Davidson, let on what she knows, which, considering she's smart and astute, is plenty. But what if she's a pragmatist, knows that Sasha will run with the story, a possible book deal for Beth, and plenty of money for both women.'

'Sasha would have milked it for all it was worth. I would have supported her, not a lot of time for Davidson, too many dodgy deals, backhanders, as corrupt as they come.'

'Would mud have stuck on you, Mr Cornell?' Natalie entered the conversation. She didn't intend to be left out if it was a time for straight talking.

Cornell laughed out loud. He started to cough, which remained unabated until a nurse came in and gave him medicine and five minutes with an oxygen mask.

'Mr Cornell needs to remain calm,' the nurse said before Bernie Cornell signalled for her to leave him with the two police officers.

'Not long to go, maybe three months, maybe a year. I was ready to go before Hannan found Sasha.'

'Now?' Natalie asked.

'I'll see the conclusion of this investigation. Ensure the person responsible is behind bars. After that, I'll accept the inevitable. Sasha's body being found has given me a new lease on life. Morbid, I suppose.'

'Not morbid, understandable.'

'Okay, get back to the facts,' Cornell said. 'Haddock, your theory is that Beth Madison is playing off Sasha against Davidson, seeing who comes up with the best deal?'

'That's where we're heading. And how do you know that we have spoken to the woman?'

'Don't worry, and don't take it personally. I'm following your movements, keeping myself up to date on where you are, what you're doing, and more importantly, who you speak to.'

'Then you know about Ingesson and Underwood.'

'I do. Conclude with the woman first.'

'Beth Madison speaks to Sasha. Probably sour grapes at first, but Sasha's enthusiastic and can see a lot of money. Beth wants money, and her primary source has kicked her out. She takes in what Sasha can do for her, a phone call to Davidson, updates him and waits for his response.

'Davidson, if he agreed to pay her off, would deal with any financial recompense swiftly, whereas Sasha is talking about one to two years, maybe longer. No point accusing Davidson of crimes committed if none can be proved, open to litigation, sued for every dollar that Beth has, and then Sasha. It could even wind up with you, Mr Cornell. Don't tell us you haven't pushed the limit, bought people off, or circumvented the law. Not sure if having us followed is strictly above board, but we'll let it go for now.'

'Well put,' Cornell said. 'It wouldn't have got back to me, although, yes, I pushed the limit. Grey areas, there always are, but I was surrounded by the best legal and financial minds that money could buy. And Sasha would have been protected if the situation had occurred. But Beth Madison, playing Sasha and Davidson off against each other, sounds plausible. The man would have paid, almost impossible to prove after so many years.'

'Capable of murder?' Natalie asked.

'I'm not certain I can answer that question,' Cornell said.

'You knew of his corruption?'

'Not back then, but I've done some checking since.'

'Why not at the time?'

'No reason to. It's not endemic in this country, but more than a few politicians are looking for the opportunity to make money. Maybe advice on what shares to buy, special loans to

90

purchase real estate, influential persons in business and banking, always handy to have a politician who owes you a favour.'

'Did Ralph Davidson?'

'Not me. Although others did, their snouts in the trough.'

'Your opinion of them?'

'Neutral. Some I liked, others I didn't. Not illegal, maybe unethical, but those who don't understand aren't involved, never likely to be valuable enough to be of concern.'

'We've not met Ralph Davidson. Your opinion of the man would be appreciated.'

'Capable prime minister, politically astute, understood the electorate's mood. He served this country well but used his position to personal advantage. No issues with that, and if he did sway the occasional mining lease and received a pat on the back from the mining company, a donation to his charity of choice, I didn't see much wrong with it. Political office is complex, factions to deal with, other countries, especially the USA, trying to impose their will, and then business leaders wanting something, banks wanting something else, an economy in the ascendancy, an economy in decay, always another election.'

'His reputation, all-important to him?'

'That's the crux of the matter, isn't it? Could he have been involved in Sasha's death? Unfortunately, not that I have any reason to believe it, but he could.'

As they left Cornell's mansion for the drive back to Sydney, the problem both could see was that Bernie Cornell did not intend to leave it to the police to conduct their investigation, but to be interventionist, spying on their movements, interceding where he could, pressuring if required. And there had been no resolution as to whether the heavies had come in from America, and if they had, where were they, and more importantly, what they might do.

Bernie Cornell was closing in on the final chapter of his life. He would not wait for the police to work within the law to find the murderer, but might take control of matters, pressure people violently if required, and then would the murderer ever see the inside of a prison cell?

A diversion to State Crime Command in Parramatta before heading back into Sydney, a meeting with Superintendent Payne, who needed to be updated on developments.

Natalie and Haddock realised they were running one race, and Cornell was running another. Who would arrive in the home stretch first and win the race was unknown.

Chapter 13

Attempts to contact Ralph Davidson had proven fruitless. Representations to his office had met with an initial rebuff, then a detailed explanation as to why he would not meet with two police officers who were investigating Sasha Cornell's murder. Although the one positive had been that the office acknowledged that Davidson had met the woman, known her since she was a child and had great respect for her.

Natalie had coordinated with Victoria Adderley in Legal at State Crime Command on the paperwork, but as the lawyer had questioned, 'You want to set up a meeting with a former prime minister of Australia. To discuss what?'

Natalie knew it was a good question, for which she wasn't sure of the answer. She tried to explain to Victoria that he could have been instrumental in Sasha Cornell's death due to his association with Beth Madison and his possible but unproven corruption. The more she explained, the weaker her reasoning sounded.

'Can't be done,' the lawyer said. 'Sure, he might be involved, knows more about that period than you and Inspector Haddock, but he'll not want it resurrecting. And how are you to know that Beth Maddison is not stringing you along? Judging by what you've told me, she doesn't come off well. A gold digger who attaches herself to men who can give her a good time, further her career, and make her rich. Her husband, the current one; any others?'

'No others. No dirt against the woman other than her association with Davidson when he was prime minister. No idea what his wife thought of the arrangement, but we assume she knew.'

'She did,' Victoria Adderley said.

Natalie had to agree. Even before the incident with the live-in boyfriend, she had suspected he had been playing up, the late nights, working late in the office, he had said, the shower before coming to bed, and clothes in the washing machine. Too busy with policing to question him, hopeful that it was her imagination and that as policing had given her heightened observational skills, she saw the worst in every situation. But in the end, proven correct the night he had come home for the office party, the admission, the attempt at reconciliation, the inevitable tears and then the lonely nights, her solace, a bottle of wine and late-night TV.

'I understand that approaching Davidson is fraught with issues, but he must have known that finding Sasha Cornell's body would recreate interest in the woman's movements, who she spoke to, deals she had in the offing, deals she was hopeful of putting together.'

'He would have, and what's he been doing since Pinchgut? You know the answer, covering his tracks. You'll not prove anything against him or his association with Beth Madison unless you can find photos of them together. A spiteful woman, Beth Madison might have some, but don't bank on it. If she was paid off once by the man, she could be playing that card again.'

'Dangerous, if he was involved in or knew of Sasha Cornell's death. I would advise her to approach him at her peril, but you've met Beth Madison. What's she like? Likely to heed your advice?'

'Confident, self-assured, pillar of society, gives to charity. No, she won't heed my advice, probably regard my opinions as inconsequential, not sure I blame her.'

'Okay, my suggestion,' Victoria said. 'Meet with Beth Maddison, explain the various scenarios, get a reaction, observe the body language, and find out if she's got proof other than innuendo. Easy to slur, difficult if you're after money from the slurred without proof. And remember, a prime minister or former still comes with credibility, reputation, security, and protection from others involved. You're walking a tightrope, not the first time, either. You were lucky with Justice Kline. It could have ended badly. You might not be so lucky the second time.'

Natalie was appreciative of the advice, but she was resolute. She had chanced it during another murder investigation when a Supreme Court judge was under investigation, his son arrested for murder, serving his time in a minimum-security prison, a minimal sentence, aware that strings had been pulled. But a former prime minister was a man who knew state secrets and activities the government and Australia's Secret Intelligence apparatus had been involved in. Ralph Davidson would be protected, regardless of his guilt or innocence.

That night, in his office, Superintendent Payne sat behind his desk, the vista of Parramatta to his rear, sprawling urban and commercial high rise. Haddock held a can of beer, as did Natalie. Victoria Adderley drank orange juice. The mood was cordial.

An astute man, Payne knew that Sergeant Natalie Campbell was more competent than Haddock, and he had told her several times that she only had to say the word and she would be promoted to inspector, possibly chief within another year, another department if she wanted it, Haddock as her junior if she chose to stay with Homicide.

Her reply, even at the current time, was to stay with Inspector Gary Haddock to learn from him what he, as a detective in Homicide, had honed over the years. She was armed with a degree, which she acknowledged was theoretical, but the practical was learnt with a seasoned performer, and none was more seasoned than Inspector Haddock, living in Parramatta in a one-bedroom apartment, wanting to move back to his wife and daughter, realising it was not possible, not when policing and family shared equal priorities.

'We've been down this road before,' Payne said. 'This time, a former prime minister. Sergeant, how do you intend to handle it?'

Over the months, Haddock realised that Payne looked to his sergeant for updates and advice more than him. At first, he thought the man was making a play for his attractive sergeant, but then he realised that he was stuck in his ways, whereas she was the future, computer-literate and personable. In a previous case, he had seen her with Russell Harding, a secretive and ageing man who knew where all the skeletons were, who was sleeping with who or involved in illegal activities. A man who kept his own counsel and never revealed secrets, but he had told her hitherto unknown facts which had advanced the investigation immeasurably.

'I'm discussing it with Victoria. Unsure would be the answer,' Natalie said.

'Expound,' Payne replied.

'We've nothing on him, only what his former mistress has implied. He might be as pure as the driven snow, and barging in on him, with nothing more than a possible vengeful woman, would be counterproductive.'

'Not to mention the heat I would have to take. You and Haddock, throwing me in the deep end more times than I can remember.'

Haddock could see that the man was in a good mood, why he helped himself to another can of beer.

'Approaching Ralph Davidson will open us to potential difficulties,' Victoria Adderley said.

'I assume you've checked if the man's mistress is to be believed,' Payne asked.

'Apart from an entry in Sasha Cornell's diary to meet with the woman and Beth Madison telling us that she was aware of the man's improprieties, then no,' Natalie said. It was an admission that she and Haddock had not thoroughly checked out Davidson. She expected Payne to blow up; the man's nature, hot and cold, with no in-between. Experienced in how the man ticked, she waited, knew that he would soon calm, conscious that he would then listen and advise.

However, sublime nothingness worried her more than the man's wrath. She had experienced the male chauvinism at State Crime Command, subtle rather than direct, after she had reported Haddock's paramour for unethical activities, spying on her colleagues with her laptop, casting aspersions at her in the canteen at Paramatta.

She had been warned to be careful of the superintendent, the probability that he would at some stage put the hard word on her, favours given, favours granted, but he had not, so far.

'I suggest you tighten up on this. Can it be done?' Payne asked. He had taken Haddock's lead, opened another can of beer for himself, given one to Natalie, a rum and coke to Victoria, who would have refused if anyone else had given it, but thanked the man instead.

'Not easy,' Haddock said, aiming to enter the discussion.

'Still on with her downstairs?' Payne asked.

'Trying to work it out with my wife.'

Was it a disarming tactic, Natalie wondered, pushing the inspector into an embarrassing corner and allowing the women to speak. She wasn't sure she was comfortable with the situation, the possible elevation in status, whether promotion up through the ranks based on merit, for which she qualified, or for another reason.

'Good, focus on the reality, not the illusion, greener grass around the corner.' Metaphors didn't sit well with Payne, a rough man when working in the outback, a small town with not much for the youth to do except sniff glue and the men to drink copious quantities of beer. Natalie thought the man had mellowed, associating with a different class of people, urbane, cosmopolitan, and not out in the bush, the Australian vernacular for anywhere distant from the main population centres.

'I'm trying,' Haddock said, taking a swig of beer from the can.

'Back to what we were talking about,' Payne said. 'Any chance of proving anything the Madison woman was saying? It's easy to throw the dirt, harder to make it stick.'

'I'm working with Natalie,' Victoria Adderley said. 'If she can find me the specifics she doesn't have, I can research them, probably get hold of documentation, cross reference, and look for anomalies. I can deal with the legal, could do with help from the Fraud Squad.'

'Anyone you can trust?'

There was only one person in Fraud whose name came to mind, and nobody trusted her, certainly not Natalie, who had reported her and Haddock, who had had an affair with the woman.

'No, and if we find someone, can we trust them? Bernie Cornell has eyes in every corner, and Davidson's bound to have people in this building who would keep him informed.'

'Okay, I can trust you three. Victoria, work with Natalie and Haddock, find yourself an office in the building, closed door, encrypt your work, and do not communicate what you're doing with your department.'

'I have a superior; she'll want to know,' Victoria said. She was enjoying the rum and coke and thought to ask for another, but she wasn't a drinker, drunk too often in her teens, easy with her virtue back then. She wanted to drink but would not, not in the superintendent's office, but would when she returned to her place and her girlfriend.

'I'll deal with her. Due to the sensitivity of the matter, you'll report to me. She might not like it, but it can't be avoided.'

'Can she be trusted?' Haddock asked.

'She's aggressively ambitious,' Payne said. No more needed to be said.

***

Beth Madison squirmed when Natalie phoned her the next day. The reaction was not unexpected, as the woman, still holding residual antagonism against her former lover, had said more than she should have on the first meeting with Natalie. If she had said nothing, lied that she was meeting with Sasha Cornell to reveal details of an affair, that was one thing, but corruption in high office was more serious. There were no details back then, but now, with the full weight of a homicide behind them, the police would not be dissuaded.

Beth Madison had little option but to comply: meet with Natalie and Haddock at Parramatta or at King's Cross Police

Station, closer to where she lived but not as discreet as Parramatta. She chose the former.

The woman's previous exuberance was absent as she sat across from Natalie and Haddock. Natalie had updated her and told her that direct answers to direct questions were required, and if she wanted to bring legal representation, she was free to do so.

'Does your husband know of your past?' Natalie asked.

'Not in detail, and I prefer it to stay that way. You're making this difficult,' Beth Madison replied. There was hostility in her; so much the better, Haddock thought.

'You stated to Sergeant Campbell when you met with her in Rose Bay that Ralph Davidson was involved in corruption,' Haddock said.

'I inferred anger with how he had treated me.'

'It makes no sense,' Natalie said. 'You live in the Eastern Suburbs, not far from the man. You must have met him occasionally.'

'I have. I'm friendly with his wife, not too chummy, no hidden signals, no recognition from one to the other of the past.'

'And you hide your anger?'

'It's a weak emotion. Negative, does no good. But I am guilty of it on occasions, and his treatment riles, even to this day. Unlike Ralph, my husband is a good, reliable, solid man who cares for me and the children but is not dynamic or exciting. Power is an aphrodisiac, and Ralph had it in plenty.'

'Even though he was much older than you?' Haddock asked. Natalie thought it an inappropriate comment, insensitive and would possibly rile the woman. Haddock did not. He wanted the woman edgy, liable to blurt out something in the heat of the moment, a titbit that could become useful.

'Not to me, he wasn't. Meet the man; you'll understand.' It was a gentle putdown. Natalie found that she enjoyed the sparring.

'You mentioned a mining lease, probable illegal activity?' Natalie reminded the woman.

'I did, but I don't remember the details, only that Ralph was pleased he had pushed it through. The environmental lobby opposed, but then, they're against everything.'

'You don't hold with their views?' Haddock asked. He had leant back and let his sergeant take the lead role, which she increasingly gravitated to. He had sensed Payne's preference for her opinion over his. His wife wanted better for their daughter and a husband by her side, but he knew he had reached his career pinnacle. From here on in, it would be a gradual decline in health and cognisance, incremental salary increases, always slightly less than required to maintain a standard of living. Retirement would be easier with superannuation, enough to live on, to sit and reminisce over murderers he had known, a pale figure of the man compared to when he had joined the force, slim and athletic, with a full head of hair.

'Do you? The current debate is along political and ideological lines, not rational and unbiased, no consensus on the scientific, focussing on a myriad of values, some good, some bad, others nonsensical.'

'Could it be that Ralph Davidson took a pragmatic approach, made a good decision, and benefited the country?' Natalie asked.

'He probably did. Although he gained favour from it.'

'Politically, no crime in that. Financially, there might be. Which is it?'

'Both. I can't remember the details, only that it happened.'

'Queensland?'

'Something to do with runoff, damage to the Barrier Reef.'

'Which is damaged already, the crown-of-thorns starfish and warmer sea temperatures.'

Haddock thought the interview was drifting. Environmental issues were one thing; corruption was another. The first concerned him; the second was more immediate. 'The name of the mining company,' he asked.

'I can't remember.'

'Can't or prefer not to?'

'I don't want to be involved. Likely to cause friction, which I don't want for my family and me.'

'It's murder,' Natalie reminded her.

'Sasha's, a long time ago. We've all moved on, got older, and hopefully wiser.'

Haddock called time for a break, ten minutes to get a coffee, a bite to eat from a machine in the hallway outside Homicide, long enough for Natalie to surf the internet to find out the name of the mining company and the environmental issues. With the name, hopeful that Beth Madison might remember more. The woman was cornered, and her affair would become public knowledge.

An affair was not the most damaging aspect. It was how Ralph Davidson would react, forced to defend himself against scurrilous media articles, whether true or not. Beth Madison was cognisant of the fact, and knew her lifestyle was threatened, a reason for her to say no more, although she had implicated herself initially with Sasha Cornell out of bitterness and then with Natalie after one too many alcoholic drinks. She thought she might live to regret it, conscious of the situation's fragility.

Against her better judgement, aware she had no other option, she phoned her husband. A bitter argument. Natalie, who was close by, could hear one side of the conversation, able to interpret what the husband was saying. The words spoken by the woman were not those of a loving wife. They were the utterances of a disturbed woman, attractive and intelligent but unbalanced. The question remained, was Davidson guilty of a crime or only of political expediency? When updated about what had transpired, Haddock thought the latter, but Natalie remained sceptical.

Natalie had researched and found out that the place was Mackay in the north of the country, in Queensland, not far from the Barrier Reef. It had figured in other disputes about mining leases, but now, Atlas Mining Company was front and centre.

Upon their return from the break, the three sat down, a red-faced woman, anger seething, an astute police sergeant, and a seen-it-all jaundiced inspector. No more was said, not even a response to a question. Beth Madison had exercised her right not to implicate herself further in what might be a red herring or a crime.

Chapter 14

Two possible motives had become apparent, but neither had any underlying proof. It would be extremely hard to prove if Ralph Davidson had been taking backhanders for services rendered in facilitating a mining lease for Atlas Mining. A prime minister does not allow himself to be open to an accusation, and the mining company would have been subject to corporate law, investigation of their books, an exhaustive audit conducted biannually, and adherence to legal, financial, and environmental regulations and statutes. Nobody involved would have been an amateur, but the most skilled persons in their field.

Victoria Adderley was reviewing the lease and how the mining company had secured it. It was contentious at the time. Mackay was the port where the extracted coal would be sent worldwide, although most would go to China, and Atlas Mining was owned by a Chinese consortium, another bone of contention, selling the farm, or in this instance, the mining lease.

Natalie had researched it on the internet: a prolonged battle, balancing the financial returns to Australia and the potential damage to the Barrier Reef, but in the end, all arguments had been whittled down. Then a uranium mine was about to start up in Western Australia, more frightening to the environmentalists, who in bulk had moved over there to protest.

Natalie understood the concerns and realised that the equilibrium between fiscally responsible and environmentally sound was difficult, too often marred by heightened emotions and extreme political views. Even so, the lease had been granted to Atlas Mining in a shorter time than others. If Sasha Cornell had died due to intimate knowledge of corruption, that would have had to come from Beth Madison, and she wasn't talking, not even answering her phone.

Regardless of the argument at Parramatta, which Natalie had overheard, the husband was protecting his wife, fielding off requests from the police, and a lawyer had been appointed as the point of contact. Natalie knew that was Catch-22. Beth Madison had not, in all probability, killed Sasha Cornell, and interring Sasha's body at Pinchgut, would have required someone with knowledge of the place. A murderer with construction skills or more than one person, and Beth Madison did not have those skills.

The other motive was the moviemaking antics of Gustav Ingesson and Terrence Underwood. Homegrown gay adult movies for their select group in Sydney was one thing, but they had expanded, become mainstream, and that would have aroused the interest of organised criminals in Australia and overseas.

The first motive indicated that Beth Madison would have been the appropriate target for removal. However, Natalie understood, as did Haddock after they had spoken about it at a café on the street, close to State High Command, that Beth didn't have the contacts or the knowledge to pursue retribution, to bring down the man who had used her and then cast her aside. Or had he had feelings for her? They needed to know, but how, not with Davidson hiding behind a veil of secrecy, sharp lawyers, and the Official Secrets Act.

Clarification of which of the two was important to the investigation would assist. But that depended on someone giving a direction. Only one person knew the key players, the dead woman's father.

Haddock thought that meeting again with Bernie Cornell was fraught with issues. The man was well-connected, his daughter had been murdered, and he was desperate to find the person or persons responsible. And not only might he have suspicions about the guilty, but he might also have been involved with Sasha and the adult movies, and he could even be aware of Davidson's involvement with the lease for Atlas Mining. Natalie couldn't dispute her inspector's logic, sound on all points, and that meeting with Cornell was a risk, not even calculated, as that implied a risk/reward factor, and neither of the two parts of the equation was known.

Looking substantially worse than the last time they had met him, Bernie Cornell was confined to his bed, his condition monitored by a battery of equipment, a full-time doctor and two nurses. He was dictating notes to an assistant, actions to be taken in the event of his death, a lawyer in the far corner on his phone.

If the man had been religious, Natalie wouldn't have been surprised to see a priest in the mansion, ready to administer the last rites, but Bernie Cornell had been clear on that issue. 'You get one chance at life, make the best of it,' was his adage.

Cornell looked up at them. 'Not yet, not until the bastard who killed Sasha is behind bars.'

Natalie thought he wouldn't make it, but the man was a fighter, determined to survive for a while.

'A few questions,' Haddock said.

'Davidson or the two moviemakers? Which probability looks the stronger?'

'Both are possible; not sure we can answer definitively which one is responsible.'

'Davidson took a backhander, money for services rendered. Too many years in the past to pursue. Political dynamite at the time if it had been revealed, but now of little interest.'

'It could have got Sasha murdered,' Natalie said. She had sat close to the bed, and Haddock continued to stand.

'If the Madison woman had given Sasha details, or others thought she had, why had she survived?'

'We need to know if what Beth Madison knew was sufficient to warrant Sasha's death. Also, why she's still alive.'

'I reckon you're wasting your time pursuing that line of enquiry, although she'll talk if necessary.'

'Rough-arm tactics?' Haddock asked.

'Not rough arm, but power. I know her husband, met him a couple of times. One phone call and his wife's yours.'

Haddock could see complications, a weakened case if Cornell interfered in due process. Although he knew they needed clarification on whether Sasha had been updated with details of Atlas Mining and Ralph Davidson. There was no option; he said yes.

Involving Bernie Cornell was a strategic move, good in theory, risky in practice. Cornell's business practices were open to debate, and now the man was, once again, taking direct involvement in the investigation.

Two days later, Beth Madison sat across from the two police officers in the interview room at King's Cross Police Station. She had wanted Parramatta, but her want was no longer important. It wasn't Davidson who would clarify the events of seventeen years previous, but the woman.

Natalie could see she was uncomfortable with the situation, there were rings around her eyes, and she had been crying. For a resilient woman, she now displayed frailty.

'I gave Sasha Cornell a synopsis, but no detail, not enough for her to run with it,' Beth Madison said. She had dressed casually for the interview, wearing jeans and a woolly top as it was cold. She had arrived by taxi, her car at home in the garage. Natalie could admit to sympathy with the woman and the tenuous position she was placed in, but it was a murder, and people, innocent or otherwise, become compromised, forced to reveal facts they would prefer not to.

'Do you believe Davidson's corruption could have been responsible for her death?' Haddock asked. He knew that his sergeant would empathise with Beth Madison. It was in her nature to feel compassion, but not his. If guilty, the full weight of the law applied; if withholding evidence, condemned by him. And it was clear that the woman, under extreme pressure, the hand of Cornell evident, would talk now.

'I knew more than I told Sasha.'

'Did you have the means to take advantage of it? Would they have believed you? Sasha Cornell had the contacts, and so did her father. You didn't. The discarded mistress of a protected man. How did you survive? And this time, the truth.'

Beth Madison squirmed in her seat, picked up her handbag, put it down again, and put a hand through her hair. 'I phoned Ralph and told him what I intended to do.'

'His response?' Natalie asked.

'He laughed, told me not to be foolish.'

'Polite, angry? What was the mood?'

'From him, conciliatory, arranged to meet me at a hotel.'

'You went?'

'I was in love, or I thought I was. I told you once before power is an aphrodisiac.'

'How did he arrive?'

'A nondescript car with another man.'

'To do what?'

'I signed an agreement, no more talking to anyone about our time together and what I knew.'

'In return?'

'It was non-threatening but not romantic. I was paid off with two hundred thousand dollars.'

'The money from his account?'

'Who knows. Probably, but it could have come from others.'

'Financially, you were secure. No threats against your life if you didn't honour the agreement with Sasha?'

'None. The other man had the paperwork. I read and signed it. I accepted the inevitable and got on with my life, and I had enough money to make a substantial payment on a place in Woollahra. Six months later, I met my husband.'

'I heard you arguing with him at Parramatta,' Natalie said.

'Raised voices only. He knew of Ralph Davidson, not in detail. I owed him that much when we got married. He didn't like it and thought I had been a tart, which was true. Ours is a successful marriage, argumentative at times, loving at others. He doesn't want me to be here any more than I do, and let's be clear, I didn't give Sasha details.'

'Sasha could have deduced something from what you said, or her father did. Davidson's astute and figured you could be paid off, but Sasha couldn't. Maybe idealistic on her part, although she was financially supporting a couple of men and their business, not strictly legal in the excess, questionable in the minority.'

'It's possible,' Beth Madison admitted. 'I've honoured my side of the agreement, told you what I've had to.'

'Pressure from Bernie Cornell?'

'In part. I phoned Ralph, had to, no option. I'm sure you don't approve, but I had to. I have a family now, and I don't want them involved, not that I believe Ralph would condone murder. That's not his style.'

'Yet he arrives with another man. Any idea who or what he was?'

'Lawyer, government, possibly a member of ASIO, can't be sure. He didn't give a name, stood outside while Ralph explained the situation, came in afterwards, and showed me where to sign. He didn't speak more than a few words.'

'And you weren't nervous?'

'Shocked, maybe. I still trusted Ralph and understood why he ended our relationship, forced to accept the inevitable.'

'One moment you hate him, then you understand. What is it today?' Haddock asked.

'Ambivalence. Pure love is wonderful, but there is a reality. My husband won't do wrong by me; I won't do wrong by him, end of story. What more do you want from me?'

Natalie thought there was no more. Without either Beth's or Davidson's cooperation, it was up to Victoria Adderley to determine if it was worth pursuing.

***

Terrence Underwood arrived in Sydney on a Qantas Airways flight from London. He presented himself at State Crime Command in Parramatta one day later, a Thursday, at 10 a.m. He had not been summoned to return to Australia or to present himself to the police, which came as a shock to Natalie and Haddock.

Natalie was in with Victoria Adderley, going through the mining lease granted to Atlas Mining and the case reports of Underwood's and Ingesson's enterprise. Time was dragging, and

Bernie Cornell was getting anxious. The Grim Reaper was nearby, kept in abeyance by Cornell's iron will and the best medical care that money could buy.

Haddock was out of the office, meeting with Superintendent Martin, the senior officer at Kings Cross Police Station. The men were longstanding friends, and the chance to have a meal together and to talk over old times was something that Haddock needed. Life was tough for him; a desire to be at home with his wife and daughter, the imbalance as a detective in Homicide, and impossible to reconcile the two.

Natalie met Underwood first, shook his hand out of civility, remembered where that hand had been in some of the movies, excused herself, and washed her hands. On her return, she escorted the man to a conference room near Homicide, organised a coffee, and phoned Superintendent Payne. It was a major event in the investigation, unexpected, and Payne needed information to impart to his superiors, who were anxious for a resolution to the death of Sasha Cornell.

'Sasha's father,' Underwood said. He was taller than Ingesson, although not in as good a physical condition. His hair was prematurely greying, and he had a look of poverty about him, threadbare jeans, a tee-shirt, and a tweed jacket. On his feet, he wore a pair of trainers.

'He paid for your trip?' Natalie asked.

'More a command, but it is not an issue. Sasha was a good person; not sure I can help. Have you met with Gustav?'

'In Brisbane. He seems to be doing well but might be involved in low-level crime. How about you?'

'Not crime, not now. To us, what we had been doing was not criminal. Sure, we were pushing the boundary between acceptable and perverse. Maybe we got carried away with our success, cut corners, were not as diligent as we should have been, can't blame us for that.'

'The judge did when he sentenced you.'

'First offence, the maximum sentence. A couple of queers locked up in a prison full of men starved of affection. I don't need to paint you a picture, do I?'

'You don't. Ingesson appears to have thrived inside.'

'I didn't. Gustav's hardcore; I'm not. Bisexual, and I don't like violence, which they wanted in prison. Beaten up more than a few times, a couple of times in the prison hospital.'

'And now, in England?'

'A brief interlude as a fraudster, conning old ladies out of their inheritances. Did time for that in prison. I now teach English part-time, and plenty need the tuition. I live frugally, spend little, and live over a shop in a room the size of a shoebox. Gustav and I got carried away with what we were doing and saw ourselves as invincible.'

'Fun for a while?'

'Exciting. We were in demand, money in our pocket, and Sasha was our friend. It was a buzz, and believe me, you tend to forget what you're doing, looking for the next opportunity, thought we were producing Oscar-winning material rather than sleaze. I couldn't watch one of them now; not sure how you did without throwing up.'

'Nor am I. At least we can agree on that. Inspector Haddock is on the way. Why are you here? Apart from Bernie Cornell. What can you bring to the table? Why was Sasha murdered?'

'She disappeared; that's all we knew, anyone knows. There were rumours of a secret lover, tired of the bright lights, joining a commune, living in the bush. You must have read back to the time. It was a great mystery. Attractive, an important father, successful, and had plenty of friends. It made no sense to anyone, least of all us.'

'What did you believe?'

'That she had come to harm, but what could we do? We didn't know anything, no reason to believe it was to do with us. She never came when we were filming, helped us because we were friends.'

'You said you were bisexual. Did you?'

'With Sasha?'

'Yes, exactly.'

'Never. I found her attractive, but I was with Gustav, one person at a time. If she had been free, who knows. But she had Josh Costello and occasionally Howarth. They were macho, I'm not; only swing both ways if the opportunities arise. I was out of her league, and I knew it, and so did she. We used to joke about it, but nothing more. Sorry that she's dead, a truly good person.'

Natalie was confused. After the initial surprise of his appearance at the police station, she was determined to dislike him, but now, she found him charming, even if his appearance was disarming.

'Where are you staying?'

'A cheap hotel in Sydney, a daily allowance, enough for food and transport. Cornell might suspect we were involved in her death, but we weren't. Neither of us would have harmed her. Helped us out when needed, a true friend. If you make pornographic videos and pimp out men, some profess to be your lifetime friend, and others despise you, but with money comes respect, grudgingly given, soon taken. No one came to visit us in prison besides Gustav's mother.'

'Your parents?'

'Disowned me, never saw them again. My mother's died since. I might try and meet with my father one last time. One week maximum in Australia, then back to England.'

Chapter 15

The situation remained the same. One murder, two possible motives, and no recent evidence to give direction.

Time was moving on, and people were getting anxious for a result, the usual complaint about budgetary overrun and key performance indicators, complicated by a man close to death who continued to make his presence known.

The investigation weighed heavily on Inspector Gary Haddock, and the return to the family home on an infrequent basis was not working out. He still took the pressure of work home with him, unable to detach, not wanting to talk about the maintenance of the house, the cost of their daughter's schooling, the unsavoury boyfriend she had acquired, and whether she was sleeping with him, and why couldn't he get some of his police buddies to check the boy out, to frighten him off, and so on. The last visit to the house had been difficult; the next would be impossible, and besides, a man needs relief, and he wasn't getting it.

Natalie worried for him and could see that he was about to fall off the straight and narrow, not that he had ever really been on it, not totally. Not a drinker, Haddock was unique in that regard, the curse of too many police inspectors. For all her faults, Theresa de Klerk had calmed the man, but she wasn't around.

'Can't go on like this,' Haddock confided.

It was just the two of them, late at night in Homicide at Parramatta. They were going through what they had, which was precious little. Until the reason for Pinchgut had been clarified conclusively, the realisation that the murder could not be solved.

Terrence Underwood had spent three hours that first time at Parramatta, going over in detail what he knew, how adult movies were produced and distributed, and the market size, which was staggeringly large. Underwood denied they had been in contact with dubious persons, mafia-type characters, claiming that most sales were online through distributors overseas who they had never met, and some had been distributed at the clubs they frequented. He further clarified that he and Gustave Ingesson had been lovers for four years and had lived together for three. But with all relationships, the romance had withered, condemned to obscurity after both had been arrested, and in England, he had a steady girlfriend and an occasional male friend.

Apart from the movies, Natalie and Haddock found the man pleasant, as they had with Ingesson, although Underwood had no intention of contacting the man, preferring to wait out his time in Sydney, answer questions asked, assist if he could, genuine in his desire to see satisfaction for Sasha.

He had met her father after her disappearance but didn't have a strong opinion about him other than his reputation, which he felt was unreliable. The man had been concerned for his daughter, curt and to the point. He never condemned the two men's activities or Sasha's financial assistance.

Natalie understood Haddock's predicament; life was complicated and a hectic lifestyle, snatched meals, reports to file, budgets to consider, and evidence to sift through did not marry. No clocking in at eight in the morning, going home at five or six in the evening, or weekends off. Homicide was either full on, seven days a week, fifteen to sixteen hours a day, or when there were no murders to solve, time to relax. But with an adolescent daughter and a demanding wife, Haddock didn't have the luxury to sit alone, sleep in late, and not worry.

For Natalie, it was easier but not agreeable. At home, in her small apartment, she could turn on the TV, a glass of wine, a good book, and switch off. Devoid of love, but it did have its benefits, whereas her inspector had none.

'Not sure I can advise,' Natalie said. 'It is what it is. Continue; hope you get through it.'

'With our daughter sixteen years of age. Too old to send her to her room, too young to hope she'll use wisdom to deal with temptation.'

Natalie remembered back to that time, not that many years before. She understood the daughter, understood why her father was concerned. Sexually active, pushing the limit, falling in love, heartbroken more than once.

Haddock sighed and snapped out of his mood, the futility of it all. He had seen enough murders, the aftermath, the loved ones suffering, relationships damned by grief, and marriages destroyed. He resolved to get a promotion, and solve the immediate problem, although one question concerned him. It was the time to ask.

'Superintendent Payne is determined for you to go up a rank. What's the issue?'

'No issue, prefer us to stay as a team for now, more to learn from you. If I accept the promotion, I'll be in the office more than I would like. Administrative tasks, which I can do, don't excite me, not as much as finding a murderer.'

'Take it, get an agreement from Payne that we'll continue to work together. You can't deny that you're competent and due for promotion.'

Natalie appreciated Haddock's confidence in her but knew she would become the senior officer if she stayed with him. She didn't want to do that, appreciative of the man's encouragement; his expertise and willingness to impart it had taught her a great deal. It had only been a short time, less than one year, from being a sergeant at King's Cross Police Station to the offer to become an inspector. She wasn't sure where she was heading, unsure if she was suited to high office. Her qualifications were fine, her ability was sufficient, and she knew she could do whatever position was assigned.

Later that night, Superintendent Payne was in his office, and Victoria Adderley was sitting on a chair on the other side of the room. Natalie had her suspicions after she had knocked on the door and entered, unwilling to speculate or to condemn.

'I want it to stay as it is,' Natalie said after Victoria had discreetly left the office.

'Don't make it out to be something else,' Payne said. His manner was curt, official, and final.

'Not my concern, Superintendent.'

'You were in conference with Haddock; Victoria's found anomalies with Atlas Mining and Ralph Davidson. She's sent you an email, pleased with herself, needed to tell someone.'

Natalie accepted the explanation, aware that an investigating officer is always suspicious. She liked Victoria, respected Payne, and hoped she was wrong, although it would not diminish the two in her eyes if she was right.

'Bypass senior sergeant, accept inspector?' Natalie asked.

'Subject to review, but you'll receive the promotion. Is that it?'

'Inspector Haddock?'

'He'll remain as an inspector.'

'The man's under pressure, financial and emotional. He needs help.'

'Are you asking me to intervene directly? Not so easy, considering the latest investigation. Give me something, and tell me what you want.'

'Chief Inspector.'

'Agreed. Once you solve Sasha Cornell's murder, you'll both receive promotions.'

'Victoria?'

'Leave it alone,' Payne said as Natalie left the room. She realised why he hadn't put the hard word on her, surprised that Victoria had succumbed. She didn't want to know the details but needed to support Victoria if the proverbial hit the fan. The next time they met, she would ask.

***

Bernie Cornell had fought valiantly, but in the end, his money and medical care had not saved him. He died at two in the morning, three days after the last time Natalie and Haddock had met with him. They could not admit to feeling great sadness at his end, although he had earned their respect. He had been encouraging yet demanding, helping when required. Whether he had been truthful was a question that had not been answered and probably never would be.

Hovering vultures in suits would soon gather, clutching cases, lawyers mainly, some financiers. The man's empire was extensive. The breakup into its constituent parts would take months, probably years. The man had assisted the investigation, although Haddock wasn't sure how much as Sasha Cornell's death appeared to have no motive. Underwood and Ingesson had met in Brisbane, even though the former had said they would not. There was more to consider with them, the involvement of organised crime in the distribution of what they had produced.

However, the old man's death wasn't attributable to crime but age. Nothing suspicious in how he had died, and Sasha, if she had been alive, would have claimed the inheritance.

At Cornell's residence in the Eastern Suburbs, once Natalie and Haddock had run the gauntlet of the media with thrusting cameras, they attempted to enter the house, a security guard halting them.

'Police,' Haddock said.

'Not the first,' the guard said. 'We've had a couple using that, even one who said he was a family friend; another reckoned he was from a funeral director's.'

Natalie showed her warrant card. 'We're the genuine article,' she said, not condemning the security guard who had only been doing his job.

'Can't be too careful,' Haddock said. 'We knew the man, Homicide, dealing with the death of his daughter.'

'What about him?' the guard said.

'Not unexpected. Old age, but he was hanging on, hopeful that we would solve his daughter's murder,' Natalie said. 'Are you here for the day or longer?'

'I used to be his chauffeur a few years back. I lost my licence for the second time, driving under the influence. I've not been here that often in the last year or two, but Mr Cornell respected my confidence, looked after me, gave me a job as security, and I stayed in the house when no one else was here.'

'You could tell us more than he did,' Natalie said. She could believe in the man's discretion. In his sixties, carrying more weight than he should, the guard was articulate. He saw a lot and kept it to himself, but this was a murder.

'Surprised he didn't tell us about you,' Natalie continued. 'A mine of information, observing from a distance.'

'I hadn't spoken to him for some years, not out of animosity, and if he saw me, he'd shake my hand, but not a word.'

'Unusual.'

'I knew of the skeletons, and Mr Cornell had a few, and so did Sasha. He looked after me; no need to talk.'

'Discretion needed now?' Haddock asked.

'It depends. If it's related to Sasha, we can talk.'

'You knew her?'

'As a child, I picked her up from school. Difficult days when she disappeared. I suppose it was around that time that our communication started to wither.'

'You reminded him of her.'

'Never thought about it like that, but it could be true. There was a bond between us, and even if he was Bernie Cornell and I was Dan Stretton, a knockabout guy from out west, there was a camaraderie.'

'Your relationship with Sasha?'

'Great. We used to talk a lot when she was younger; tell me about her day at school, her friends, that sort of thing. As she got older, less, but she was very respectful, and I would have done anything for her.'

'If you had found out who killed her?'

'Nobody thought she was dead, not for a long time, least of all Mr Cornell.'

'Even so, a lot of effort was put into finding her. What did you reckon?'

'Initially, I thought she'd taken off with a man. She lived with Costello, having it off with Howarth or someone else. You could never be sure with her.'

'Out of character?'

'It was, but what could anyone else think? Nobody wanted to consider that she had come to harm, especially her father.'

'Disappearing with a stray lover? What did he think about that?'

'If she had phoned, he would have accepted it. Bernie was not one to condemn his daughter, might have told her she was a bloody fool.'

'He accepted Josh Costello?'

'Steady hand, pliable, understood he was onto a good thing, not the jealous type.'

'Malleable?' Natalie asked.

A ruckus outside the front door. The guard moved away to deal with it. Natalie and Haddock moved further into the residence, surprised to find Duncan Howarth outside at the rear, smoking a cigarette.

'Paying your respects?' Haddock asked, looking at the cigarette. Currently not smoking, he would have taken one if offered, which it wasn't.

'I am.'

'No more than that?' Haddock's animosity was obvious. Natalie was sure that Howarth had seen the slight, conscious that he wouldn't care. He was a superior man, arrogant as she and Haddock knew, devious, hiding behind lawyers when asked to come out to the murder site.

'If you mean, have I come to gloat, the answer is no. I had business dealings with Cornell. Protecting my interests. He knew about Sasha and me, not the only person, either. Costello knew, but then he was unfaithful to her too. Don't judge others by your morality.'

Natalie could see it was more than animosity; it was a seething hatred. Howarth was a man who had risen to the top through his sporting achievements and academic brilliance, whereas the inspector who questioned him was almost beneath contempt. How he viewed her, she wasn't sure, but she had attributes Haddock didn't, young, attractive, and female. She drew Haddock off to one side. 'Leave him to me,' she said.

'Makes my blood boil, his petty-bourgeois putdown, "let them eat cake" mentality.'

Haddock's literary quote revealed that he was highly intelligent but rarely displayed it as a police officer, the occasional insight, the literary, historical, and oblique putdown of a person he did not like.

Upstairs, Cornell's body lay. Due to his position in society, and doubly so due to his integral involvement in the murder of his daughter, an autopsy would be carried out. Haddock saw it as a formality, as he had known the man in the last few weeks and seen his physical being slowly reducing in vigour. Initially, after Sasha Cornell's body had been discovered, he had been agile, walking with a cane, his brain alert, helping the police, conducting his own enquiries, but that had lapsed, and he had died.

Haddock reflected that for a man with such a fearsome reputation, he had been civil with him and his sergeant. He had to admit to liking the man, self-made, but retaining a humility, whereas Howarth had not.

Downstairs, Natalie spoke to Howarth, who was charming and polite with her. Her intuition told her this was not a man to trust or like. What you saw was not what you got.

'I have been involved with Bernie Cornell for years, asked him for financial advice, and given him mine when requested. There are a couple of endeavours we were involved in, needed to show my respects to the great man, ensure that his legacy endures.'

'And that you're not out of pocket,' Natalie added.

'Bernie would not have expected any different with the vultures hovering. Lean pickings from him.'

'We weren't aware of family members except for a couple.'

'Both will be here soon enough.'

'To take control?'

'Tentative control. Bernie set up a complex series of measures and counter-measures to protect his legacy.'

'Where did Sasha fit into this?'

'When she was alive, it was clear that it would have been her in control, but she would have needed support.'

'Support Bernie and Sasha could rely on?'

'Nobody could be trusted, not even me. Too many hands in the cookie jar, too much temptation. Sasha wasn't interested in taking over from him and preferred to be involved in public relations, advertising, and promotions. Big business is dirty, too much for Sasha. Bernie brought me in to take responsibility for the day-to-day running of his empire while he looked at the bigger picture and the next opportunity.'

'Was he aware of you and Sasha?'

'He would have preferred me to Costello, but he knew he couldn't control me. Costello was putty in his hands, do the right thing by Sasha, even though he played around.'

'It seems that most of you do,' Haddock, who was within earshot of the conversation, said. There was sarcasm in his voice.

'No more than you, Inspector, from what I've heard,' Howarth replied.

It was confirmation to Natalie that Cornell had had her and her inspector checked out and that Howarth was privy to the fact. Which raised another issue. The man had been involved with Sasha Cornell before her disappearance. And since the body had been found, unwilling to cooperate with the murder investigation but still part of the father's inner circle. It was suspicious; Natalie had not formed a judgement but registered it for further enquiry.

Regardless of his alibi, Howarth had to be a primary suspect, the man to gain the most from Sasha's death and Bernie's demise.

Chapter 16

On the other side of the Pacific Ocean, in an office in New York, another of Sasha Cornell's lovers was emptying the contents of his desk.

It would be ten days before Natalie and Haddock became aware of the situation, with a disgruntled figure sitting in Homicide when they arrived in the office.

'Summarily dismissed, one hour to clear my desk, hand over my laptop and return the car,' Josh Costello said.

'How long back in Australia?' Haddock asked.

'Five days.'

'No fancy hotel, no fancy woman?'

'The hotel, not now, although I did receive severance. No financial issues for a few months, possibly a year if I'm careful.'

'Not your style,' Natalie said.

'Not really, and my wife doesn't want to come to Australia, and I don't have citizenship in the USA. My status there depended on working for Bernie, but he's dead, and others are calling the shots.'

'Duncan Howarth? We're suspicious of him. Seems to have popped his head up at Bernie Cornell's death,' Haddock said.

Natalie preferred the down-spirited Josh Costello to the exuberant person they had met before. Back then, Cornell had been looking after him.

'Your plans now?' Haddock asked.

'Flexible, moved in with a friend for a couple of weeks, try and come to a decision.'

'Your children? Your wife?' Natalie asked. 'The friend, the same as the one before?'

'Another, known her since we were at school.'

'Platonic?' Haddock asked.

Natalie thought it a foolish question. There was nothing about Costello that was platonic, not with women. Even she was susceptible to his appearance, manner, and soft accent. He was a magnet to women.

'Mostly. Not saying I'm a saint, but there's my wife and the children. Catch-22, not sure which way to turn, and with Howarth exercising control, I've not much hope of a solution. Besides, Bernie paid me above my worth. I'm capable, professional, and trustworthy, but paid more than I should have been, upset some of those in New York.'

'Upset you?' Natalie asked.

'To some extent, but I wasn't going to say no to it, was I?'

Natalie would have said that he should have maintained his dignity, not be beholden to someone else, although it was fifteen seconds before she responded. There was an itch that needed scratching, and it required an answer. 'Why?' she said.

'Bernie was a sentimentalist,' Costello replied.

Natalie observed a nervousness in the man, and he avoided eye contact. Haddock, not as astute as her, did not recognise the signals.

'We've always gone along with that theory, but her father had no reason to care what happened to you. He knew what you were and looked after you because of Sasha. Did you know something? And if you were so important, why has Howarth ejected you the moment Bernie Cornell died?'

'Howarth is a hard-nosed bastard, and Bernie had no obvious successor. It had to be Howarth who would take control.'

'Why Howarth? Is he the only one involved, and if there are more, why only you? Surely Bernie would not want his empire to end up in the hands of unscrupulous persons?'

'Howarth is trustworthy, a wise decision for Bernie. The man will protect his legacy, not for altruistic reasons, but because it benefits him. I was a fly in the ointment, someone to be removed.'

It wasn't making sense in that nothing was solid or believable. Natalie knew something was missing, and she was determined to find it. Costello's future required open and frank discussion, and if Howarth had been overseas when Sasha had gone missing, Costello could have been elsewhere than the Horizon building. Two men, one who had gained by Bernie's death, the other who had not. There had to be something tangible, but what was it? Could the two men be in collusion, although that made no sense, or was there antagonism?

'The truth,' Natalie said. 'Why are you here?'

Natalie could see the truth of it. Costello had been dumped from his position in New York on Bernie's death, although Bernie had kept him in the company, working for him for seventeen years, not out of a misplaced trust in his daughter's beau, but something more significant.

Bernie Cornell had only one weakness, his daughter, but he would not have cared for Costello, not after her disappearance, not unless there was something unseen, so unexpected as to not make sense.

What Natalie and Haddock had accepted before no longer held as valid. Howarth would play his cards close to his chest, hiding behind his celebrity, intelligence, and lawyers. Costello had no such protection and would talk once broken. That time was now, the man at a low point in his life, visiting with the police to tell them what was happening, to look for sympathy. If he wanted that, a church, the salvation army, not a grizzled detective inspector and his astute sergeant.

'It's either you or Howarth,' Haddock said. He had let his sergeant speak, conscious that their time as partners was possibly ending, not that either wanted it. He was a pragmatist, recognised the limits of his ability, and that she had the potential to be a finer police officer than him, somebody who could, in time, sit in Superintendent Payne's office if that was what she wanted, but he knew – she had told him on several occasions – that she wanted someone in her life, someone to love. Long-term relationships and dedicated policing were fraught with issues, too many hours, time away from home, the possibility of straying as he had, or alcohol. The mental anguish, the insensitivity after seeing the worst of humanity, what one person could do to another, did not get left at the office but often would be taken home – sullenness, mood swings, unwillingness to talk, and the most sympathetic of partners would struggle with the situation.

'Whoever killed Sasha, it wasn't me. I intended to marry her,' Costello said.

'Why did her father look after you?' Natalie said. 'Did he like you? Even if we accept that you were important to his daughter, she was missing. Did he always believe she was coming back?'

'Always. I was his ally, not that I could do much, and I grieved as much as him.'

'But you soon found another woman. Surely Bernie must have reacted and said something about that situation? If he believed she was returning to him and possibly to you, he would have regarded your behaviour as unforgivable, but he protected you for seventeen years. Why? You're not here in Homicide to pass the time of day, and if he looked after you for his benefit, not yours, that doesn't apply now. Or does it? Josh, level with us; none of this beating around the bush. Howarth or you? Is Inspector Haddock making sense? What's the great mystery?'

Haddock wasn't sure there was one, but Natalie was determined. Costello was full of contradictions; the loving husband in New York, but in Sydney, playing the field, and when he had been with Sasha, he had been two-timing her, the same as she had him. Which of the two was the worst? Natalie wasn't sure.

'Okay,' Costello said with a sigh. 'I knew more than I told you. Sure, Sasha used to see Howarth occasionally, and I wasn't a shrinking violet, more than my fair share of women. Sasha was cool with it and knew her father had cheated on her mother. For me, it was ideal. Money in my pocket, a good place to live, and Sasha as a bonus.'

'Why did Bernie Cornell keep you on?' Natalie asked, realising that the man was skirting the truth.

'If you remain that close to the action, you pick up knowledge of what was going on. The two movie directors and their pornographic movies. Bernie also knew, waiting to see how it panned out. There's plenty of money in the distribution, not so much with gay porn, but heterosexual. He was letting Sasha suss it out, and then he would decide if he wanted to become involved. It's nearly a hundred billion dollars globally, up to fifteen billion in the USA. A small share of it could be worth in the tens of millions, and all Bernie had to do was let Sasha check it out and for Ingesson and Underwood to run the movie side of it. Easy money for Bernie. Not strictly legal, not strictly illegal. It's a grey area, but easier enough to relocate the studio, bring in models for the day or the week, promote online, advertising revenue, join a club, stream it free or on a subscription basis.'

'Organised crime, seriously nasty people, kill you as soon as look at you,' Haddock said. 'Did Cornell know this?'

'He did. Most of the time, he was legitimate, but when business was tough, he ventured to the other side of the track, dealt with criminals, and became one himself. Sasha reckoned he had financed adult movies forty years back.'

'You know the man better than most. Was she right?'

'Probably. He didn't pay much tax and reckoned you were a mug if you paid more than you should. He knew all the loopholes, and Sasha was tarred with the same brush. A different morality, dog eat dog, winner takes all.'

'And you?'

'I didn't care. With the lifestyle, why should I care? Would you?'

It was an interesting question. Haddock knew he might not have cared because of his parlous marital and financial situation. Natalie, more idealistic, did. With a close family upbringing in the country, it had been easier to maintain discipline, not misbehave or get into trouble with the law. Apart from her late teens, when youthful curiosity and overcharged hormones made her sample some of the local lads. After that, the police service, and it had been a long time since she had felt the touch of a man, the reason she looked at Costello, not dispassionately, but critically. His morals were not hers, but he had the looks of a seducer, a man that women lusted over, and he was opportunistic, and now he was destroying any chance of reclaiming any of it back.

The day was getting long, eight in the evening, and Costello was starting to yawn. The man was talking, opening up to some extent but holding more back. So far, he had hinted, but the detail was required, the detail that both police officers were certain that Duncan Howarth was privy to.

'A meal,' Haddock said. 'The local pub or a restaurant? Your choice, Josh.'

Natalie could see the ploy, ply the man with a few pints of beer or a bottle of wine, loosen the tongue, act as a friend, and then tease out additional details. She approved of her inspector's approach. Hadn't she done the same with a Supreme Court judge on a previous murder enquiry? Although the man was a lecher, playing a game with her, she had backed off before it became compromising. Unfortunately, it had been his son who had been arrested for murder subsequently, serving time, learning new tricks or minding his own business. Natalie imagined it would be tough for him, the son of a man who had imprisoned many over the years.

Not far from the office, the Commercial Hotel on Hassell Street, beer and good food, although Natalie would have preferred a restaurant. Haddock was buttering up Costello, and it was known from when they had met him that first time, the Lord Nelson in The Rocks, that he appreciated a drink of beer.

'My shout,' Haddock said.

Natalie hoped it would not be a round-robin, each taking turns to buy a round. 'I'll stick to orange juice,' she said. Someone had to retain control of their faculties, and Haddock could walk to the small apartment he had rented. She still had to drive to her apartment in Potts Point, where she enjoyed the cosmopolitan atmosphere of the area, not the concrete jungle of Parramatta Central.

The two men bought each other drinks for over an hour, and Natalie, not wanting to be seen as standoffish, ordered as well. By the end of the evening, she knew she would not want to see another squeezed orange for a long time and would have preferred a glass of wine. Haddock was steady on his feet, just a slight wavering of his body, a slurring of speech. Clearly a more seasoned drinker, Costello appeared sober, although there was a redness in his face and a need to relieve himself after every drink.

'Medical condition,' Natalie said.

'Or scared of the truth, frightened that what he wants to tell us could go pear-shaped. The man's stuck between the devil and the deep blue sea; damned if he does, damned if he doesn't.'

Traditional pub fare, heavy on the quantity, not so on the flavour, pedestrian food, Natalie thought. Although Haddock enjoyed himself, as did Costello. After the meal, further questioning. Drunk as he was, Haddock maintained the instincts of a police officer, hopeful of a breakthrough, quick to question Costello.

'We know about Sasha and her father, involved in pornographic movies, not that he would admit to it, not sure we pressed him on the matter, oversight on our part,' Haddock said, calling over to the bar to set up another couple of beers.

Natalie wasn't sure he would be able to find his way home even if it was only two blocks away, although the former mistress was closer, having returned to the area in the last few days. Natalie only wanted the best for Haddock, but if he was about to shoot himself in the foot, there was only so much she could do.

'You're saying it was more than knowing about Sasha's financial assistance, but active participation,' Haddock continued. 'Did Bernie have the contacts? Wouldn't it have affected his credibility?'

'What credibility? What you read in the newspapers or see on the television? Old boys' network, or, in Howarth's case, new boy. It's a club, members only and very select. The high flyer, new money, old money, they didn't care. And then the media was in their pockets, lackeys who write the news and those who recite it in front of a camera. Do you think government and elite control is a modern phenomenon? Bernie was smarter than most, smarter than anyone else I had ever met; the reason I was with Sasha. She was a beautiful woman with his genes, but her skills were not honed.'

'Her father protected her?' Natalie queried. What's good for the goose is good for the gander, or was it the other way around? She wasn't sure, not certain if it mattered. She caught the eye of a waiter hovering, not so difficult as he had been giving her the eye all night. 'A glass of wine,' she said. Her voice was stern; there was no need to get the waiter any more excited than he was.

She knew she was attractive, but no man asked her out, apart from a fellow police officer in Kings Cross, who she fancied from afar, but close up and after a few drinks, he was pawing her as if she was his personal property. She wanted someone dependable and decent who would not get drunk, screw around, and would treat her with respect, a partner in life and in love. Sitting in that pub, she realised that she wanted the attractiveness of Josh Costello, the inherent decency of Inspector Gary Haddock and the commanding presence of Superintendent Payne, who, regardless of Victoria Adderley's warning, had never acted flirtatiously towards her.

Distracted momentarily, she refocused on the two men. Haddock was well over the limit, but Costello, who had drunk as much, was still coherent, even if his eyes were closing; another thirty minutes before he was out of it.

'What is it?' Haddock repeated, attempting to get an answer from Costello.

'Bernie knew all about it, was heavily involved, organised the distribution, dealt with those who attempted to muscle in. Not sure if Sasha knew how dirty the business was or the types of people out there, not so many in Australia, a lot more in the USA and Eastern Europe.'

'Why?' Natalie asked. 'All that money, why risk reputation and fortune with an industry that most people abhor.'

'Why not?' Costello replied.

It was a glib answer. Did it reflect the man's attitude to making money and life, Natalie wondered, or was there something more sinister.

'Did you approve? You're a chancer,' Natalie asked, taking over the subtle grilling of Costello.

'The law changes, one year illegal to produce pornography or to distribute it, other years legal. Bernie knew how to work around it.'

'Howarth?' Haddock asked, momentarily revived.

'He was younger back then, fancied himself as a stud, might have acted in one or two.'

'Acted?' Natalie quizzed. 'He was well-known back then. Surely he wouldn't have risked his Mr Clean image.'

'The camera's not focused on the face, is it?' Costello smirked.

'And you? A reluctant participant, or did you relish the chance to have sex with other women?'

'Not me. I had enough as it was. I visited the production once, a threesome, a stud and two women, took one of them to a hotel afterwards.'

'You're a charming man, attractive to women,' Natalie said. 'Women come easy, Sasha was your meal ticket, but you could have spread yourself around, plenty for the taking.'

'I could have, sometimes did. I'm a louse. But there was Sasha, and she was screwing Howarth.'

'Which her father knew. Why you? Why not Howarth? More Bernie's style of person than you.'

The conversation was becoming frustrating. Costello was starting to wither; the waiter was still eyeing her, and her inspector had drunk more than he should have. It was clear that Inspector Haddock's life was a mess. She had attempted to help once before, had spoken to his wife and calmed her fears about another woman, even picking him up from the mistress when it was proven that the woman's fears were well-founded, taken him to her place, made sure he had a shower to remove the other's woman's scent and put him in a taxi back to the family home, but it had all been in vain. Should she take Superintendent Payne's offer, dump her inspector, accept the promotion, transfer to another department at State Crime Command, or take Haddock's position and transfer him to another location, somewhere far enough from Sydney? Was Payne genuine? Or was it a ploy to get her onside, then seduce her?

She was anxious for promotion, deserving of it, but Haddock was a millstone around her neck that she wasn't ready to get rid of. 'Focus, Natalie,' she murmured to herself. 'Get Costello to talk.'

'Josh, the truth. Was Sasha's death related to her and her father's involvement with pornography?'

'It could be.'

'Is this why you came to State High Command? Did you want to tell us something, frightened of the consequences?'

'Frightened, who wouldn't be? I might not have known the full details, but I knew some. Bernie was in serious financial trouble, not that you'd notice it, but that's how the man's wired, the cut and the chase. He needed fast money, and there was plenty in adult films. There was a recession, property prices were down, and the cost of servicing the loans was becoming an issue. He told me one night. Sometimes he'd talk to me. "Josh", he said. "I might have to move Sasha out of the Horizon building, the love shack you and her are living in." That was how he said it, sometimes formal, sometimes casual. He knew about her and me, her indiscretions and mine. I was certain he had private investigators watching us; he needed to know everything. Not that he had a problem with Sasha or me. He told me that he needed cash and fast, the reason he had thrown in his lot with the devil. Oh, yes, he was clear in what he was doing, knew the risks to life and limb.'

'And it was Sasha that paid with her life.'

'Was it? I can't be sure. It might be unrelated. What else did Sasha know? What about the prime minister's floozy? Have you spoken to her? She must have a few hidden secrets, and according to Sasha, the woman would spill the beans.'

'Soon after, Sasha disappeared,' Natalie said. 'Is it possible? We've considered it, aware that Davidson was using his position to advantage, feathering his nest, taking Beth Madison at the taxpayers' expense around the world, whispered secrets over the pillow of a night time.'

'And now, Beth, respectable, an Eastern Suburbs matriarch, pure as the driven snow.'

'You know her?'

'Not well. I met her a few times, purely social, nothing more.'

'Did you like her?'

'I didn't know about her and Davidson until Sasha told me, came as a shock. According to Sasha, Beth had plenty on her former lover, enough to blow the lid off his respectability, possibly destroy his marriage, an honourable political career down the gurgler, and possibly a corruption charge, although I would have thought all of those were unlikely.'

'Why?' Natalie asked.

'It's a club, I told you. They would have rallied around the man, protecting him at all costs. Not out of loyalty or decency, but what do you reckon half of his political colleagues were up to? Looking out for themselves, most of them. Davidson had probably done it better than most, and having Beth as a mistress, they would have admired him. Not publicly, if it couldn't be contained, but privately, they would wish it was them. If you want devious and corrupt, look to our politicians; a few decent people there, but many aren't. And Davidson might have been into more than a few dodgy land deals and mining leases.'

'Adult movies?'

'Not as a performer.'

Natalie thought the idea was ridiculous and laughed so much that the waiter realised his chances were slim. He walked away, no longer ogling her.

Haddock offered a comment but was ignored by the other two. His evening was over, and he had to get home and sleep it off. Beth Madison would need to be spoken to again. And why hadn't the messenger been killed? After all, according to

Sasha, no details had been given to her, and intimation of something more would have been squashed, Official Secrets Act, privileged information, a flurry of lawyers, letters sent to the police, back off or else.

Superintendent Payne would have discounted the threats and told Haddock and her to get on with it and not to bow down to pressure. She liked that about the man, willing to take a stance and defend those who worked for him.

'Howarth, where does he stand in all of this?' Natalie asked.

'How will you get him to talk? Granted, he would probably know it all. A confidante of Bernie's, Sasha's lover, and the man who has connections, privy to Bernie's paperwork. There must be a record of the adult movie business somewhere, although under a different name; take an army of accountants to find it. Talk to Ingesson and Underwood, not that they would have been able to deal with the overseas distributors, but they must have sensed something, known something.'

'Your movements from here on in?'

'I'll stay in Sydney another month and make a decision. I'd prefer my wife and our children here with me, but if she won't come, there's not much I can do.'

'No chance of a green card?'

'It's possible. I'm not sure I want to return, and if I do, on less money than before. Bernie paid me well. I'll give him that.'

It seemed that there were more questions now than answers. Natalie knew that the next week she and Haddock would be busy. She thought the adult movies offered the best possibility, but Davidson and his shenanigans were homegrown and easier to pursue, although there was bound to be political interference. Nothing was clear; Howarth had the answers, and Beth Madison had some details.

If Sasha had been murdered for what she had known seventeen years prior, was the reason still relevant? Would there be another death? To Natalie, it had all the markings of further violence. She was excited on the one hand and afraid on the other. Even though it was late in the evening, she would have to walk her inspector home to ensure he was safe; it was not a good idea to have a police inspector asleep on a park bench.

There was an adrenaline rush that she could feel. It was what she liked about policing and Homicide, rarely a dull moment, and then rapid momentum, the chance to drill deep, to pressure some, to coerce, to get others drunk.

'I'll grab a taxi,' Costello said as he left the pub. The two police officers followed soon after.

Chapter 17

It was a remarkable recovery. The next morning, Haddock was in his office at State Crime Command for a seven o'clock meeting with Superintendent Payne.

Early morning meetings with Payne were not the norm, a reason to believe it was important. Natalie received the message on her phone at midnight, sent by Victoria, with no explanation or callback other than to be in the office promptly.

In Payne's office, the man sat at his voluminous desk. Victoria sat alongside Natalie and Haddock on the other side.

'Update,' Payne said. In one hand, he held a mug of tea.

'Our current investigation centres on two possibilities: adult movies and a former prime minister,' Haddock said, aware that the evidence for either was slim and depended on two gay men talking or an Eastern Suburbs socialite willing to risk ostracism from those she regarded as important.

'Treading on toes,' Victoria said. Natalie and Haddock regarded her as competent and ambitious. They had worked with her before – willing to take a stand when required to go the extra mile. Natalie also knew she had separated from her husband and was living with a girlfriend. The woman was bisexual, which didn't worry Natalie unless the woman came on strong to her, which she hadn't. The relationship with Payne was indeterminate, and Natalie thought, in Payne's office, that it might be her seeing wrong when there wasn't any. A police officer, as competent as she had become, saw possibilities in any situation, not least that of Payne and Victoria, or the two gay men, Ingesson and Underwood, or Beth Madison and Ralph Davidson.

'And incurring the wrath of others,' Payne added.

'Davidson?' Haddock asked.

'Official Secrets Act, the usual. I'm being pressured for us to back off. Even if he's involved in corruption, it might be suppressed.'

'Why?' Natalie asked.

'Politics. Deals are made, some above board, but embarrassing if the details are revealed. Let us assume Davidson took a backhander. But what else occurred? Was an environmental impact statement altered? Was there a rare breed of frog or bird not mentioned? Some might have been sanctioned by the government, employment, and a boost to the local economy. It's happened before, still does, and Davidson was a pragmatist, saw the bigger picture, and took the opportunity to line his pocket.'

'Do we continue?' Haddock asked.

'It's murder. You know the answer,' Payne said.

It was the answer Natalie and Haddock expected. Payne would not kowtow to political or legal pressure. To him, solving the murder took precedence.

'What can you prove?' Victoria asked.

'Not a lot, no names if it's adult movies, a lot of money there. We don't believe that Bernie Cornell would have been averse to financing such an operation, the hidden man, a sense of the dramatic. Costello told us that sometimes Cornell was short of cash, money tied up, and probably adult movies were exciting, a sense of adventure, which is how Sasha saw it, and so did Duncan Howarth, a star in one or two if we were told the truth,' Natalie said, conscious that in a discussion at State Crime Command, it was her who spoke more than her inspector, who the others looked to for discussion.

'Duncan Howarth, the mind boggles,' Victoria smirked. 'Any idea which movies?'

'Victoria, keep it serious. Howarth's a suspect, close to Bernie Cornell. Titillation is not appreciated here,' Payne reminded her.

'My apologies. I've met Howarth on a couple of occasions. It's hard to imagine.'

'Hard is the operative word,' Natalie said, surprised that she had said it.

'Okay, everyone's had their fun,' Payne said. 'Get serious. What was his involvement?'

'We've not seen the films,' Haddock said. 'No facial shots. It was seventeen years ago when he was a lot younger. The sporting hero, the great man, probably saw it as a lark, something to shock if anyone knew. Not that anyone did, not that we've asked. Costello told us last night after more than a few drinks.'

'You and him, blind drunk?'

'More than I should have, but we needed him primed. It was Sergeant Campbell who got him to talk.'

'Natalie, what's your take on this?' Payne asked. In his office, a degree of informality was acceptable when discussing a case. He could see Haddock holding her back, but she had been adamant that they were a good team. He admired people who took a stand on principle, even when it was against their best interests, and he knew she was ambitious and could use the extra money.

'Howarth could open this case wide, but he won't talk, and we can't get near him without concrete evidence that he's concealing Bernie Cornell's involvement in pornography and possibly Ralph Davidson's corruption.'

'If it exists or it's true. We're talking about a period almost two decades ago. Any evidence is possibly not there, and there's a statute of limitations. Victoria,' Payne said, looking over at her, 'you're the lawyer. How do we deal with Duncan Howarth? Any ideas?'

'He's already resisted requests from Sergeant Campbell and Inspector Haddock. Not sure he would respond to anything I might produce. I would need something firm for him to answer.'

'Which we don't have,' Natalie said.

'Then I suggest you get it,' Payne said. The meeting ended with no conclusion, just acknowledgement that the superintendent would keep the wolves at bay, Victoria would research how to get Howarth to talk, and Natalie and Haddock were on a flight to Brisbane that afternoon.

***

An informal approach for the first meeting at a neutral location, a restaurant not far from the police station in Brisbane. The reunited lovers arrived, holding hands. Haddock didn't like it, but Natalie was ambivalent, pleased for the two men who had rediscovered their love for each other and sad that she hadn't found anyone to replace the live-in boyfriend who had cheated on her.

'Are you staying?' Haddock directed the question at Underwood.

'Uncertain, we might go overseas, somewhere cheaper, and Gustav needs a break from police harassment.'

'From us? Not sure it's harassment,' Natalie said.

The four ordered, the two men, no longer holding hands, adamant that they would pay for their meal. Haddock didn't object.

'It is, but Gustav had a run-in over under-the-counter steroids. He wasn't involved; we both learnt our lesson after a few years in prison.'

The man was guilty of the crime, Natalie and Haddock were convinced of that, but neither commented. The crime was unprovable, but the police in Brisbane were persistent, even if incompetent.

Haddock drank a beer, Natalie a house wine, and the two men ordered a cocktail each, a cherry on a stick, an umbrella propped inside the glass.

It appeared to be a friendly get-together, which it was – for now.

Once the meal had been eaten and Ingesson and Underwood had swooned over each other, Natalie decided it was time to talk.

'We know you are both anxious to discover what happened to Sasha, and we believe you're not involved.'

'We loved her, a true friend. We were sad when she disappeared, but like everyone else, we thought she had just taken off, a new lover, time out from her life,' Ingesson said.

'When did you worry?'

'After a month, maybe six weeks. Sasha had a wild side to her, the same as her father.

'You met him?'

'On a couple of occasions. I can't say I'd liked him; his reputation was dreadful, companies he had taken over, people he had dismissed.'

'Enterprises he had funded,' Haddock chimed in.

'Including ours,' Underwood responded.

Natalie could see her inspector destroying the mood of the gathering. The softly-softly approach had been her idea. Gay men like Ingesson and Underwood could be sensitive and would not respond to being berated by a forceful heterosexual male.

'What we need to know is, was it your idea to expand the business from gay to heterosexual? From locally distributed to worldwide?' Natalie said. 'We have no proof of this, and we don't believe you would have dealt with the distribution. That's cutthroat, nasty criminals involved, and you two couldn't hold your own.'

'If we were?'

'We want to find Sasha's murderer, not revisit other crimes from long ago. You were sentenced for your crimes; no more to answer.'

'Sasha saw the possibility, used our expertise, and set up another studio, another production team. We wrote the scripts, assisted occasionally, no more than once or twice. After that, we were paid as consultants, would get to look at the final product, quality control, give our stamp of approval, and send it on.'

'Distribution?' Haddock asked, taking the lead from his sergeant and keeping it calm, although sickened by the open displays of affection by the two men.

'We weren't involved. You were right. We couldn't negotiate. Our clientele before had been within the gay community, word of mouth mainly. It was good money, even on that scale, but Sasha had admitted that her father was interested in becoming involved.'

'Shocked by that revelation?'

'Confused. Her father had money, but he had a reputation, ruthless but honourable. Why would he want to become involved in our seedy little operation?'

'He saw the possibilities, the untold money to be made, tempt even a saint.'

'Not us. Heterosexual pornography offends us as much as gay porn would you.'

'Duncan Howarth?'

'Sasha told us he did it for a laugh, the great hero, debased and appearing in a porno. Not that we could see the joke, but then Howarth didn't like us, no more than we liked him.'

'You met him?'

Underwood replied, 'We did. A soiree at Sasha's one night, a couple of mincing queers and the macho man. He made his dislike of us obvious, didn't say it out loud, but we were used to it, learned to ignore.'

'Why did Sasha tell you so much?'

'She trusted us. We would never have told a soul, not even on trial.'

'Did Bernie look after you in prison?'

'Not that we saw. It was rough, beefy men with tattoos. We were there to satisfy them, no matter if we didn't want it.'

'Okay,' Natalie said. 'Here's the crux of the matter. Sasha was killed for a reason. It's either the pornography distributors, heavy-handed with Bernie Cornell, or political corruption. Bernie's not likely to buckle under the threat of the distributors and will take them on at their own game. But he's out of his league. Business in Australia is kiddies' play to what some of them get up to overseas. Mafia in the USA, rogues and villains of the worst kind in other countries. He's pressuring the internationals, or they're pressuring him. Neither side will back down, but they have a lever, Bernie's daughter. Everyone has an Achilles heel, and she was his. She's a bargaining chip; make a deal or else. But Bernie doesn't believe they will do anything, just keep her safe and secure for a few days, or maybe he offered her as collateral, maybe she had agreed. Something goes wrong, and she ends up dead. Then someone with knowledge of Pinchgut reckons it's an apt place to bury her, in sight of Bernie's mansion, sees her every day but doesn't know.'

'It sounds implausible, burying her out there,' Ingesson said.

'It is,' Natalie agreed. However, it was a position from which to postulate.

Nobody thought that the reason for Pinchgut for the burial of Sasha's body was plausible. Not Superintendent Payne, not even Haddock's wife, nor Victoria.

Haddock had spent quality time with his daughter the previous night at the family home, but she was sixteen going on twenty-five. At least, she thought she was, but without the calming influence of the father in the house, there was a wildness about her. The love bite on the neck confirmed heavy petting, but Haddock had been around the block. He knew the current generation of teens does not consider virginity a virtue, but when did they? Hadn't he and his wife, her mother, rushed up to the altar before the pregnancy showed? He had spoken to his wife, who realised what their daughter was up to, unsure how to confront her other than to advise her to be careful.

Haddock's approach was more direct. 'Don't do it,' he said, a scowl from him, his daughter looking away from him. He knew she didn't want a parent advising or commanding, turning to her peers, equally young, equally naïve and stupid, for advice. Advice that was given freely and in abundance was counterproductive. How many lives were wasted due to a foolish act when the child transitioned to an adult? At the back of the house, he had a room for him to stay in, his wife's bed off-limits, although the first night he had spent there after their separation, they had made love, but not now, not until the situation settled and their daughter was wiser. Which, to Haddock, would be a long time. Hadn't he been foolish in his early teens, getting into fights, aiming to prove that he was a strong man, taking on all-comers, standing in front of a magistrate for unruly behaviour, receiving a fine and a lecture from the magistrate and his father, and then at the age of twenty-one, wising up and sorting himself out? He assumed his wife had a similar history to his daughter, but they had never discussed it. The past was best left back there. However, a female can become pregnant. The most a young man can get is a bunch of fives, a severe fine, and a belting from those stronger than him. Although he couldn't remember anyone beating him, realising he was digressing, best to deal with the issue front and centre.

In his room, father and daughter. One made a conciliatory speech, the other, averting her eyes, embarrassed to hear her father talk about matters so personal, and yes, she wasn't a virgin, but he was a good person who wouldn't let her down.

He tried to explain that he would, and at their ages, final decisions on a life partner couldn't be made. He emphasised that he wasn't criticising, not telling her to stop, but advising that love eternal at sixteen is the fodder of soppy movies and make-believe. The boyfriend would want other women before deciding on one, and she would have other men, some who would break her heart, others who would treat her badly. It was part of life, the growing process, the transition from child to adult, and a traumatic time for those who went through it.

In the end, they hugged, his daughter appreciative of her father's concern and glad he was in the house. 'Taking protection?' his final words.

'Yes, Dad.'

As an overly protective father, he wanted to lock her in her room and give the boyfriend a smack around the head, but he knew that wouldn't work and only create tension. Best to be an ear to listen if she needed advice. His wife appreciated what he had done, kissed him on the cheek, and opened a bottle of wine. It was good in the home, but it wouldn't last. A police inspector, dedicated to his craft, coming home at all hours, sometimes the worse for wear, was what she had signed up for when they had got married, but now, she wanted more than he could give.

Ingesson continued. 'We were in the backroom, not dealing with the heavies.'

'Were they?' Haddock asked.

'We saw one of them once, swarthy, dressed in a suit.'

'Australian?'

'American. We didn't speak to him; he preferred watching a couple going hell for leather.'

'Gay porn?'

'Regular, male, female. An attractive woman, the man had another attribute.'

Both officers understood.

'Why come to Australia? Why did he want to visit? Who was he?'

'We don't know if Bernie knew he was there, and we didn't tell him. Sasha might have known, but we didn't tell her either.'

'Why?'

'Low profile. It was obvious that Sasha and her father, especially her father, were dealing with unsavoury characters. Before, it had been fun, and our distribution channels had been friends, but now, we could see it was not. We had produced movies for those discerning few who were appreciative, but now it was sordid and dangerous. It never came out at our trials; I don't know why, assume the production continued without us, another location, and possibly another production team.'

'Did you think that Sasha was playing with fire?'

'I told her to be careful,' Underwood said.

'Her response?'

'She told us not to worry. Implicit trust in her father. Maybe she was right; who knows? Only that we kept out of it, never visited where they were making the movies again, backroom boys as we said.'

'Paid well for your efforts?'

'Well enough. We enjoyed gay porn and made money from it. But the business had become crass commercialism. The performances had become mechanical, grunting and grinding.'

'And yours weren't?' Haddock asked.

'You wouldn't understand. Our movies were made with love and kindness.'

Haddock hadn't seen either of those commodities in the gay porn he had watched, but he was a police inspector investigating a murder, not an arbiter of what constitutes art, and adult movies attracted the wrong kind of people, the American, for instance. And the two who could elucidate were both dead. Only one person who might know remained, and he was conspicuous by his absence and the barrier between him and the police.

Chapter 18

Two days later, back at State Crime Command in Parramatta, Victoria Adderley was working hard, trying to get Duncan Howarth to talk, and Natalie and Haddock were sifting through what they had so far. Searches were out for the production team that had taken over from Ingesson and Underwood, but it was difficult as a long time had passed since then. Addresses had changed, possibly names, and the performers had names reflecting the industry.

Natalie found one of the performers, slim and pretty with pert breasts when performing, but now Crystal was in her forties and living in the Blue Mountains, a two-hour drive to the west of Sydney.

'A long time ago, crazy in the head,' the woman said. No longer slim and pretty, but overweight and dressed downmarket.

'Why?' Natalie felt she should ask, not that it would advance the investigation but to find out what made women debase themselves in such a visible manner.

'Drug addiction. Not everyone is, but most have an issue, psychological, an abusive childhood, or drugs. Most don't live to a ripe old age.'

They were in a three-bedroom house in a middle-class area of Katoomba, the main city in the mountains, not far from the unusual rock formation known as the Three Sisters, the area's primary tourist attraction, overlooking the scenic vista of the Megalong Valley.

'But you sorted yourself out.'

'In time. I would prefer the videos not to be out there; not much I can do about it. Nobody recognises me, not now, old and frumpy. I could make myself look better, but I prefer anonymity.'

'Family?'

'A fifteen-year-old son, a daughter of thirteen.'

'Husband?'

'Boringly middle class, which suits me fine, and yes, my husband knows. I had to tell him before we married, let him know what he was getting into, reformed drug addict, ex-porn star.'

'His response?'

'Love conquers all, or words to that effect. It's not discussed in this house, and the children don't know. I hope my son doesn't find any of my movies online. That would be tough; I might have to tell the children one day. Hope I don't have to. But you know what children are like.'

Natalie did.

'Three hours,' Crystal, or Anne as she was now called, said.

'Before your children arrive home from school?'

'I don't want them to see you here, although I could introduce you as a friend. They'd be excited to know if I was assisting in a murder investigation, but that would require more answers. I can't avoid telling them some of the truth one day. I've been putting it off for a long time, but today's not the day. You, Sergeant, represent trouble.'

'We could have met somewhere else.'

'We couldn't. I've committed no crime, and I don't intend to hide away from the police. I was young and confused, heroin-addicted. People do stupid things in their life, and I have done mine. And yes, I knew Sasha, Terrence, and Gustav but never met Sasha's father.'

'How well did you know them?'

'In passing. The two men didn't appreciate the finer aspects of heterosexual sexual activity. A couple of bum boys is what the producer said, not maliciously, as he was gay. But he wasn't the mincing type. Is Terrence mincing? I've not seen them for a long time, don't want to, no reunions of long-lost workmates for me.'

'Fear of a relapse, inject yourself again?'

'Not me, not now. The demons have been vanquished. Anyway, I knew Sasha, but not well. We would chat occasionally, not about the videos, but about life. I liked her, a kindred spirit, mixed up, unsure of herself.'

'A wealthy father, a successful business, plenty of friends, a man she loved.'

'She cheated on him. Did you know that?'

'She told you?'

'Once, she did, not that she mentioned a name.'

'Sasha was murdered for a reason. Adult movies bring in unsavoury persons, and the money generated is mind-boggling. Did you see anyone who was suspicious, or did you hear anything untoward? Ingesson and Underwood aren't involved, but we believe that Sasha's father was behind the scenes, dealing with distribution through his contacts or others he had made. Persons who might have killed Sasha. And any idea why a small island in the middle of Sydney Harbour would be significant?'

'Duncan Howarth. He came along once and took part in one of the movies. Maybe you know that already.'

'We do. No headshot, though.'

'There was, edited out. Find the original.'

'How and where?'

'Melbourne, Bill Sharples, not the name on the movie credits, but that's his name now. Runs a video production company, privately-funded movies, no pornography, music videos, advertising videos, totally legitimate and above board. He might not like to be reminded of the past, but he would be your best bet.'

'In contact?'

'Not for a long time. I saw him interviewed on television a few years back and recognised him, although he's balding now. He was an archivist, a stash of early Australian movies, who thought retaining the country's history was important. I wouldn't be surprised if he doesn't have a stash of us cavorting in front of the camera, and then there might be a facial of Howarth.'

'You were in the movie with him?'

'I was the other half of the duo. No idea why he wanted to be involved, but then a walk on the wild side might have appealed.'

'Not much of a walk,' Natalie said. 'Afterwards, did you hook up with him?'

'If you're asking, did I spend the night with him, the answer is yes. Just the once, an impressive man.'

'Did Sasha know?'

'Probably, but I don't know. Talk to Bill Sharples, don't mention my name if you can avoid it. And don't come here again. I'm sure you understand.'

'I do. We won't meet again, and do enjoy your boring middle-class life and your boring middle-class husband.'

'I will,' the former Crystal said.

***

The consensus was that the adult movie angle seemed the most likely reason for Sasha Cornell's murder, although the reason for Pinchgut hadn't been established. Sure, it was highly visible, the Manly ferry passing it every day, the ocean liners in the harbour steaming close by, disgorging their passengers into Sydney in the early morning, most days before six o'clock, leaving by five or six in the evening, a tug boat at the rear to steady them as they negotiated the harbour and its traffic.

The arrival of Duncan Howarth at Parramatta came as a shock. Victoria Adderley had been jubilant when she had told him that information had been obtained that tied him to a video production company almost two decades earlier and that it might be appropriate for him to clear the air rather than wait for a couple of police officers to be outside his office with a piece of paper in hand. She also said, one professional to another, that State Crime Command leaked like a sieve, and the case file was in Homicide, and more than a dozen people had access to it, and his name was in it, and it would be embarrassing if it came out.

She had never heard of Homicide leaking like a sieve, but she had added it just in case and enjoyed getting one up on Howarth.

'Off the record,' Howarth said.

A conference room had been set up for his visit. Natalie had to admit that he was an impressive man, and although his manner had been curt and demeaning to them at Bernie Cornell's house, he was agreeable at the police station.

'Thanks for coming,' Haddock said. He didn't like the man; too good to be true and dismissive of his inferiors. To Haddock, being born with the silver spoon in the mouth, and winning the genetics lottery, didn't impress. He was working class, a Western Suburbs snotty-nosed kid who had gone from being a smart-arsed street fighter to a police inspector, a greater achievement than being given all the ammunition for a successful life at birth.

'We need to clear up certain matters.'

Natalie knew that professional and personal embarrassment would result if Howarth's starring role, complete with his face visible, became known. Ridicule would result, and the video would go viral, a man known for sporting and business prowess revealed as a porn star.

'Two issues concern us,' Haddock said. 'One is what you knew of a video production company seventeen years ago. The second is your relationship with Bernie Cornell, which seems incongruous, in that the man appears to have made no contingency plan to ensure his legacy.'

'I'll answer the first issue. Sasha and, subsequently, Bernie became involved with Ingesson and Underwood. Sasha was fond of them, unsure why, as I found them obnoxious.'

'So do I,' Haddock said.

'Something in common,' Howarth said. 'However, she was involved and saw nothing wrong in what they were doing, but ultimately, they paid for their crimes. Sasha's involvement was hushed up, but she gave them money. It could have been argued that it was an unsecured loan, nothing more. Anyway, I was spending time with Sasha, not often, but we were good friends. Both of us had come from privilege, and both were successful. Josh Costello was the man she loved, but he was not of her calibre or class. I told her she should leave him and move in with me, but she wouldn't. She thought that Costello would do the right thing by her, but I wouldn't.'

'You wouldn't have,' Natalie said.

'You're right, Sergeant. I would have been unfaithful, but I would have stayed with her, been the father of her children, son-in-law of the great man. Bernie knew it, approved of me, but Sasha wouldn't have a bar of it.'

'The video?' Haddock came back to the first question. What Howarth said was important and could be crucial information, but the inspector feared that the man would direct the conversation and confuse, a manipulator of people and the truth. Even now, he was being magnanimous, almost friendly, which was not his usual demeanour, although it might have been with Natalie but not with him.

'Stupidity, what else can I say. My persona is carefully woven, ensuring visibility in the media and that any negatives against me are negated and the positives enhanced. I pay a public relations company a lot of money to deal with it.'

'Sasha's company?'

'No, although I would have if she was interested. But she had been honest with me, knew my foibles, a short temper, lewdness, and other bad habits.'

'Drugs?'

'Back then, cocaine. Nowadays, whisky. No serious vices against me, but back then, I went to see the videos being produced. Curiosity, I would say if pressured. Anyway, I was there for whatever reason. The producer was short of a male stud and asked if I would be interested. No face shot. I agreed, don't know why, and my public relations company would have had a fit, but no one ever knew.'

'Ingesson and Underwood knew, but they would never have revealed it, no matter how inconsequential you think they are,' Natalie said.

'No one else, apart from them. I might be harsh, but I don't approve of their behaviour or the videos they produced. The one I saw and participated in was vanilla, heterosexual, man, woman, the way it should be. I thought, why not? So I agreed, and besides, the woman was very attractive.'

'After the shoot, you took her home with you.'

'I did. No idea what became of her. We did the scene. I took her home, made her a meal, and she spent the night. She left the next morning; I never saw her again.'

'Except the producer lied. There is a facial shot of you and her, and it's clear what she was doing to you.'

'You've seen it.'

'We have.'

Natalie had made a phone call to an inspector she knew in Melbourne, the capital of the state of Victoria. He had been out to meet Bill Sharples, obtained the video, and checked it before leaving. Sharples had been adamant that it wasn't for public distribution, but it was evidence, and it was secured in Melbourne, edited highlights sent to Homicide in Parramatta.

'I might have been worried back then, but not now. The folly of youth might portray me as more human. I'll let the PR company deal with it. I would have preferred it to remain hidden, but I'm interested in discovering who murdered Sasha. That is more important than humour on social media and daytime television at my expense.'

'Two motives we keep returning to, adult movies and political corruption. The first you were involved in, a willing participant, or were you more? What type of persons was Bernie contracting with overseas and here in Australia? Dangerous individuals, who use violence and death as a negotiating tool?'

'My involvement was benign. I was aware of it, and dealt with the financials, read through the contracts negotiated, ensured money was paid, money received.'

'Offshore accounts?'

'Always. Bernie used them, and so would most people if given the opportunity.'

150

'Did you meet some of the people?'

'In America, sleazy gangsters, not that they said they were. I recognised the signs, the expensive suits, the battery of lawyers, and the reams of contractual paperwork, hidden from the authorities in their country. I warned Bernie to be careful, not that he was always squeaky clean, but he wasn't into murder or kidnapping, which was Bernie's fear when Sasha went missing.'

'He never told the police that,' Natalie said.

'It would have raised a cavalcade of questions for which there was no answer. And besides, no one came forward with a demand. A kidnapping would have had to have a reason, and no contact meant it wasn't that. He thought, so did I, that she had taken off with a guy she had met. Pretty certain I wasn't the only stud she slept with. Free-spirited, saw life as for living, not dwelling on, or rotting in suburbia.'

'If not kidnapping, then why did she die?'

'She must have known something, I don't know what, or seen something. You mentioned political corruption.'

'We did. Any thoughts?'

'Nothing to do with me. I would have thought politics and corruption were one and the same, small-minded people, inflated with their opinions of themselves, making sure they're well-compensated, over the table or under it, ensuring they stay elected long enough to receive their generous pension for service to Australia.'

'You don't reckon much to them?'

'Most are marginalised by factional politics, catering to vocal minorities in their electorate, staying elected and cashing in. No, is the answer.'

'Your relationship with Bernie Cornell. How did he intend to preserve his legacy?'

'You met the man, what do you reckon?' Howarth asked.

'Straightforward, no airs and graces, concerned about his daughter,' Haddock said.

'That was the man. He had only one weakness, Sasha, and for seventeen years, he held onto the belief that she would walk in the door one day. A workman at Pinchgut finding her body destroyed that illusion. He had one purpose left in his life, to find her killer, but in the end, old age and ill health finished him off. As for the legacy, it meant little to him. His assets will slowly be dissolved, a library at a university with his name on it, a school somewhere else, a hospital maybe. Seventy to seventy-five per cent of his wealth will be used for the good of the community; his name will live on, and his empire will slowly wither, consumed into other empires.'

'Yours?'

'There are complex legal agreements duly signed by Bernie and endorsed by me. I will not cheat him or anyone else, no reason to, and besides, Sasha's murder affected me too.'

Howarth's face showed a visible sorrow as he left the police station. Natalie thought that maybe he had loved Sasha, but discounted it. Duncan Howarth would not be capable of intense feelings for another person.

Chapter 19

Sydney Harbour became the scene of another drama. Leo Hannan had found Sasha Cornell's remains, but a young boy found the second body at Watson's Bay, not far from the Gap, an ocean cliff at South Head in the Eastern Suburbs, facing out to the Tasman Sea, infamous for suicides. But this was not suicide. It was murder, a nylon cord around the man's neck. Natalie had been to Watson's Bay several times, a ferry ride from Circular Quay, the Watsons Bay Hotel, fish and chips and a bottle of wine. It was an idyllic spot, full of tourists at the weekend, devoid of any on a rain-sodden and windy day.

As the two police officers looked down at the body, brought ashore on an incoming tide, they knew who it was. It was the man they had dined with at the Commercial Hotel in Parramatta; it was Josh Costello.

It was a further complication in an investigation that had consumed more time than expected, but it was possibly the breakthrough they were looking for.

Neither officer was fazed by the scene, even though the man was known to them.

'Why?' Haddock said as he moved away from the body. The crime scene investigators had erected a tent, and they were busy. There was no need to ask what had killed him. Over in the distance was the young boy who had found the body. They would talk to him at some stage. Judging by the state of the body and the cord around the neck, Josh Costello had been in the water for several hours. Where he had died and how far he had drifted might be relevant. Did his murderers know he had been speaking to the police, getting drunk with them, and saying things he shouldn't have? Were they being watched? Was Costello? Who were these people? Gingerly, Natalie turned her head, looking for someone suspicious, but she could not see anyone.

'Don't bother,' Haddock said. 'We'll not find anything on Costello's body or anyone lurking unless luck is on our side, and I don't hold with that. It hasn't done me much good over the years.'

Natalie thought Haddock was downbeat and negative. There was no reason to feel concern for the dead man. He had been there when Sasha had disappeared, a link with the past, but he wasn't a prime suspect, not back then, not now, and he was dead, killed by either the person who had killed Sasha or someone different. The question was always the same: why?

Beth Madison couldn't help. She was called into Homicide at six that evening. A report on Costello's death would be forthcoming from Forensics and Pathology, but it was unlikely to assist constructively, although the talkative and cooperative woman opposite the two officers might.

'Frightened?' Natalie asked. She had given the woman a cup of coffee to calm her nerves, but she still shook.

'My husband brought me. I couldn't drive, not after what happened to Josh Costello.'

'You knew him?'

'A long time ago, but not well.'

'An attractive man.'

'He was, but I had Ralph. To me, the prime minister of Australia had something that Josh would never have.'

'We know that Sasha could be liberal with her favours when young. Were you?'

'Prudish, but with Ralph, that was something different.'

'Even though he was married?'

'I saw it as love, pure and simple, what should be, and his wife is a shrew, not that he will tell you. They pretended to be a loving couple at the book launch, but it was separate bedrooms at home, and they barely said a word to each other. Strange that he dumped me; not sure why. Why would he have? You're police officers; surely you must have thought about it.'

'We were pursuing another possibility. We still think it's the stronger motive of the two, but hard to prove. Too many years have passed.'

'It was Ralph or someone else; systemic corruption at the highest level.'

'Are you certain?' Natalie asked. 'Can you prove it?'

'It's unlikely you will find anyone to corroborate my story, and those who might have are either dead or dying. Seventeen years, people get old, their memories aren't as sharp, or they discover amnesia.'

'It might be best if you give us a statement, as much detail as you can. Dates, people, actions, leave it to us. No guarantee it will come to a satisfactory conclusion, too many people with a vested interest to distort the truth. And you've been holding back. Why?'

'The answer was fished out of the harbour today. Why ask a question when you know the reason. Why do you think I didn't meet with Sasha, and then she's dead, and Ralph's on the phone, telling me it will be me next if I don't take the money and keep my mouth shut.'

'Had you told her anything?'

'Enough for her to create waves, and her father had the clout to find out. Ralph was frightened, knew him as a shrewd operator, but Bernie Cornell was politically opposed, saw a better future than Ralph and his cronies, and would have taken the opportunity to bring him down.'

'Why would he be concerned?'

'Elder statesman, ambassador to the United States, all the perks. Then there's the ego, not shy of it, not Ralph. Me, in his bed, a wife at home, a reputation to protect at all costs.'

'But who would have murdered Sasha and given her a burial on the island?' And why are you still alive? If Bernie had known that what you had was political dynamite, why didn't he contact you?'

'His daughter is missing; concerned about her, not me,' Beth Madison said.

It was a logical answer that the daughter's disappearance had taken the emphasis away from Davidson and placed the focus on a missing woman. Beth Madison's disappearance would not have had the same impact, and those who knew of her and her relationship with the prime minister might use it to their advantage. Indiscretions by politicians had not been spoken of in the long distant past, but seventeen years ago, they were. Official Secrets Act and security had kept a lid on the PM's romantic interludes, but they could not have been too secret, others must have known, and if there was corruption, it would not have been the prime minister on his own ramming through approval for the mining lease, treading others underfoot. Australia was a functioning democracy, a political process with a percentage of irradicable corruption and irradicable incompetence. And then there were the various departments and organisations concerned with the environmental impact, wildlife preservation, the quality of life in the affected areas, pollution, real estate prices, the cost of the infrastructure, and whether it was technically feasible, and also about the Barrier Reef, the world's largest coral reef, threatened by the crown-of-thorns starfish, rising sea temperatures, and tourism. It was a quagmire to wade through, and it would take more than a prime minister to resolve the lease issue. A cabal would be needed, palms would need to be greased, promises broken, people sidelined, and others elevated.

What was Beth Madison scared of? Howarth had a support network, Beth did not, other than the Eastern Suburbs socialites that would offer their sympathy but do no more, essentially neutered by the need to maintain their social standing, their wealth, and their reputations, which meant a lot to them, but not to the two police officers. Outside the room, Barnaby Madison waited. Neither Natalie nor Haddock had met the man, unsure if he was important or just a bit player in the saga. However, there had to be an answer to why Pinchgut.

Although Beth would have abhorred the reference, Juanita Neilson, another socialite, had lived in Kings Cross. The granddaughter of the founder of a retail empire, she would have inherited a fortune in time, but instead, she devoted herself to conservation, highly active and visible in the seventies, due to her opposition to the urban development on heritage Victoria Street in Potts Point. It was a time of organised crime and police corruption, rumoured political but never proven. She had disappeared in July 1975, and her body was never found, either buried under the developments she opposed or weighted down and thrown into the harbour. But Sasha Cornell had been found, not at sea, but incarcerated in a place that one day might be discovered. There had been multiple occasions when the discovery could have been made, but why did it take seventeen years? Was there a reason?

Barnaby Madison came into the room and sat alongside his wife. He was tall and striking, with greying hair, although still in his forties. Natalie could see affection between husband and wife; Haddock could not.

'You're aware of the situation?' Haddock asked.

'My wife's past, the current situation, Costello's death? Yes, I am. My wife is worried, and so am I. We are dealing with people we do not understand, who regard violence as a solution.'

'Pacificist?'

'Not particularly. We want to sleep easy at night, and now I've had to pay for security to protect Beth and our children. When will this end?'

'When we get answers. Your wife is privy to certain information, but, with time, it has lessened in importance, probably not even prosecutable now. Although with Sasha Cornell's reappearance, it could be. Is it related to Davidson and political corruption or another line of enquiry we're pursuing? What's your take on this? You're a real estate agent in the Eastern Suburbs. Have you heard anything or suspected something? No matter how insignificant, it could be important.'

'It could be that someone decided it was time for the body to be discovered before her father died,' Natalie said. It had just come to her that, with Cornell close to death, it was opportune to throw a spanner in the works, to distract the man, and to strike a deal that would be advantageous to the person behind the deception.

'Any more to add, Mr Madison?' Haddock said, aware that his sergeant was one step ahead of him. Momentarily, he felt inadequate, the inspector outsmarted by his sergeant. He wasn't sure what he thought, the realisation, yet again, that she was the lead investigator in ability, if not in rank.

'Another restaurant to open on Pinchgut, but it's not the first time; the last one closed in 2007. Why she hadn't been found then makes no sense. I never knew her, but Beth said she was capable. Apart from that, there's no more I can add.'

'One thing,' Beth said. 'Ralph spoke about the island once, a partnership with a company interested in taking over the lease. This would have been around the time of her disappearance, but he could not have put her there, no intention of getting his hands dirty.'

'A possibility,' Haddock said. 'Is there more?'

'Proof of Ralph's corruption.'

'Are you sure?' Natalie asked. 'You're in deep, as it is. Are you prepared to go deeper?'

'I am. I've spoken to Barnaby; the children will visit my sister in England until this calms down. We'll stay here and see it through. I suppose I owe it to Sasha, and Ralph, not that I'm bitter, not after so many years, and now I've got Barnaby and our children.'

Haddock did not think England afforded more protection but was unwilling to say so in the meeting. He was, however, interested in Beth Madison explaining more of what she knew. 'Detail what you know, what you can prove.'

'Political corruption at the highest level. Documentation which I can supply, although it's old. At the time, it would have caused Ralph embarrassment, caused him to be deposed, and a Royal Commission set up if the opposition had won the upcoming election. But now, it's irrelevant.'

'Has he contacted you recently?' Natalie asked.

'We see him from time to time. Polite conversation, nothing more, no threats. I don't believe he is behind Josh's death.'

'Then why are you a threat? Our other line of enquiry has nothing to do with you, or does it? Gustav Ingesson, and Terrence Underwood, are the names significant?'

'Not to me,' Beth said.

Natalie didn't think they would be. When younger, Beth Madison had erred with the prime minister, flattered by the man's attention and power. But now, a devoted wife and mother, nothing more.

'I'll make sure a police car drives past your house every few hours,' Natalie said. She would phone Kings Cross Police Station and pull in a few favours for the woman.

***

It was a hunch, but Natalie thought it to be good. Not the relevance of Pinchgut, but why the body had been discovered after seventeen years. Other people had been on the island over the years, renovating, modifying the kitchen and the facilities, laying in electrical cables and sewerage from the mainland, and restorative action on the ageing construction of the fort, but no one had attempted to remove a wall in a room underneath the tower, not until Leo Hannan, alone on the island, had.

Due to the seriousness of her concerns, Hannan presented himself at State High Command at 9 a.m. the following day. He was dressed casually, in jeans and a white shirt. Natalie had initially liked the man, but then she found that he had taken some of the money in Sasha's handbag, along with some documents, and he had hidden them in his apartment, unbeknown to his wife. No charges had been laid, but he had received a stiff warning. One more time, and he would be charged with a crime.

'Not sure I can help you,' Hannan said.

'You can,' Natalie replied. She had adopted the softly-softly approach in the past with him, but this time the hunch was strong, and she was not in the mood for his procrastinating or avoiding the question.

'I'll do what I can.'

'Fine. First question, why were you alone on the island? Surely health and safety would have required more than one. What if there had been an accident?'

'Bert was there with me, and so was Graham. Bert's wife had been rushed to the hospital, and they had taken the boat to Garden Island. Graham was coming back for me.'

'I never saw another person and was there for a few hours.'

'Graham's had run-ins with the law before. He saw you, then the commotion, and decided not to return.'

'You messaged him.'

'As a mate. No reason for him to get into more trouble; enough as it is. He was doing it tough, drug addiction, and we'd been covering for him for a few days.'

'Where is he now?'

'Unsure, and that's the truth. After it became a crime scene, our company laid off most of us and kept me on, as I was the witness who had discovered the body. They reckoned my getting the sack would have reflected badly on them.'

'It would have. We'll need Graham's details, also confirmation from Bert.'

'No problem. I've got his phone number.'

'Even if we accept your explanation, there remains the issue of why you discovered the body when other persons have worked out there.'

'Lucky, I guess. I wasn't looking for anything untoward, but there I was. I hit the wall; it cracked and crumbled. Can't say any more than that.'

'But why you? Was there a plan to enlarge the room? It's heritage. You can't go damaging the place, excavating or tearing down the tower without a detailed plan and someone signing off on it.'

Natalie wasn't sure about the construction and renovation process of a heritage-listed building and was testing if Hannan did.

'Convenient you finding the body, don't you think?' Natalie continued. 'For seventeen years, the body had been there, a cannon firing at 1 p.m. for some of the years, vibration and shockwaves from it, the pounding of the sea, people in the restaurant, guided tours of the fort, and then, you come along, pickaxe in hand, and the wall gives way. Too convenient.'

'That's what happened. Okay, I stuffed up before, took some money from the handbag, but I didn't kill her, just a child back then, and I didn't find her because I thought it was time. Hell, I didn't know who she was. I had never read the story about her, the daughter of Bernie Cornell, a rich woman. I searched on the internet before you arrived. The woman had it made, and then someone killed her. Why, I don't know. She was attractive, a lot of class, a shame that she died, but don't look to me for an explanation.'

'But I am, Leo,' Natalie said.

Haddock came into the room. 'Got it,' he said.

'Proof?'

'Conclusive. Our man here is lying through his teeth.'

'I'm not,' Hannan protested. 'This is a setup.'

'A phone call, two days earlier, that Leo Hannan was to go into that room and expose the body, money into his account,' Haddock said.

'One day, not two,' Hannan blurted, painfully aware he was correct.

'The truth, Leo,' Natalie said. 'Unless you want charges laid. Withholding evidence is a criminal offence, and perverting the course of justice carries a maximum of two years imprisonment. If you want to leave here today, level with us.'

'We're doing it tough, a child on the way, bills mounting up. I met a man, or I should say, he met me and told me how I could make an easy five thousand dollars. I said I wouldn't do it if it was illegal, but I knew it was.'

'You heard him out?' Haddock said. He had taken a seat and would support his sergeant as she pressured a cowed man.

'Five thousand dollars, he said. He frightens me more than you. Lock me up, but I've no criminal record, mitigating circumstances, and under financial strain. What might he do?'

'Did he threaten you with repercussions if you spoke to the police?'

'Money in my bank account, and yes, he did. What was I supposed to do? What would you do if you were desperate? There were complications with the child, and I needed the money. I won't do time, but what if this man finds out?'

'It depends if we get to him first. Who was he?'

'Gazza Blake, heard of him?'

'I have,' Haddock said.

'So have I,' Natalie said. 'Standover merchant, extortion, insurance fraud.'

'Did you know who he was?' Natalie asked Hannan.

'Not then. I found out later.'

'He was acting on instructions from someone else,' Haddock said. 'He's my age; know of him from my misspent youth. Murder's not his game, nor is subtlety, and Sasha's burial was subtle. What did he tell you?'

'He knew I was out at Pinchgut. Told me that if I broke down a wall, I'd find something that might shock me, which it did. Scared me witless. He didn't say it was a body, only that I needed to do it within a couple of weeks, time of my choosing, and that I was to contact the police.'

'Did he give you his name?'

'Not when I met him. I found out later. You can find anything on the internet. Entered a few parameters: height, age, appearance, tattoos, and accent. I found one that matched the man and got a name.'

'That's what we would have done,' Haddock said. 'Why would he be so conspicuous?'

'He probably thinks he's invulnerable.'

'He might be. He associates with serious criminals and needs to be careful with them, and now you've told us his name. He probably didn't kill the woman, so why tell you? Why not go out there late at night with a few mates, break the wall, and let you or someone else find the body?'

'I can't answer that question. Do I need police protection?'

'We can't give it to you, and then there's your wife and child. If Blake's not cooperative, we'll consider it. For now, go home, get on with your life, and we'll give you a rapid response number for your phone.'

Chapter 20

Gazza, only his mother called him Gareth, stood at the hotel's bar in Bankstown. It was an area that Haddock knew well, having grown up there. The two men had known each other as children, but it was not a friendship. Haddock had found the police, but Gazza Blake had not. He was a squat man, barely to Haddock's shoulders. On each hand were rings, and his arms were covered in tattoos. If someone had decided Hannan needed to be approached, choosing Gazza Blake would not be a good choice. He was distinctive by his tattoos and the leather pants, and the jacket he wore. As a child, he had been rough and tumble, a schoolyard bruiser, taking on all-comers. As an adult, he had joined a bikers' gang, the reason he dressed in their uniform. His language was coarse, his voice was deep, and his capacity to down copious amounts of beer was well-known.

At school, the young Haddock had never liked the equally young Blake. It was a feeling that had continued through the years.

'Who put you up to it?' Haddock asked. The old friend routine wasn't going to work. Blake had little time for overt friendship, especially not from a police officer, a class of people he despised. He had spent time in prison; once at Long Bay Jail for robbery with menace, another time at Bathurst, a five-hour drive from Sydney, close to Mount Panorama and its motor racing circuit.

'A friend,' Blake said as he pushed his glass over to Haddock. 'Same again.'

There was no need to spell out what they were talking about. Blake knew but did not seem concerned.

'Good, bad, evil, a saint? What sort of friend?' as the two men clinked glasses.

'The type that doesn't ask questions. Not a person you would like, Haddock.'

Haddock knew he wouldn't and wasn't expecting much from Blake. They could have brought the man into the station, given him the third degree, and charged him with complicity in a crime, but that came with two problems. First, Blake was a seasoned criminal who had been in prison and knew his rights. He would have clammed up, unwilling to incriminate himself, and then there would be the increased possibility of violence towards Leo Hannan. Second, what crime had he committed? He had paid Hannan to break through a wall. Did Blake know what was on the other side? He only had to say he didn't; no one could contradict him. Blake and Hannan were guilty of crimes, but they were minor compared to the main event. Who had killed Sasha Cornell? And now, why had Costello died? It could only be because he had spoken to him and his sergeant that night in Parramatta. Haddock didn't feel guilty about being responsible; collateral damage was not unexpected. Besides, had Costello been truthful? Had he known more? And what about Ingesson and Underwood? Although the kingpin was Duncan Howarth, smart enough to now control Bernie Cornell's empire, smart enough to arrange a murder.

Even so, minor or major, Blake knew something, and it was vital and, yet again, another piece of the jigsaw.

'I'll tell you this,' Blake said. 'Let's say it's for old times' sake, which it isn't. Leo Hannan's got a big mouth.'

'He is looking at two years maximum in prison for perverting the course of justice. You must have had enough time inside; you would not want to return. Young boys in the showers, your idea of pleasure?'

'You know it isn't.' Blake, for all his faults and disarming appearance, was a family man, a homely wife of sixteen years, a couple of children doing well at school, polite and well-behaved. It seemed incongruous, but Blake was a complex person, hard on the outside, mellow inside, with strong family values.

'He needed the money,' Haddock said.

'So did I. Offered him good money, and he was a puppy at my heels. A kid in trouble that needs medical treatment. He couldn't resist. I didn't know what was behind that wall, only that someone wanted it knocked down.'

'Who is this someone?'

'Well-spoken, never met him, only talked to him on the phone. We agreed on a deal. He transferred the money, and I transferred what was agreed with Hannan to him. Knocking down a wall, five thousand dollars to me, five thousand to Hannan, easiest money I ever made.'

'Phone number?'

'It didn't show. Might recognise the voice.'

'Why choose you as the messenger?'

'I didn't ask.'

'Or you've worked with him before.'

'I might have, can't say. Although if he knew there was a body, he might have put it there.'

The body had been hidden from view for seventeen years, and now the possible murderer was making mistakes. It didn't make sense, but murder rarely did. Did the murderer want to be discovered? Was there a psychosis eating away at him? The need to make amends for the past, a terminal illness that made it necessary? Haddock realised that theorising served no purpose; his sergeant was better at it than him.

Haddock didn't want a repeat of when he and Natalie had met the recently-deceased Josh Costello. He decided to slow down his alcohol intake to maintain the pressure on Blake, who could be talking himself into an arrest but seemed ambivalent.

'Why?' Haddock asked.

'I never knew about the young woman behind that wall. Nobody deserves that. Recompense for a sinful life, I might say, but you would not believe me, not sure I would either.'

Haddock's phone rang. The voice on the other end asked him and his sergeant to meet in his office at two o'clock the following afternoon. As the man spoke, Haddock held the phone close to Blake, the man listening for a while before nodding his head. One question had been answered, and now the man who had paid Blake to pay Hannan, whose actions had resolved what had happened to Sasha Cornell, was not hiding but asking two police officers into his office, a place barred to them before.

Instinct told Haddock that they were in the home run, that the murderer or murderers of Sasha Cornell and Josh Costello would soon be revealed.

***

Duncan Howarth had long been regarded as the person who could provide the impetus that would allow a resolution to Sasha Cornell's death, although now, there was Josh Costello to consider.

Why he had used Gazza Blake and how he had come to know of him remained unclear. Hopefully, Howarth would clarify.

As befitted the man, Howarth's office was resplendent, a sweeping view of Sydney Harbour out at far as the heads, Pinchgut in the foreground, the key to the woman's death. On one wall of the office, the trophies he had won, the medals he had worn around his neck on the podium.

'We'll let you go first,' Haddock said. 'It seems you have a lot to explain.'

'I did not murder Sasha. How I came to know where she was buried is important. It's hard to believe, uncertain you will. Before Bernie's death, I learned certain facts that could only result in one conclusion.'

'These facts, where from?' Natalie asked.

She could see the man squirming, attempting to be the police officer's friend, when he was anything but. His demeanour changed as needed. A man of success in multiple fields, critical of a police inspector who was not. Howarth was in the hot seat, and there were reasons why he should be considered a strong contender for Sasha's murder and, by default, Costello's.

'You're our prime suspect,' Haddock said.

'Bernie knew where she was,' Howarth said as he sat back in his seat.

A fact not thought possible, but Natalie believed the man, unsure why. It answered many questions, but the primary answer had not yet been given.

Haddock was more circumspect. He didn't believe a word of it. Howarth, the worm, was trying to wriggle off the hook but was held firm. He had to prove his innocence, not attempt to deflect with confusion, hearsay, and innuendo. 'Can you prove this?' Haddock asked.

Howarth sat up, took a sheet of paper from a right-hand drawer of his desk, and slid it across. 'Read that,' he said.

'Genuine?'

'I know where the original is. Your forensics people will verify it once I have given it to you.'

'Why's it not here?' Natalie asked. 'You realise what you've just said?'

'I do. I had no intention of giving it to the police, destroying the man's legacy, but what's in that letter will be distorted and incorrectly reported. Possibly the police will never make its contents known.'

'They might not,' Haddock said.

'Read it,' Natalie said.

'It's formal, on a letterhead. Any idea what it means?'

'The letterhead, no,' Howarth replied. 'Incredulity on your part, Inspector. You came here to arrest me or for me to confess to a murder.'

'Something like that. Before I read it, tell us why you arranged for her body to be found.'

'Bernie was ailing, no longer able to maintain control. He trusted me, asked me to work for him, and laid out a plan for his death. He was meticulous, kept anything, even a scrap of paper if it might be important later.'

'This letter, one of these? It reads like a crackpot wrote it to me,' Haddock said.

'Of course it does. Except it's not the writing of a crackpot but an educated person. Also, the original is on embossed paper. It might be possible to find out where it was embossed and who purchased it, although I have a shrewd idea. Read it.'

When you arrive at Sydney, sailing up
The harbour, a small central isle you'll see;
With two or three low huts, but not a tree,
Nor blade of grass,-upon't; and, on the top,
A score of men, in coarse habiliments,
Hewing the rock away. You may remember,
Among the many evil-traced events
Of a town life, some robbery, when December
Brought on the long, dark nights-a neighbour's boy
Tried for't, and banished. He, perchance, is one,
Who yonder lift the pickaxe in the sun
To level Pinchgut Island! If e'er joy
Gladden'd your heart on England's shore, oh! Never
Forget that Englishmen are banished here for ever.

'No more,' Natalie said.

Haddock's reciting of the sonnet did little to enhance it, but for the first time, the name Pinchgut was mentioned. 'I don't get it,' he said.

'It's obscure, I'll grant you that. The sonnet was written in 1842 by a senior politician in Australia. The longest-serving premier of New South Wales, a man of great importance. Surely you've heard of Henry Parkes.'

'I have,' Haddock replied.

'But why did you believe it means that Sasha was buried there?' Natalie asked.

'The letterhead is from a company that Bernie once owned.'

'Are you saying…?'

'I'm not. Bernie would not have killed her, but he had long suspected she was dead, the only conclusion given that she had been missing for so long. He received the original three months before Hannan found the body.'

'Why and how?'

Natalie and Haddock were confused, unable to comprehend what they were being told, the realisation that there was an element of truth within the incredible story. But how and why, and by who? It beggared belief, but they had to believe.

'I had not intended to reveal this letter out of respect to Sasha and Bernie. However, I am forced to do so.'

'The truth is always best,' Haddock said. 'So, what does it tell us?'

'Only one person could have written the letter, which would have been long ago. It doesn't tell you when it was sent and by whom. That is more important,' Howarth said.

'Who wrote it?' Haddock asked.

'Sasha. It's handwritten. When the letter was received, it was a clue to where she was. She wrote the sonnet in her handwriting; someone has had it in their possession for seventeen years. For whatever reason, we can assume Bernie's imminent demise, it was sent to him. A regret from whoever killed her, or a final act of vengeance against the man.

'Bernie trusted me and asked my opinion, although how Sasha knew she would be incarcerated in Pinchgut, I can't answer that question. It took me several months to find someone I could trust. Someone who would visit Pinchgut with me and had expertise in where a body might be buried. He also had to have a good knowledge of construction.'

'How did you find Gazza Blake?'

'I put out feelers through contacts. Blake was a criminal, rough side of the track, seen it all, done it all, a person who would not talk, and he had known Sasha. I went out to Pinchgut one day with him and spent a couple of hours. He found the place, and then he found Hannan, a man with financial troubles but no criminal record and no criminal intent. The man was desperate for money and said he would do it.

'Hannan's innocent of all crimes, phoned the police as soon as he made the discovery. Blake committed no crime, nor did I. The only intention on my part was to give Bernie closure, to ensure Sasha was buried with respect and dignity, and to never reveal the letter to you or anyone else. Written with a steady hand, its contents indicate a woman conscious of her tenuous situation. Whether she realised that death was imminent or not, we can't know. That will be for you to resolve, although I don't believe what has been said here tonight will help you.'

Chapter 21

The focus was on Sasha Cornell's death. The murder of Josh Costello did not receive the same attention, but it was recent and should be easier to solve. His wife, who had flown into Sydney, identified the body, and it had been released for burial. She intended to have the funeral in Sydney, and her children were due in Australia within two days.

Natalie met with the woman. They sat in a restaurant in The Rocks, which still maintained many of the area's original buildings, but not the squalor of when it had been a convict settlement. Now, it was upmarket, with restaurants and shops, souvenirs of Australia made in China, and an abundance of items to buy to remember Australia, but invariably confined to a drawer back home, along with the selfies taken with their phones, looked at once or twice and then deleted.

'It wasn't always easy,' Costello's wife said.

'His amorous adventures?' Natalia assumed.

'He was a good father, devoted to the children and me. I might have tolerated his philandering, but he was troubled.'

'Do you know why?'

'Sasha's father looked after him, made sure he was financially comfortable, paid more than he was worth. I asked him once why, but his answer was noncommittal. Something to do with what had happened in Sydney. He thought she had come to harm, but what could he do? Time moved on, and people tended to forget, but it gnawed at him. The usual. Why didn't I go for a run with her? What if she had stayed at home that day? Not uncommon to consider events you had no control over, but we all do it, turn in the road, left or right.'

'You knew more?'

'Insatiable curiosity. I was keen on Josh; who wouldn't be? Who Sasha's father was, who Sasha was. A beautiful woman, more so than me.'

'Don't put yourself down,' Natalie said. 'Sasha disappeared a long time ago; people age. Beauty is skin deep; a person's soul is more important.'

'From what I read of her, she had a good soul. And then a massive search for her, but she was never found. Where did she go? Any ideas?'

'None. We know where she was taken from, or we're convinced we know, due to low visibility from nearby houses and lack of traffic at an early hour. She left the Horizon building, ran up Forbes Street, and turned onto Liverpool Street. So near to safety, so far away. We believe we understand why she was buried at Pinchgut.

'We were with your husband the night before he was found. It might be related to his death, although we cannot see why.'

'What did he tell you? He would talk about Sydney, wanted to come back, but could not, not with Bernie paying his salary and my reluctance to come.'

'Why wouldn't you come? You have been here before, met Josh here. You know what it's like, a good place to raise children.'

'An ailing mother. I will not leave her, not for Josh or anyone else. I would have come if it hadn't been for her. But Josh knew it was a pipedream. He could not afford it and would have been unable to maintain the lifestyle. And then Bernie dies, and he's out, shown the door courtesy of a sanctimonious bastard.'

'You know of Duncan Howarth?' Natalie said.

Costello's wife smiled, the first sign of ease since she arrived in Sydney. 'Almost a swear word in our house. Apparently, Sasha spent time with him.'

'Did you speak of her often?'

'No, not at all. But we couldn't ignore her. Her father used to come to New York occasionally, and we would meet with him. The man liked to reminisce and talk about her. I couldn't blame him, as Josh had lived with her. Only natural that Bernie wanted Josh to talk about her as well.'

'Jealous?'

'Not particularly. He was the ideal husband and father. Give and take in a relationship. If you're looking for Mr Perfect, he ain't there.'

Natalie wondered if that was her problem, looking for someone who did not exist. She put it out of her mind and focused on Costello's widow.

'Did he have any qualms coming back to Australia? Initially, he had come due to Bernie Cornell. But after that, did he raise any issues?'

'Not with me. Said he missed the family, which I can believe, but nothing more. He told me about the investigation and even phoned me the night he met with you and your inspector. He said he spoke more than he should have and realised he had to help you find the murderer. We argued about his determination to stay in Australia, as he did not have citizenship in the USA. He could have gotten it from me, but he didn't like the country and felt homesick for Australia.'

'Were you the love of his life or Sasha? Not sure you appreciate the question or want to answer.'

'He had loved Sasha and saw a future with her, the son-in-law of Bernie, an easy and affluent life. With me, it was more difficult. My family was conservative; churchgoers, strong ethics, and no adultery. I learned to deal with it; my parents never would if they knew, which they didn't, and now, it's only my mother, and she's fading, vague a lot of the time. She wouldn't understand if I told her.'

'Who killed him? Any thoughts?'

'Only one, that bastard Howarth. That's who Josh would have said, how he referred to the man. Have you met him?'

'On several occasions. Fuelled by his own brilliance, he is friendly when he needs to be. We don't trust him, but he's given us information about Sasha's death which we are following up on. Vital information, but nothing on Josh's death. That's a mystery.'

The reason for Costello's death was uncertain. He knew Beth Madison and her relationship with Ralph Davidson, but did it matter? Was the man's reputation so important that murder would be committed to protect it? Natalie had come across politicians before, the local member in the town she had come from. He made promises and eloquent speeches but did little more. Her parents suspected him of corruption, but nothing was ever proven.

'We're no nearer to the truth,' Natalie admitted. 'Josh knew more than he revealed, and he paid for that. The question is, what was it that he failed to tell us? You are his wife; you knew him better than anyone else. Anything said over the breakfast table or late at night, or did he talk in his sleep, blurt out a name? Why didn't he come forward if he knew why Sasha had disappeared, even if he was not involved? Her death might not have been expected, her disappearance pre-planned, and then something goes wrong, playing a role that turns nasty, someone taking advantage, and then her death, either accident or intentional. Persons were frightened and confused, and why did Sasha write a poem after her disappearance, which provided a clue as to where she might be buried? Duncan Howarth's the key, but we've got nothing on him. His support of Bernie Cornell and then discreetly finding the body, using a cryptic clue in Sasha's letter, indicates that we should give him a degree of trust.'

'Are you sure you can?'

'Too smart for us, could be running circles around us. Met his type before, their minds function at a different level, calculating the odds, formulating plans, and being able to envisage the outcome. We would not have made sense of Sasha's letter. We could be pawns in a chess game, only able to move one square at a time, while Howarth and Bernie were free to roam the board.'

'Josh was a pawn like you and your inspector.'

'But what did he know? What is it, no matter how insignificant? Think hard and long. Whatever we don't know got him killed.'

'If you believe that, I'm not blaming you. Why did Sasha's father ask Howarth to follow up on the letter? Surely the police would be better, and why be suspicious of a poem. It's bizarre.'

'Pieces on a chess board, clues are given, open to interpretation. We know it was Sasha who wrote the poem. Her handwriting's been confirmed, and the ageing of the original letter coincides with her disappearance. Someone had held on to the letter, sent from a letterbox in Sydney.'

'Josh never said much about his time with Sasha out of respect for me. He didn't like Howarth and thought he might be involved, but that might have been because Sasha preferred him but didn't see him as marriage material. I've seen photos of the man and read about him. She might have been right. Is Howarth as charismatic and attractive as Josh?'

'Oozes success and might be charismatic if he wanted to be. He did not tell us more until he felt threatened. Even now, who knows?'

***

A one-day trip to Melbourne: an early morning flight out of Sydney and then the grindingly slow drive in Melbourne's early morning bumper-to-bumper traffic. The focus was still on the adult movie productions as the reason for Sasha's death and now Josh Costello's. The connection to Ralph Davidson, the former prime minister, was tenuous. And if Sasha had died, why hadn't Beth Madison? Beth wasn't the daughter of an influential and powerful man but the daughter of a dentist. Her death would have been newsworthy for a week and would have barely rated mention in the media after that.

Even though the connection had been made to Pinchgut, the cryptic letter from Sasha, had she expected to die? Was it a suicide pact? But surely it could not have been, knowing the woman's zest for life. The woman had everything to live for, and suicide pacts required two. It was still murder, and Josh Costello's recent death made less sense. The man had said more than he should have at the pub, but it was old news. Howarth's explanation had been plausible, and even if Haddock detested the man, and Natalie found him obnoxious, a snob living off his reputation and achievements, there was no way they could lay a charge unless it was the minor charge of perverting the course of justice, for not coming forward earlier with Sasha's letter and the poem in it, his visit to Pinchgut, the payment to Hannan to break the wall.

The chain of events was illogical, but then, so much had been with Sasha's disappearance, her murder, and then her discovery. Although there was one certainty: Sasha had not died the day of her disappearance, as the letter had been written two months after that date. Forensic analysis had revealed that the paper on which the poem had been written was a limited run, a company in Sydney, and their records gave the dates they had commenced production and the date they ceased.

Further clarification of where she had been, in good health or not, incarcerated in a darkened room, chained to the wall, or reclining on a chair in the sun, was impossible. Analysis of Sasha's writing in the letter did not show distress, but Haddock did not place too much credibility on that. Drugs could have calmed the woman enough for her to write the letter of her own volition or forced by another. It had not been spoken about before, but Howarth had confirmed it in a phone call from Natalie to him. Terse but polite, telling her that Sasha often read poetry at the end of the day, and she could have known Henry Parkes' sonnet from memory. Eidetic, he said, but no one else had mentioned that fact before.

'Sasha was the front that we saw,' Sharples said. He was a man in his early sixties, balding on top, with a ponytail down his back. He looked like an ageing hippy, but this was not a man who eschewed wealth. Outside, there was a top-of-the-range Toyota Landcruiser, and they were not cheap. Inside the building, the trappings of affluence, of a business making a lot of money. It was clean and modern, and the production facilities were impressive.

'High demand,' Sharples said. 'Advertising, video, and still.'

'Adult movies?' Haddock said. He had no issue with Sharples, apart from the ridiculous haircut. The man was making good money. He did not have the airs and graces of Howarth but was polite and affable.

'The money was good; set me up. Purely a financial decision. Besides, it wasn't difficult, with little concern about continuity and minimal script. You saw some?'

'I did,' Haddock said.

'Sergeant?'

'I saw them,' Natalie said. 'Although we need to know what else you can tell us. We're interested in Sasha Cornell and now Josh Costello.'

'Sasha would come in occasionally, chat to me, to the performers, watch sometimes. No idea why she stayed, but later I found out that she had been cheating on Costello, screwing Howarth.'

'Did that worry you?'

'Not particularly, none of my business. I've been around long enough not to be offended by people's behaviour. We've all got a hidden side; pornography lays it bare.'

'Did Duncan Howarth perform in one of your movies?' Natalie asked. She knew the answer as Sharples had supplied the movie but wanted to know if the man would attempt to distance himself from it.

'He did. One time. It was late at night, and the stud was incapable.'

'Erection?'

'Precisely. Howarth was adamant, no shot of his face. Although when there's action, we have more than one camera. We didn't release the movie with his face but kept the pre-edited film. That's what I handed over to the police.'

'Have you ever wondered why he agreed to be part of your production? After all, he had a reputation to protect. If it had been revealed he had been involved in pornography, it would have reflected poorly on him.'

'It was late at night, only myself, Crystal, a cameraman and Howarth. Maybe the great hero was tired of living up to the image. Is there a dark side to the man?'

'We don't know, although he is deeper than we first thought. He was responsible for the body being discovered but had not told the police until he had no other option. Why he did, we can't be sure.'

'Something to hide,' Sharples said.

'And you? Your past making adult movies?' Haddock quizzed. He was certain the man was hiding something.

'I don't make it known that I had made those movies, but it's not a secret. If asked, I would admit to it. Very few people are that prudish that they would reconsider doing business with me.'

'Has Howarth?'

'I only saw him once. I don't know why he came; he said he had expected to meet Sasha there, but I knew she wouldn't be.'

'How?'

'She had gone to meet him, a hotel somewhere.'

'Proof?'

'She phoned me, told me where she was, and that Howarth hadn't shown.'

'You didn't mention this to Howarth?'

'I didn't want Howarth to know that Sasha had told me about her affair with him.'

'Heroin?'

'With Crystal and some of the other performers. Not my concern. Production schedules were tight, and I wanted to wrap the movies, supply and demand, a hungry market, and distributors to satisfy.'

'Which distributors?'

'Long time ago, no reason to keep it secret. Warren Uxbridge. Have you heard of the name?'

'I have,' Haddock said.

'He was the man back then. I wasn't supposed to know, but he was a sleazy character who couldn't resist coming to the studio for a perv. Not sure if Bernie Cornell knew, although Sasha did. She seemed to like him, don't know why, wrong side of the track, rough and ready. But then, Howarth wanted some of the rough and ready we supplied. It might be that Sasha did too. She was living with Costello but sleeping with Howarth.'

'Uxbridge would be the man. I haven't seen him for a long time. He must be in his seventies now,' Haddock said.

'Who is he?' Natalie asked.

'Uxbridge? He had a chain of adult shops: kinky underwear, sex toys, leather outfits, bondage gear, and whatever else. Behind closed doors, nothing illegal, steady clientele, and made plenty of money. Sells online these days.'

Chapter 22

Natalie thought the investigation into Sasha Cornell's murder was drawing to a conclusion, and it was only a matter of time before the pieces would fall into place. Haddock wasn't so sure; hitherto unknown facts kept being revealed, unwilling to believe an arrest was imminent and that something was still amiss.

Natalie thought that what they had each said was effectively the same. Warren Uxbridge might be the lynchpin, but he would have to wait. Victoria Adderley had been working late at night, following through on what was known about Ralph Davidson and his shady dealings. She had discovered disturbing insights into the political process, deals made with unscrupulous persons, information that would prevent a desired action, for the good or the bad, and the Official Secrets Act used too regularly.

A mining lease, the primary focus, as Beth Madison had mentioned to Sasha, was not the only anomaly she had found, but it was the focus when the three met.

'Twenty-two billion dollars, eight thousand new jobs, there was no way it would not be approved. The environmental lobby put forward a good case, and there would be damage, inevitable considering the scope of the operation. However, towards the end of one of the mining company's submissions, almost an addendum, recognition of the possibility of damage to the Barrier Reef, and that they were mitigating that by advanced technology, monitoring on land and at sea. It was bogus; the company they intended to employ was false, a website, manipulation of its credibility, and they did not have any knowledge of the environment, not one boat, not one piece of equipment.'

'Could others have discovered that?' Haddock asked. 'How did you?'

'Long hours, and the prime minister, intended to push it through parliament. Others might have discovered it, but the final submission, released to those interested, had omitted that contentious part.'

'The mining company or the government.'

'The government. The original was submitted, probably to show they were responsible citizens when they weren't. However, the government, namely Ralph Davidson, had suppressed it. Also, there had been a one-off payment to a bank account in the Cayman Islands, which can be linked to a company in Australia belonging to Davidson's wife.'

'Would it stand up in a prosecution?' Natalie asked.

'How I found out about the bank account in the Cayman Islands wouldn't.'

'Not strictly legal?'

'The information is correct, but the bank in the Caymans will not corroborate. Davidson could never be charged with a crime, but the man's fuelled by his ego and reputation, and it is more damaging to have those destroyed than a prosecution. The man took a bribe, or he might call it a commission for services rendered. It can't be proved, but if Beth Madison had held to the story and Sasha had used her PR skills to maximum effect, serious embarrassment for Davidson. The man might have reacted, and who else might have been involved. Could Sasha's death have been political? Or is that too much of a conspiracy theory?'

'It's not,' Haddock said. 'We're not pursuing corruption, but two murders. What did Costello know?'

A lingering doubt remained about which of the possible motives had been responsible for the murders. Haddock had his money on political, and if national security was at stake, then there was the Official Secrets Act, persons expendable in the national good, although the citizenry of Australia wouldn't have the opportunity to decide if it was the right move. That would be determined by their leaders, backroom deals, money under the table, a nod and a wink, a person destroyed, a life forfeit.

A part of Haddock's reasoning was to do with Warren Uxbridge, a good businessman, not long on ethics, crude and rough, as he had been described.

Of the five shops he once had, one had been in Kings Cross, up a flight of stairs, a sign as you entered informing of the shop's contents, failing to mention the live show in the rear. Seedy and banal, Haddock had been in a few of the shops and seen the toys and the costumes, Uxbridge egging him on to try one. A little humour between a villain and the police never went amiss. Uxbridge had always steered a fine line, ensuring that he adhered to the current legislation, one year different from the next, dependent on social mores and the political party in power.

'Online, these days,' Uxbridge said. He was a pug-faced little man who dressed shabbily and worked from a ramshackle building ten kilometres from the centre of Sydney. 'Drop shipping, no need to keep any stock,; just get the orders, send them to the manufacturer, and let them ship. Low risk, maximum profit.'

Haddock had not disliked the man years prior, no reason to now. Even if he was not a person to invite to the family home, he was agreeable company. Natalie, not excited by the merchandise on the man's website, could not find him offensive. He looked like a rag and bone merchant, dealing in one person's rubbish, another's treasure. Yet, he was known to be wealthy, with a large house on acreage and children that had been educated privately.

'The shops?' Haddock asked.

'Sold four, closed one down. No demand for strip clubs and gyrating females. If you want an easy woman, Tinder, take your choice, a couple of drinks, buy them a meal and go back to their place. Dead easy.'

'Not for you?' Natalie asked.

'I deal in a commodity for the more adventurous, the broad-minded. Does little for me, but I don't have to watch or partake. Offend you, Sergeant?'

'Not particularly. Each to their own. We're not here to discuss your business. Something more important: murder.'

'Sasha Cornell?'

'Yes. What do you know about it?'

'I knew her, met her a few times. I liked the woman, a healthy outlook on life. As long as no one was offended, and no kiddies got to see what they were producing, what did it matter. I didn't go much for Ingesson's and Underwood's videos, although I'm not meant to say that in this enlightened age. How about you, Haddock? You must have watched a porno; offend you?'

'No. Ingesson and Underwood are pleasant enough characters if you meet them, but what they produced doesn't work for me. Those steps leading up from Oxford Street in Paddington, the exclusive clubs for those of Underwood's and Ingesson's persuasion, who knows what happens there.'

'You know, we all do, even your sergeant, who doesn't approve.'

'Not of what you're selling. Do you bring any of your items into Australia?'

'Not a lot. The manufacturers deal with it. I facilitate and prefer not to bother with stock or live shows. Too many of them with addiction or psychological issues.'

'You dealt with the distribution of the videos that Bill Sharples produced. Is our information correct?'

'It is, in part. I came in after a couple of months. Sharples made out that he was in charge, but he wasn't. He had no clue about profit and loss, margins, percentages, or how to sell the product. I figured that out in five minutes. The two gays were better at that and had a good network. Not that they could have expanded it by much, but credit where credit is due., a good business model.'

'Is this?' Haddock asked.

'Low overheads, minimal profit, low percentage return on the item cost, but no hassles, no interaction with the customer. And no damn employees, bar a couple of people that have worked for me for over twenty years. Florence, in the corner, you might recognise; John, you have seen before. There is another couple out back in the warehouse.'

184

Natalie saw a woman in her fifties with frizzy red hair, a knitted cardigan, and threadbare jeans. The man wore a suit. He was of a similar age to the woman, his hair combed back and sporting a voluminous greying beard.

'Florence, I do.'

'Good to see you, Inspector,' the woman shouted out. 'No more poles for me. Who is the pretty woman with you?'

Haddock was embarrassed he had been caught out and that visiting Uxbridge's shop in Kings Cross wasn't always official. Natalie wondered if his visits were only to watch or whether he and Florence were more than casual acquaintances.

'Sergeant Campbell.'

Natalie waved at the woman and looked over at a sheepish-looking Haddock as if to say, a friend of yours?

'John was the other half of the duo,' Uxbridge said.

Natalie understood what the man meant;, but she found it hard to imagine a stud in his twenties oiled up for his performance on the stage with Florence. Haddock knew that the ageing process was inevitable, certain that he had aged as they had. He found it a depressing thought.

'Why were you brought in?' Natalie asked.

'I didn't know, not at the time, that Sasha was keeping a watch on the productions and that her father, a long way behind the scenes, was doing the numbers, concerned that he wasn't making the money he wanted out of it.'

'No one else did.'

'Your inspector knows me, knows I'm a straight shooter. My shops were run correctly, I paid my taxes, broke no laws. Okay, pushed it with a few of the shows. Florence, John, and the others were paid a decent wage, nothing to complain about. Friends more than employees.'

'We always thought you should have been breaking the law but never proved it,' Haddock agreed.

'Bill Sharples approached me and asked if I would be interested.'

'How did he know you? He said he hadn't produced adult movies before and hasn't since.'

'A venture of mine a couple of years prior. He had produced a few for me. The man's mainstream now and got himself a solid business in Melbourne. He doesn't want it known that he had been down and dirty, producing sleazy movies. With me, they were, but I wasn't that much interested, produced a few to see if the market was there.'

'Was it?' Haddock asked.

Florence had come over, winked at Haddock, smiled at Natalie, and thrust mugs of tea into their hands.

'Six months, maybe a bit longer. Sales were down in the shops, and margins were tight. I had been selling videos in the shop years before. DVDs. But then, it was the early days of online streaming. There was not much plot to worry about. Sharples was good at what he did, but I didn't have the quality equipment, so I bought it second-hand off eBay. Sharples did his best; I covered my costs, and that was it. I doubt if any of what he produced exists today.'

'They do,' Natalie said. 'In the ether, it might take time to find. Depends if they are important.'

'They aren't. Regardless, Sharples had produced adult movies before, might even be now, but probably not. The competition is fierce.'

'Sasha?' Haddock asked.

'Sharples had recommended me to Sasha, which means, by default, Bernie. His decision was good, as my confidence was inviolate. Enough rogues in the sex industry, but if you play fair, the word gets around. After a couple of weeks, Sasha introduced herself. Not that she needed to; I knew who she was.

'Social pages, the internet, up-and-coming public relations company, socialite, daughter of Bernie. She watched the occasional production, and I was making headway with the distribution. It was going well. I never met Bernie, though. Money was flowing in, and my bank account looked healthy.'

'Why here?' Natalie asked. 'You must have plenty of money.'

'A man's got to do something. Sitting at home or playing golf would drive me crazy. I work eight hours a day, weekends for the family; life could not be better. Not much fun for you two; horrendous hours and paid a pittance. Not sure how you can do it.'

Natalie wasn't sure either, but she wasn't about to change. Warren Uxbridge was talking, and they hoped he would reveal a hitherto unknown fact.

'Pinchgut?' Natalie asked. 'Any meaning to you?'

'Bernie was negotiating to get the lease for the restaurant out there; more than a few vying for it. Sasha was interested in taking control, but it was tough. Bureaucracy, legislation, hoops and swings, bribery, and corruption. He was determined, and Sasha told me, knew that I was discreet, that it was likely to be secured in time, and she thought the place romantic, a high-end establishment with horrendous prices. I had seen the figures she showed to me.

'Apparently, her father approved of my frugality, business ethics, and discretion. He thought I would be a good person to advise Sasha. She was smart, but she would get over-excited about the possibility. I couldn't see it; that much work to make a return. My shops were doing well; Sharples' movies were selling well.'

'Who did you distribute to?'

'A company in the USA, West Coast. Another in the Netherlands. They would receive them, put them on their servers, and ensure that major websites had them. If they were viewed, a minimal cost back to the two companies I mentioned, then money back to me and the Cornells. I never met the people overseas. All done online and with phone calls. Nobody wants to be too visible. The law changes, and what was legal could become criminal, and it was a juggernaut that could not be stopped.

'Gangsters or legitimate business persons?'

'I could never be sure. It wasn't for me to know or care, only to ensure we were rewarded for what we supplied. Sasha was pleased with the results and assumed Bernie was. A great deal of money in a short period.'

'What caused it to end?'

'Sasha disappeared, and Bernie never came forward. I can't blame him for that. Three months after she disappeared, the business was closed.'

'And you went back to your shops?'

'I carried on at another studio. Sharples was handling production, Ingesson and Underwood, up until their arrest, dealing with the plots and the scripts, not much of either, need to go through the pretence that the female is the step-sister, that the young virgin next door is chaste. Nobody believes any of it. I kept it going for another nine months, but I had enough money and couldn't be bothered, and there was a growing demand for more depraved acts. I wasn't interested, nor was Sharples. He went to Melbourne. Very capable, doing well now, by all accounts. You've met him?'

'We have. No reason to believe he's involved, but you've raised an interesting point.'

'Pinchgut. Unsure how many people would have known about her interest. Hardly seems to be a reason for murder, not that it helped the company that obtained the lease. From what I can remember, they lost a bundle of money.'

'Not something you would have done, Warren,' Haddock said.

'Profit margin was too tight. You need room to manoeuvre. Single-digit percentile profit after outlaying a fortune makes no sense. Videos, we were making thirty per cent.'

'You could have set up your own distribution channel, a website, payments for the full video, free highlights to entice them in.'

'We did, website on a server overseas. It's a lot of work, and those overseas would hack it. They are probably persons you would not want to meet. And it costs millions to promote.'

'What did you think when Sasha disappeared?' Natalie asked.

'I'm not sure what I felt. Friendly when we met, but what did I know about her? Attractive and obviously capable. Her father had a reputation as a tough man, but I hadn't met him, never seen him. Did he play dirty? I was sure he did; goes with the territory.'

'No rumours? You've got your ear to the ground; move in dodgy circles. You would have come across villains over the years.'

'Speculation. She wanted time out, gone overseas, a lover somewhere, wrong side of the street. Or maybe it was her father. She adored the man, and he treated her well. I sensed that the relationship with the live-in boyfriend was strained.'

'Is there any more?' Haddock asked.

'Not that I can think of. Considering the business I was involved with, I always played it as straight as possible. I don't know whether Bernie and Sasha did. My opinion of her wasn't based on her looks. She hadn't been concerned with what Ingesson and Underwood had been producing, whereas I was.'

'Did she mention her other businesses? Beth Madison? A prime minister?'

'Not to me. Just social if we met, which was rarely. Can't help you more.'

'Did she ever speak of somewhere she would go if needing time out? A casual remark.'

The meeting wasn't going well, Natalie thought. Haddock's manner with the man was conciliatory, possibly due to their previous interactions and Haddock's indiscretions.

'Mr Uxbridge, Warren, you've been skirting the law for years, and you know that,' Natalie said. 'You might have avoided prosecution but sailed close to the wind. And the women putting on shows at the back of your premises were for hire. Maybe we won't be able to charge you, but you clearly treasure your good name. You're villainous, no doubt a heart of gold, but it won't wash with us. You know more than you're saying. Josh Costello knew more and ended up dead. Duncan Howarth's playing a smarter game, but he's not immune, and I don't think Florence and John will put up much of a fight if the heavies come in here. Biker gangs, hardened criminals, more their style dealing in drugs and pornography. Online, selling drugs? If you don't open up, I'll have the Fraud Squad, Drug Squad, and the thought police down here to announce that you're a lecher, pervert, and you sell women for profit and debase society with your wickedness.'

Haddock sat down stunned, as did Uxbridge. Over in the corner, Florence's mouth was open in astonishment; John was laughing out loud and enjoying the spectacle.

'You can't talk to me like that, Sergeant,' Uxbridge said once he had regained his composure.

'I can and I will. Two people dead, more possibly, and everyone acts as if they're saints when we know they are not. Ingesson and Underwood aren't, and certainly Howarth isn't. What do you know?'

'I met Bernie once. He was in trouble; we all were. He needed my advice; I needed his solution.'

'Where was this?'

'Blue Mountains, that monster place he calls his weekend retreat. It was a couple of days before Sasha disappeared. He was worried about her. We were being hassled by another group in Sydney, threatening their movie productions which were cheaply produced and tasteless. Sharples was a stickler for quality, artistic merit, lighting, and atmosphere.'

'Who was muscling in? And why did Bernie hold onto believing she might still be alive?'

'That's what fathers do.'

'But why be concerned about third-party threats. He had intended to bring in heavies from America to deal with anyone recalcitrant after Sasha's body was found.'

'Did he?'

'We never saw them, nor did Bernie mention them after we clarified our concerns.'

'Can't help you with that. Only those pressuring us wanted us to cut a deal, or they would close us down.'

'Did they?'

'After Sasha vanished? Never saw them again, but the business soon ended. Without Bernie's commitment, no one had any interest. We've discussed this before.'

'Who was hustling?' Haddock asked.

'Blake knows who,' Uxbridge replied.

'Did he kill her?'

'I don't know. You know him, what do you reckon? He's rough around the edges, but I've never considered him violent.'

'Nor did we,' Natalie said.

'Was he involved, or does he know more?'

'Not involved, but he knows who they are.'

No more was forthcoming from Uxbridge. He wasn't involved in either murder but knew who might be. Discretion on his part would be the safest course, he had decided, a guiding morality that had allowed him to circumvent the law when he had broken it, to deal with violent criminals when confronted, to have ensured a profitable and self-satisfying life.

Chapter 23

The focus was on adult movies and nefarious characters. Uxbridge had been polite and obliging, but he knew more. He might reveal more in an interview room under bright lights, a man who had his ear attuned to the gossip, able to decipher the verbiage from the fact, but he was a man who enjoyed his life and was unwilling to commit a heinous crime. Besides, what was the gain to him? He had made money from adult movies and sex toys, and now he was into mail order on the internet, the manufacturer to ship, and limited stock in the warehouse in Sydney. Easy, three people in the office, a couple out back in the warehouse, one of them a young woman in her twenties, whippet-smart, an ace at designing websites, organising the graphics, dealing with the SEO, and ensuring the technology was working to perfection.

Ralph Davidson's appearance in Homicide came as a surprise. Some people in the office shook his hand, and even Haddock admitted that his presence caused him to miss a beat. The man who had led the country for seven years was well-respected but might be a murderer. How to address him when it was impossible to be impartial?

Natalie took the lead, shook the man's hand, and invited him to the conference room, ensuring he had a cup of tea. Haddock, his politics diametrically opposed, shook his hand and thanked him for coming.

'I believe my name had been mentioned concerning the death of Sasha Cornell,' Davidson said.

'It has,' Haddock said. 'We have two avenues of enquiry. Your earlier relationship with a person of interest and her possible revelation of that relationship and irregularities while prime minister. Your visit has caught us off guard.'

'Superintendent Payne informed me that you would be here. Also, the NSW police commissioner has advised me that it would be opportune to meet both of you to explain the situation and the current status.'

'Are the allegations true?' Natalie asked.

'Did I have a relationship with Beth Madison? Yes, it is true. A sweet girl, young and naïve, an imaginative mind. She knew what the relationship was, but power is seductive. She confused it with love.'

'You took advantage.'

'Inappropriate, inadvisable, but Beth was never treated with disrespect. You have spoken to her; does she reflect negatively on me?'

'No. With age comes wisdom, and she realises that the past was long ago. Why here? Why not in your office or your home?'

'I will make a statement to the media after we finish today. I will mention my indiscretion.'

'Does Beth know?'

'She does. So does my wife. You will continue to investigate, to implicate me in a murder I did not commit or authorise.'

'Authorise?' Haddock interjected. 'That sounds as though you could have used government officials to quell enquiry, to remove the irritation.'

'Inspector, I was the prime minister. Authorise was a word I might have used. It does not indicate wrongdoing on my part or my government.'

Natalie could see what the man was doing. At some stage, his name would be mentioned, and it was better to pre-empt the negative press at a time and place of his choosing. If he was open with the police and the public, then opinion would favour him, and the indiscretion by a senior politician would be excused.

'Beth Madison, is she to support you with this?' Haddock asked.

'She will issue a statement if necessary.'

Haddock realised that the woman was no longer viable as a witness. She had been nobbled, whether from Davidson's bank account or the government coffers. It was going to be a whitewash, but he was not surprised. He had a healthy disregard for politicians, whichever persuasion they were, left-wing or right-wing, centrist, libertarian, or green. In power, virtually all were seduced, the hand in the cookie jar, a free run in the sweet shop. Christmas came early for more than a few of them, and Davidson's mansion in Vaucluse, the wealth he had attained, had not come from judicious investments but from other income streams. Haddock knew the man was guilty, but there would not be a crime against him, and even if Beth Madison had held to her story, what would it have meant? Would she have been another body in the harbour, a wire around her neck? And what of her husband? Would he be pleased with the revelation that his wife had been a powerful man's fancy woman, his whore? Salacious tittle-tattle, the talk of the town in the Eastern Suburbs where the well-heeled gathered to brag about their wealth, the charities they supported, those they had helped, where they were off to for a vacation: Barbados, Monte Carlo, Mauritius, Hawaii, a myriad of places catering to those with the money, to a former prime minister who had been paid handsomely for services rendered, to a woman who had sold her soul to the devil, to be regarded as a whore by the impoverished, a whore by those with the money, but the first would soon forget, and the second would forgive.

Regardless of what Davidson said and did, the immunity he felt did not obviate the fact that two persons had died. One had had knowledge but without the detail to pursue the man. The other, Sasha, was not after justice but the opportunity to get a ghostwriter to write Beth Madison's story, then publish, fast and hard, six weeks maximum. But Sasha disappeared, Beth lost her determination, and Davidson was off the hook. And then, Natalie and Haddock had resurrected the case, and Davidson was magnanimous, a man of the people. In the police station, shaking hands with those who approached, an arm around those who wanted a photo.

Natalie had wanted to tell those who warmed to the man that this person was subject to a criminal investigation, a lecher who had taken a young woman, heart, mind, and body to his bed and discarded her like old clothing. He had given her money and told her to sign a document stating that she would not raise the mining lease publicly or privately. But she had, with Natalie and Haddock. Had she violated a solemn oath or committed an offence under the Official Secrets Act? Or was seventeen years long enough? And why was Davidson determined to make a speech to the media? Owning to his sin with another woman, discussing the contentious lease, convincing those of his political persuasion that he was innocent, realising that the opposition would raise the issue in parliament and that there would be a heated exchange across the floor

Why had Davidson come to the police station? Why had he been open with the two police officers, and why make a statement? It didn't make sense to Natalie, but involving themselves in Australia's political process and governance was a battle best not fought. And if they decided to fight, pressure would be applied to back off. But that wasn't how Natalie and Haddock worked. Then had run up against the brick wall of officialdom on a previous murder investigation involving a senior judge of the Supreme Court of New South Wales. But they had pushed through and arrested the man's son for murder.

Haddock summed it up. 'Someone killed Sasha and Costello. Our duty is to them.'

***

Natalie watched Ralph Davidson on the television that night as he laid out what he had achieved as prime minister, the legislation passed, and the improvements he had wrought through diligent management and fiscal responsibility. The interviewer remained silent until he had finished.

'Why are you here, Mr Davidson?' The interviewer had been chosen well. One of the least aggressive, unlikely to take on the man, to pressure him on what he was about to say.

'To pre-empt speculation concerning persons of my acquaintance and that one of them had been murdered.'

'A person of your acquaintance? Why State High Crime Command? Why visit?'

The cameras were focused on the two persons, one of whom believed that respect should be accorded him, unaware that the woman had received instruction before the interview. The fine art of seducing the interviewee into complacency, thinking he had aced it and would soon be home with his wife, a glass of brandy in his hand, gloating about how easy it had been, and what incompetents the television station and its lackeys were.

'Open conversation was required. As an Australian citizen, I take my responsibilities seriously. I was privy to certain facts I believed should be given to assist the police in their investigations.'

'Did you mention your affair with a much younger woman when you were prime minister? A woman who accompanied you on trips overseas, a woman who was your mistress. Isn't that true?' It was a hit job, flawlessly executed.

Taken aback, Davidson did not speak for ten seconds. He wanted to wring the woman's neck but remained calm, although there was tension in his voice, a minor heart palpitation, and heat under the collar.

'I am referring to Sasha Cornell,' Davidson replied.

'Who was discussing with your discarded mistress an exposé of you, and no doubt others, about a contentious mining lease in Queensland. We have proof that you pushed the lease through, disregarding advice. How much were you paid for your troubles?'

'I repudiate this line of enquiry. I have come to your television station to make a statement, not to be subjected to the third degree.'

Geraldine Bosworth breathed a sigh of relief. Her relaxed, non-aggressive interviewing style had been fine for daytime television, but now a chance to show her mettle, to take down a politician. Davidson had agreed to be interviewed by the woman, the daughter of one of his cabinet ministers.

The knives were out. He had made an error, but he was on camera, not ducking out in a huff, making excuses about another meeting, although this was not what was agreed on. He was trapped. He had to talk his way out of it.

'Miss Bosworth, my personal life is not of concern.'

'It is when it is paid for by the taxpayers of Australia. What do you have to say about this?'

'Australia prospered under my leadership. My reputation and hard work for this country are well-known.'

'Not as well-known that you had a mistress in her early twenties, a lot younger than you, basking in the glow of high esteem. And then you threw her out, went back to your wife, and published a book glossing over the disreputable, failing to mention the woman or the backhanders you took. As a former prime minister of this country, I put it to you that you used your position to financial advantage and your charming manner to seduce a young woman barely out of her teens.'

'She was twenty-six years of age, hardly a child.'

Davidson's wife looked on in horror. The man was in his seventies now, and she had noticed a vagueness about him at times. She had known about the affair and did not care if her life was good, which it was. But now, ridicule and conjecture, a debate as to whether he was guilty of a criminal act. He would be tried and convicted by the public, the target of social media, a pariah who had taken the public purse, accepted bribes, condoned corruption, and seduced innocent young women.

Natalie knew that Beth Madison had not been young and innocent. She had confided that to Natalie the first time they met. And she had loved him and thought he loved her. Natalie thought that might have been true, and Davidson's wife was neither attractive nor pleasant. One of her neighbours had described her as a battleaxe.

'There is also concern that Sasha Cornell died because of the book she had intended to publish about your time as prime minister, the salacious details provided by your mistress, the proof of your corruption to be given to the police.'

'This station is using a denouncement of me, unfounded as it is, to bolster its ratings. I will not allow this to continue.'

'A statement from you. Your side of the story.'

'Very well,' Davidson said. 'I will admit to an inappropriate relationship, which I regret. The woman was mature, over the age of consent, and the relationship was consensual. I apologised to my wife a long time ago. She graciously accepted my apology. As to the mining lease, the government followed the procedure. All the documents had been submitted. Some were for it, some were not. I felt, and I debated this with my colleagues and in parliament, that in the country's interest and that of the people of Queensland, approval should be given. Did I talk to the executives of the company? I did. Did I accept their hospitality? I did. However, I did not take money, gifts, or other incentives to speed up the process. Records in parliament will show this to be true.'

Natalie knew the records would be true, doctored over the years since the mining lease had been granted, although Victoria Adderley had uncovered irregularities, proof that corners had been cut, and the odds were that Davidson had been guilty of corruption. But it was a long time ago, and no charges would be laid, although the media would run with the story, and they would want the woman. Did she know what had just happened? Natalie phoned Beth Madison.

'We've agreed.' The answer Natalie received. She knew that more money had changed hands and that Beth Madison would say no more.

In the days that followed, a statement from Beth on the path outside her house, an admission that she was the mystery woman and that she had loved him, but it was a long time in the past, her husband's arm around her shoulders. And yes, she had spoken to Sasha Cornell the day before she disappeared, and no, she did not think it had anything to do with the woman's murder.

It was a scripted statement, and even though the media's flashing cameras and microphones were thrust in her face, she would not be drawn to say more or defend her actions. The Madisons retreated to the sanctity of their house, a couple of bruisers by the front door blocking intrusion from those outside.

'Did you believe what you just said?' Natalie asked. She had been in the house, seen the chaos outside, aware that most would file the story, edit the video, and forget about it, but some would pursue it.

'There's no more to say,' Beth said, a handkerchief to her eyes.

'There is. Who gave the interviewer the ammunition? Who went to school with Geraldine Bosworth?'

'You know?'

'I do,' Natalie said. 'Who advised you to give the woman the information.'

'Geraldine contacted me. My affair with Ralph was not the greatest secret. Others knew, others suspected. This is the Eastern Suburbs; people gossip but rarely condemn. In a couple of weeks, it will blow over. Ralph will bask in the glow, and I'll be the innocent virgin he pursued, and my husband will just have to wear the comments.'

'It was the right thing to do,' Beth's husband said.

'You have placed the man in an embarrassing position. Have you considered his reaction?'

'We have.'

Natalie could see it clearly. Beth had the proof, and they had already taken money from Davidson. Her secrecy was contingent on another payment. It was a dangerous game. Two people had been murdered. A third would not be hard to arrange. And if Davidson had committed a crime, prosecutable or not, others were involved, and immunity was not ensured just because of their wealth and influence. But it might be a penetrable fortress, the walls high enough to repel most, but one or two might breach them.

Chapter 24

The focus had been on the production and distribution of adult movies, but Davidson's visit to the police station, his explosive interview with Geraldine Bosworth, and Beth Madison's intent to leverage what she knew for more money could be a motive for a future murder.

Whereas Sasha's murder was predominant, Josh Costello's was recent. Clues, the few they had, had not been diluted by time, although the body had revealed little other than the cause of death and that it had been dumped in the harbour. Consensus inclined towards the body being thrown over the side of a boat, which came with another question. Why hadn't the body been weighted down? Had someone intended it to be found? By whom, and when? Hit and miss, the body could have drifted in any direction, even out to sea, or eventually been consumed by sharks. Too many ifs, not enough facts.

Haddock focused on pornography as the motive for murder; Natalie stayed with Davidson and Beth, concerned for the latter, indifferent to the former. Victoria Adderley double-checked, and Superintendent Payne fretted.

'Uxbridge has put you in it, Gazza,' Haddock said.

The two men met near Gazza Blake's home, a neutral location, no distraction from others watching, no alcohol, and nothing recorded. Blake was circumspect, realising that he was in trouble, not from Uxbridge or the police, but others. He was unsure what to say or do. Despite his rough appearance, he was controlled by an ethic of morality and family, but he had sailed close to the wind, and now he might have sailed off the end of the world.

'He knows as much as I do,' Blake said eventually.

Haddock recognised the truth of what was said. Uxbridge was playing it carefully, whereas Blake was compromised. One had a lawyer and the money to pay; the other did not. One or the other would fall or talk, and if Blake was about to reveal vicious murderers, then either or both might die. It was a risk Haddock was willing to accept.

'I'll give you that, but he's not talking; you must.'

'Why would I do that?' Blake replied.

'People have died; others might. I don't want you to be one of them.'

'What's it to you, Inspector? What am I? A hustler, looking for the next deal, police informer occasionally.'

'Pimp?'

'Not me. Uxbridge might have supplied the models for the pornos, had a few around the back of his clubs, but you knew that.'

'I did,' Haddock said. He did not intend to elaborate, but in his younger days, he had had the chance to relax, drink, watch a show, and spend time with the women. He consoled himself with the fact that it was what a young police officer would do. He had not been married then; Uxbridge remembered, but how did Gazza Blake know?

'Uxbridge needed a facilitator, someone to coordinate, to meet with the interested parties. He didn't want to travel overseas, nor did he want to be seen. Not that he was hiding away, but there were a few unsavoury characters, gangsters in America, Eastern Europeans in Europe, slit your throat for the price of a good night-out.'

'You went overseas when it was necessary?'

'I did. Good hotels and great times. Uxbridge paid me well, and those I met were hospitable. No reason not to be.'

'Couldn't it have been done online?'

'It could, most of the time, but a handshake was occasionally needed, and phone calls could be monitored. Distribution could be illegal in some places, but that wasn't our concern, only how to get the product to them and the money back in return.'

'Cash only?'

'Untraceable money, not only cash. Offshore banks, that sort of thing. Uxbridge does not like travelling. Not sure if he has ever left Australia. Better to leave it to me.'

'Where did Sasha Cornell go after her abduction?'

'She wasn't abducted.'

The letter Bernie had received and that Howarth had interpreted as confirmation of where she was interred had sown further doubt with Natalie and Haddock that her disappearance might not have been an abduction but a carefully-engineered subterfuge. And now Blake was confirming their suspicion. Why was unclear. The woman had been involved in illegal activity with high rewards, but the risk was substantial. An abduction would lend plausibility to her disappearance, even though considerable money and resources had been wasted by her father and the police.

'How do you know this?' Haddock asked.

'It was me that picked her up.'

Blake's statement was dynamite, an answer to a question that had plagued the investigation, for which Natalie had jogged the route for several days before being attacked by Evershed, a man with delusional issues, a known troublemaker, who had been found guilty of the attempted abduction, his lawyer filing a claim against Natalie for excessive violence in resisting the man. Victoria Adderley had dealt with the matter, and the lawyer had backed off.

'At the top of Forbes Street?'

'Yes. Uxbridge knew but didn't want to tell you. The man's playing it close to his chest, pretending to be an honest burgher, upright and decent, while peddling in sleaze, something you used to be fond of.'

'Still am,' Haddock replied. It was an honest admission, not giving out of cordiality to the man, but because he wanted him onside. Picking up Sasha was not a crime; withholding it from the police was.

'Now you tell us. Why? We asked you enough times. You knew we wanted to solve her murder.'

'Seventeen years ago, nobody knew of me. Uxbridge phoned last night and told me to assist the police. Neither of us has committed a crime, although I suppose that's not literally true. Nobody thought that Sasha would come to harm, but she needed to go overseas to meet with various persons.'

'Why the subterfuge?'

'You've heard of Victor Wimbush?'

'US Senator, on the moral right, renowned for his strong anti-pornography stance, anti-drug, anti-everything, evangelical Christian, bible basher.'

'That's him. Seventeen years ago, an up-and-coming politician, a platform based on conservative biblical values, a preacher in his church, a dynamic orator, family man.'

'He still is.'

'He's a skilful politician who says one thing, does another. He was Uxbridge's man in the USA. The two had a lot in common, but Uxbridge was small time. Wimbush was Mr Big in the distribution of smut back then. The front the populace saw was just that.'

'His political peers?'

'What did they care? The political system in America is in tatters, always has been. Not much better here, but Australia's small time.'

'Why meet with Sasha?'

'Wimbush is an arrogant, foul-mouthed bigot when he's not in public. Sasha was intrigued by him, and Wimbush wanted to meet someone of his social standing. I met him twice. He wouldn't shake my hand and considered me beneath contempt. Probably not wrong there, but his kind makes me sick. I'm an open book, and so are you, Haddock. Your sergeant wears her Puritan values like a badge. I tolerate honest people, even if they are criminals or walk a thin line. But Wimbush, the nastiest piece of work you would ever want to meet.'

'Where did they meet?'

'Wimbush was dealing with Uxbridge through his people, rarely speaking to Uxbridge other than on the phone. It was unbalanced, can't you see? Bernie Cornell had the goods on

Wimbush, the ability to cast enough dirt his way to make the man's run for the US Senate difficult or impossible. Wimbush needed something on Bernie sufficient to make the others honourable when they weren't. Sasha agreed to visit Wimbush, and the meeting was recorded. Not sure if Sasha knew this, but she was adventurous, and Wimbush did have a certain allure.'

'Are you intimating there was a romance?'

'I'm not, although there might have been. We flew over to the USA, to Chicago, and met Wimbush and his people outside the city, close to the Wisconsin border. Private jet there, false names for both of us.'

'Were you her security?'

'Not security, but I knew the people over there, and Uxbridge insisted I go with her, which we now know was what her father wanted.'

'He trusted you.'

'He must have. I play it straight and would have done my best to protect her. She was lovely, not condescending to a grub like me from the rough end of town. We got on like a house on fire.'

'First time you had met her?'

'Not the first, but the first when I got to know her. Anyway, we are at Wimbush's place. Security around the place, dark suits, menacing. To the outsider, he was the up-and-coming politician, what the country was crying out for. Inside the compound, foul-mouthed, arrogant, and dismissive of me. He gushed over Sasha. The two spent three days together, wining, dining, discussing business, like-minded souls, united by achievement and powerful people.'

'After three days?'

'I was dismissed, taken to the airport, came home on United Airlines, squeezed between a fat man and a whining woman.'

'And Sasha? Uxbridge? Her father?'

'Uxbridge said to leave her there. I wasn't so sure. The goons around Wimbush were intimidating, and a lone woman was at risk. Although it was her that wished me well, even embraced me, and thanked me for looking after her. That was the last time I saw her.'

'When she didn't return?'

'Cornell had raised the alarm that first day, a defensive tactic, plausible denial if Sasha's visit went pear-shaped.'

'You're not implying that he thought she could come to harm.'

'I'm not. If her visit became public knowledge, or the deal with Wimbush soured, he could claim that his daughter had acted alone, made decisions he did not approve of, get her out of the country, set her up in the UK or Europe if she wanted.'

'She knew this?'

'I wasn't privy to everything that was planned. But Sasha would chat, telling me that what she was doing in the USA was make or break and that the Australian adult movie industry was too small to be consequential.'

'Why would Wimbush have been interested?'

'Legislation was tightening in the USA, making it more difficult to make movies. Why not ramp up production in Australia with less industry control? Uxbridge saw the wisdom in it; no doubt Bernie did, and Sasha enjoyed the thrill of it. She told me she enjoyed it and that Josh Costello was on his way out, but Howarth wouldn't commit. Wimbush was an option; after all, as the daughter of a well-known Australian, she had the attributes, and he had the dynamism to maybe become president. More than a few rogues have risen to the position.'

'What went wrong? When did Bernie realise that she wasn't coming back?'

'I don't think he ever did. Maybe he didn't want to believe it, but then there's the letter.'

'Written where and when?'

'Howarth had the letter, not me. I didn't know about it, not until I was contacted. I organised the trip to Pinchgut and made a deal with Hannan.'

'Howarth wouldn't have killed her, too smart for that, and why? He wasn't involved with the movies, but Sasha was. Why had she written the letter mentioning Pinchgut? Had she known? But how? None of this makes any sense.' Haddock was confused, unable to decipher what Blake was saying, not even sure that the man knew himself, fragments of information, none coalescing into a recognisable format or the truth. He phoned Natalie, aware she was more astute than him, that she might be able to make sense of what Blake was saying and, more importantly, what he was not. Was it the truth, or yet again more diversion, persons aiming to protect themselves from prosecution, to preserve their lives if they said too much.

Natalie arrived thirty-five minutes later. By then, the two men had relocated to a pub ten minutes from Blake's house.

'Mr Blake,' Natalie said. This time she acquiesced and agreed to a glass of wine, South Australian, a Riesling, which was too sweet for her. She would sip it in the spirit of cordiality, but this was not cordial. The conversation should be recorded in the interview room at State High Command. 'You have withheld vital information and are not the only person. It seems that any of you could have murdered her, and all are guilty of one crime or another. Duncan Howarth's reputation and legal team protect him. However, you, Gazza Blake, are without assistance. What you have is us, and neither Inspector Haddock nor I is inclined to do anything for you until you give us more than entertaining anecdotes about trips to America and that Sasha was a lovely woman. She was involved with unpleasant people, and these distributors in America, the sanctimonious Wimbush, were the worst of all.

'He's untouchable, protected by political influence and persons in his back pocket. If anyone's going down, it's you. And down is a subjective term. Either six feet or life in prison, hard labour, hairy men desperate for a weak man. We can't protect you, and you're guilty of a crime, withholding evidence for one, but you and Uxbridge were up to your necks in something more than pornography. Transmit them digitally. Even seventeen years ago, was anyone buying DVDs or CDs? I don't think so. What was it? Tell us now, or suffer the consequences.'

Blake picked up his glass of beer and downed it in one gulp. 'Another?' Haddock asked.

'I reckon so. No pussy cat, your sergeant,' Blake said. Haddock had to agree.

'What is it?' Natalie asked as the man drank another beer.

'Official statement. I want it on the record.'

Chapter 25

For two hours, Blake spoke. The man who said little had plenty to say. Bernie Cornell was in financial trouble and had bitten off more than he could chew.

'How do you know all this?' Natalie asked.

'I listen and observe. I was with Uxbridge at the studio where they made the movies. I could see the product in the boxes, the actors doing their thing.'

'What product?'

'Drugs. Bill Sharples knows about it, and Uxbridge was involved and still is. Check out his place, the warehouse at the back, open boxes, and focus on the sex toys. Easy distribution around Australia.'

'It makes no sense,' Haddock said. 'Bernie Cornell involved in importing drugs.'

'Why not? No one's looking that closely, and the sex industry kept away the prying eyes. Did you think about it? As for me, I didn't care either way, drugs or porn. Each to their own, and if people are stupid enough to become addicted, that's their problem. Cornell did not care either.'

'Are you saying that Bernie was using Sasha as security?' Natalie asked.

'Wimbush knew the relationship between father and daughter. She had been lured to America on the pretence of hammering out a business deal, but Wimbush held onto her once there. She was sleeping with him. Whether it was love on her part makes no difference. Bernie knew she was there but could not get her out. It was then he raised the alarm. The video at the Horizon building had been doctored, and the dates changed.'

'He contacted the police within a few days,' Haddock said.

'A private jet to America, a false passport, fake name. Do records go back that far? Check with immigration. Jennifer

Ealing. Hair dyed, dark sunglasses, dated clothing. Uxbridge will give you the date and where he got the passport.'

'This could get you killed,' Natalie said.

''It got Costello killed.'

'How? Did he know the story?'

'He knew enough. Desperate people, desperate measures, and Costello was desperate, talking to you and Haddock. Sasha was long gone; nobody wanted the police to delve too deeply. If they had, they would have found out that Bernie was a major financier of drug trafficking and sales in Australia; Sasha, the loving daughter, amoral, didn't care about the drugs one way or the other, only for her father. Duncan Howarth, the great man, out for himself, wanted Sasha, she wanted him, but they knew it would not work.'

'How do you know so much?'

'I spent four weeks in America, not the three days I said before. We got on well, and she knew she was trapped. I became her confessor, told me about her father, the two gays and their movies. How her father had financed the movies when they became heterosexual. He recognised the money that could be made, but Australia would never be a major producer of adult movies. It was a good front for drugs. Except Wimbush sidelines Bernie Cornell and sees a way to take over distribution in Australia. He's got Sasha, which plays on the relationship between father and daughter. Squeezes the father and the daughter, but there are two kinds of squeezing.'

'Did Wimbush have Sasha killed?'

'She returned after seven weeks, a house in Palm Beach, north of Sydney, with sandy beaches and expensive real estate. It was secure, and she remained there. Bernie knows where she is, but he does not visit and believes she is safe. The man's cornered, his business in unravelling. Wimbush's got him over a barrel, and he knows it. Makes it clear that any attempt to double cross and the police will receive a dossier with all details of the drug importation. No one's immune from prosecution, not even Bernie Cornell. Industrial-scale importation. I visited her. She realised the situation and kept repeating that with great risk comes great reward, which was her father's favourite saying. But this was her life we are talking about, not a few million dollars gained or lost. Wimbush wouldn't want loose ends or people he couldn't trust implicitly.'

'You survived,' Natalie said. What was it about this man, she thought. He appeared to live a charmed life. Others had died, yet he still lived.

'If Bernie knew she was there and had the politicians in his pocket, why didn't he pull in favours and get her rescued?' Natalie asked.

'How? He was up to his neck in crime. Those he could have turned to were not about to help, careful to protect their backs. He was forced to negotiate, but his hands were tied. I was let into the house and spent time with her. She realised the situation was tenuous, meat in the sandwich and her father would do what he could, which wasn't a lot, and that Wimbush, the respected politician in America, intended to go from strength to strength. She was expendable, so was Bernie; so was Howarth, who knows more than he's letting on.'

'And Uxbridge?' Haddock said. Natalie was on a roll. He wasn't about to disturb her flow, aware that Blake was about to shoot himself in the foot, pushed into a corner, with no way out unless he could deal a killer punch to his opponent. But who was the opponent? Was it Bernie Cornell? That seemed unlikely. The devotion of father to daughter was inviolate. The only person he had cared for, the only person she had cared for.

'Uxbridge knew about the trip to America, not her return.'

'Involved in drugs?' Natalie asked.

'He turned a blind eye and took profit from it. The man was interested in sex clubs, strippers, and adult merchandise. Confided to me that the people Bernie was working with frightened him. Frightening Uxbridge was difficult, but he wanted to back off and live a quieter life. As for me, Haddock knows I go with the flow. On the periphery, handy to have around, few scruples, and I keep my mouth shut.'

210

'When did Sasha die?'

Three weeks after her return. She knew the situation was hopeless and that Wimbush was pressuring Bernie for money he didn't have.'

'There is no record of Bernie Cornell under pressure after she first disappeared,' Haddock said.

'That's how the man's wired, keeps his problems close to his chest. She had gone, no trace of her. Eventually, the police exhausted all possible leads, and the investigation was put in the too-hard basket.

'That's true,' Natalie said. 'The enquiry wound down, and she remained missing for seventeen years. Why was Bernie anxious to find her murderer? Surely he knew, not that he would have ever been able to prove it.'

'He never knew who killed her, assumed Wimbush was involved, but the killer would have been local. Bernie wasn't sure she was even dead. Time moved on, and she wasn't anywhere to be seen.'

Natalie could see it clearly. Wimbush was a rogue, a possible president of his country, but seventeen years previously, he had been a major criminal, hiding behind a carefully constructed veil of respectability. A good family man with strong Christian ethics, charismatic and honourable. He had held her, probably had an affair with her, and could have arranged for others to maim and kill. But he wouldn't have got his hands dirty. Others would.

'Whose idea was Pinchgut? And the letter that Sasha had written? Forensics checked and declared it to be genuine.'

'It wasn't. Well-crafted, the work of a genius, the person who had organised the fake passports.'

'Who put her there? Who killed her? Was it you? You've worked in construction. We know you had worked at Pinchgut in the past, but what was the significance? The letter was fake. Who wrote it? Who suggested Pinchgut? An American would not understand the importance. Macabre.'

Suggesting that Blake had worked at Pinchgut came to Natalie in an instant. She had no idea if he had or not, although he had worked in construction.

Blake put down his drink, his face ashen, his hands shaking, eyes welling up. 'I did,' he said.

It was the revelation that Natalie and Haddock had been looking for.

'I didn't kill her, couldn't do that,' Blake added.

'Did you fall for her?'

'In America, I did. But she had no time for me.'

'Concealing a murder is a crime,' Haddock said.

'Charge me, but hear me out first.'

With Blake in custody but not yet charged, the two police officers drove him to Palm Beach. At the end of a peninsula, a lighthouse on the headland, the house down below, fronting the Tasman Sea. Two crime scene investigators were in another car. The house owner was surprised when Haddock knocked on the door.

Inside the house, luxurious and worth millions, Blake led the way. No need for protective clothing. If Sasha Cornell had died there, it was almost two decades ago. The CSIs were unsure what they were looking for, and the owner, a retired currency trader, was nonplussed, although having a house with history, even if violent, amused him.

'Sasha Cornell,' he said. 'In this house?'

'Was it here?' Natalie asked Blake.

'I found her outside, by the pool. She had drowned.'

'You didn't phone the police,' Haddock said.

'With what? No one else was in the house. The goons had gone, and what would have happened to me? Would the police have believed me innocent?'

'Forensic evidence would have confirmed your innocence.'

'How? She had been murdered; a leaf scooper used to hold her underwater. I would have been crucified. My appearance, a conviction for violence in my teens. No one would have been interested in what I had to say, and you know it.'

'We do,' Natalie said. She felt for the man, in love with a woman who could not love him in return, murdered at the house; those responsible, long gone.

'I panicked, tried to think of what to do. There was no one I could talk to, maybe Uxbridge, but he wouldn't have wanted to become involved, would have told me to get away from the house.'

'That would have made no sense,' Haddock said. 'The crime scene investigators would have found proof that you had been here. Did you touch the body?'

'I had to, to check.'

'Fingerprints on the recliner, door handles in the house. Your fingerprints are on record; less than an hour before arrest, and no one would believe you innocent of her murder.'

'I knew how to get into the room at Pinchgut, the only key there was, and no one went in, considered it unsafe. I had worked there two years prior. I took a small boat and went out there late at night.'

'You would have needed an accomplice.'

'I had one, Leo Hannan's father. He's dead now; not much you can do with him, but it was a favour to me, no questions asked. I didn't kill her, a homage to her. Besides, I was despised by her father for allowing her to be compromised. Sasha had tried to get the lease for the place. You know that already. I didn't want her buried in a shallow grave or at sea.'

'A monument to her,' Natalie said. Blake's actions were strange, but so was the man. He had loved the woman, and in death he didn't want her to become a curiosity, a freak in a sideshow, or the subject of salacious gossip in a magazine. Not that for her, but a place of repose, a craggy isle, a fort, a restaurant, a commanding position in Sydney Harbour.

'Did the son know what his father had done? Did Leo know you before you met with him? And why, after so many years?'

'Closure. Her father needed to know what he had done before he died, to feel the hurt I had felt for so many years.'

'But it was Howarth who had the letter. He told you to find the body.'

'I sent it to him, and then a week later messaged him and Bernie, also Costello, a phone I bought in the supermarket, explained the poem and where Sasha was buried. Remember, I spent time with Sasha, knew about her love of poetry and her fascination with Pinchgut, and she even told me she could imagine being buried there when she died. I organised the passports and the fake letter. Howarth killed her,' Blake said.

Natalie almost fell off her chair; Haddock was speechless. From this one man, the entire story of what had occurred all those years before.

'How do you know?'

'I didn't at the time, not until recently.'

'What happened?'

'I had sent the letter.'

'Did you say it was from you?'

'Howarth figured out it could have only been me who sent the letter. I've known Howarth a long time, done the occasional job for him. Bernie must have recommended me, knew that I was straight, would not speak and had no qualms about rifling through an office, digging in the trash, and finding leverage that Howarth and Bernie could use. He knew it was me from the phone message explaining what the letter meant. I told him I knew where she was and hadn't killed her. He asked my opinion, which proved that he had killed her. Otherwise, he would have contacted the police. I told him I would find a way for her body to be discovered. Leo Hannan was the obvious choice. He had access to Pinchgut, and his father had put her there. He felt obligated, although shocked that his father had been involved.'

'Does Howarth realise that you know he killed Sasha?'

'Sees me as a fool, the answer is no. That's the arrogance of the man. Sending the poem and then the SMS required some intelligence. Costello confronted Howarth after I sent the message. Sasha was using Howarth to deal with the legal, the inevitable obstructions in obtaining the lease. And Costello and Sasha used to sit on the balcony of their apartment while she waxed lyrical about Pinchgut, a clear view from there.'

Natalie knew that even if what Blake had said was true, there were seventeen years between the woman's death and her discovery. It was a long bow to stretch. All the police could do was confront the man, put forward circumstantial evidence, and aim to make him talk. But they knew Howarth was smarter than that.

Chapter 26

Two days later, time for Natalie and Haddock to write their reports, for Blake to be charged and released on his own surety, and for Leo Hannan to update his story and that he knew his father had helped Blake conceal the body, Natalie and Haddock sat down to eat fish and chips at a restaurant on the wharf at Watson's Bay, no more than twenty metres from where Josh Costello's body had been found.

The weather was clear, and the place was busy with tourists. Haddock was feeling pleased with himself; another night at the family home, his wife and daughter were glad to see him. Yet again, he had spent the night in the spare room, although he remained optimistic about a reconciliation. But what was it? he wondered. Was it the impending conclusion of a murder investigation that allowed him to relax, or was it something more? He still loved his wife, but the pressure of policing made his temperament changeable, his ability to relax and enjoy the family and taking an interest in their lives was difficult.

'Why here?' Haddock asked.

'Perspective. Visit the crime scene, try to get into the head of the murderer,' Natalie replied, who was not pleased with her choice of fish.

'Elaborate.'

'If Howarth killed Sasha, a summation by Blake, not based on fact but a perception, how does that make sense? And what is it with this letter? Cryptic, at least.'

'I couldn't make any sense of it, glad you couldn't either. Let's give Blake the benefit of the doubt and say he was responsible for her burial on Pinchgut, although that seems odd. He was right that he would have been charged with her murder and probably convicted. The man was right to be afraid.'

'Accept that Howarth killed Sasha. Why was she in Sydney? Why didn't she contact her father? Do we accept what we've been told about Wimbush? What's the Drug Squad's take on this? We've only got Blake's statement that he went to America with Sasha Cornell, and they met Wimbush. It's not evidence; too long ago to prove. We know Hannan found the body, and Blake had spoken to him and paid him good money. Circumstantial that he chose the son of the man who buried her there? And then I went to Hannan's place and found out that the man had taken money from her handbag. Not something a person would do if they received a financial windfall from Blake. And yet again, if Howarth did kill the woman, no reason to find her body unless he's arrogant enough to believe the police are incompetent and he's above the law.'

'He's not above the law,' Haddock said as he ordered another beer.

'Or he was aware of her father's parlous health, that he was getting old, not in good condition, with a weak heart and soon to meet his maker. Howarth's got the ear of the old man, the key to the treasure chest, and he can afford to speed the man's demise. He knows Cornell will come out fighting, both barrels blasting, disregarding medical advice, and soon dead. Who is to gain from Cornell's death? Only one person, although supposedly others behind the scene, but we've not seen them. Was Cornell in control of his faculties? We saw the man fired up, adrenalin flowing through his veins and supercharging his brain. What if he was suffering from dementia, and Howarth knew where the money was, how to access bank accounts, and passwords to the computers?'

'Hard to prove.'

'Not impossible. A former prime minister keels under pressure when he realises we will not let him off the hook. Makes a statement to the media, makes a hash of it, and opens himself to enquiry by the federal parliament and the media. People make mistakes when the heat is on.'

'Do we agree that Davidson is not involved in either death?'

'For now. Not convinced he's clean, and Beth Madison is a can of worms. She's not telling the full truth, nor is Davidson. And not Howarth, who knows more than anyone else. That doesn't make him a murderer, but the man's got a dark side. Starring in a porn movie? Strange behaviour for someone committed to maintaining the persona of sporting hero, all-around good guy, and, twenty years ago, Australian of the year.

'And if Sasha and Costello had died due to Davidson, it would not have been at his hand, others to do that. In the national interest? We don't want to go down the road, a bottomless pit, investigation put in the too-hard basket and we're told to back off and don't touch.'

Natalie pushed her fish to one side. 'We've got work to do,' she said.

Haddock was enjoying the sun and the harbour. He could have stayed longer, but with his sergeant, the bit between her teeth, he had to agree.

At three o'clock that afternoon, the door to Howarth's office opened. 'Welcome,' he said, shaking the hands of both police officers.

An ominous sign, Natalie thought.

'Mr Howarth, we have charged Gareth Blake with concealing Sasha Cornell's body at Pinchgut. Are you aware of this?' Haddock said.

'I am. Why?'

'According to him, he found her dead, drowned in a swimming pool. Unfortunately, Pathology could not deduce that from what remained of her, and Forensics had nothing to examine. He has accused you of the murder.'

'Impossible. I was out of the country when she disappeared.'

'Blake said she was alive for several weeks after you returned.'

'Do you believe him?'

'Elements of his story don't ring true, but he did go to Pinchgut, on your instruction. He did find Leo Hannan, who we have confirmed had a father who had been a tradesman at Pinchgut.'

'Bernie was playing a dangerous game. I told him not to get involved, the cost was too high, but he wasn't listening. Blake's got it all wrong. I didn't kill Sasha; why would I?'

'Wimbush? You've met the man?'

'Not personally. I knew who he was and saw through him. Met enough of his type over the years, promise you the world, give you crumbs when you are no longer of any use.'

'Costello?'

'Not sure. He's not the brightest, but then you know that. I was with Sasha most weeks, and he didn't suspect it. He still thought she was there for him. She wasn't. She was Bernie, a pretty face but ruthless. Alive, she would be formidable, take her father's business empire and wield it into something incredible. Bernie was fading, even back then. The edge had gone off, the hunger when he was starting up no longer there. Give the man his due, incredible determination. But he gets into pornography and then drugs. I tried to warn him, told him he was heading down a slippery slope, persons who would see you dead if you got on the wrong side of them.'

'You knew this back then? Perceptive for someone so young,' Natalie said.

'Hindsight, Sergeant. Your sarcasm does not befit you. You're smarter than that, a promising future ahead, yet your behaviour does not bode well for your future as a police officer.'

A masterful putdown, but she wasn't having any of it. Angry, she responded. 'Mr Howarth, you've misjudged us. We're not fools, and we don't respond to your putdowns. It is you who should be worried. We find you at every turn, at every avenue we head up. Not only were you sleeping with Sasha, but you were also cosying up to her father, inveigling your way into his confidence and ultimately controlling his wealth. Yours is the strongest motive that we can see. Blake feeds us nonsense, that Wimbush met Sasha with Bernie Cornell's blessing.

'He wouldn't risk sending his daughter without evaluating Wimbush's credentials. Maybe Wimbush didn't have the public profile he has now, but Bernie Cornell would have conducted checks with private investigators and business colleagues, compiled a portfolio on Wimbush and what he was up to, who he was, and whether he could trust his daughter with him. And then, she's dumped there, and Blake's on a plane to Australia.'

'Checks were made, assurances received. I told you Sasha was Bernie.'

'She wasn't, so why don't you drop this pretence. She was successful, found pornography risqué and was possibly amused by it. What we know of Bernie Cornell, and we met the man who showed no sign of dementia, was that his daughter was the most precious thing in his life. Sure, he was a rogue with others, but he wouldn't have risked his daughter. Blake spins a good tale, walks the talk, and he's there at your beckoning. The truth, the house in Palm Beach.'

'It belonged to Bernie, not that he ever went there.'

'And Wimbush?'

'That much is true. The man's a villain, amoral. Drugs, pornography, and whatever else. Incredibly smart, politically devious. A nastier piece of work you would not meet.'

Natalie knew that was not true. The sporting hero with the celebrity status and the good looks, the business acumen to take effective control of Cornell's empire, imbued her with the impression that Howarth was Australia's Wimbush. Could Wimbush be a red herring? She wasn't certain of it and knew it would be difficult to prove. As a former prime minister, Ralph Davidson had political and business influence. But Australia was not the USA. Senator Wimbush was untouchable, not open to criticism, and he would distance himself if she and Haddock, even the NSW police commissioner, attempted to coerce him into a meeting.

'If it's his house, why didn't he see his daughter? And what's with this fortress analogy? It's not America, but a large house close to the sea in an expensive part of Sydney. Hardly high walls and men in black suits carrying automatic rifles.'

'Blake's susceptible to exaggeration. Sasha was there on her own. Bernie knew this but didn't go. She wanted time out, didn't want to speak to her father, realised that he had placed her in danger in America, and wasn't sure if she was coming back to Costello or her father.'

'Who knew this? Why did Blake lie? How do we know if you're telling the truth?'

'You don't. Wimbush had tried it on with Sasha, and she had relented.'

'How do you know this?'

Natalie could see that, once again, the same old merry-go-round, each person contradicting the other. She felt that until they had something one hundred per cent certain, the case would move from person to person with nothing more than hunches. She wanted to believe that Howarth was the guilty party, but that was personal, and that Sasha had been a good person. She had no firm views on Blake, who seemed to be a minor player, a cog in the wheel, a go-to man when things needed to be organised, a word in the ear given, support for Sasha Cornell when she went to America, and that hadn't turned out well.

Howarth contradicted Blake, and Leo Hannan had been cautious about what Blake had said to him, and yes, he did have a father who had worked on Pinchgut in the past, and the dates tallied. Natalie felt they were going in a circle, and it seemed illogical that if Bernie Cornell had owned the house in Palm Beach, he had stayed away. The relationship between father and daughter had been strong, and then, she was back in Australia, hiding in her father's house. It made no sense.

Superintendent Payne made a representation to his counterparts in America but received nothing in reply other than there was no investigation into Senator Wimbush, nor had there been in the past. Payne thought he had been fobbed off, and if Wimbush was politically powerful, he would be protected, another of those above the law, protected by their class, political influence, and wealth.

Another wasted visit with Howarth; the man was too smart to give much away and unlikely to let hitherto unknown facts slip if it was not to his advantage.

The golden boy, his halo slipping, in a desperate attempt to maintain his image commenced a public relations campaign in the following week, with interviews on the television about his sporting prowess and how he was to shape Cornell's legacy. A hospital to be dedicated to him, donations to religious bodies, and ethnic studies at one university. Sasha's name was to be given to a scholarship and to a ward at St Vincent's Hospital in Darlinghurst, fully equipped with the latest equipment to research heart disease.

Natalie made a phone call outside Howarth's office in response to a message on her phone.

'At 6 p.m.,' Victoria Adderley replied.

'Anything?'

'It could be important.'

***

Victoria met with Natalie; Haddock was upstairs in the building, updating Superintendent Payne. Natalie thought it would be a short conversation, although the two men alone would down more than a couple of beers each.

Victoria sat close to the wall in her office, her arms folded, with a smug look.

'That good?' Natalie said. She was sitting on a hard chair, attempting to remain alert. The office was too warm, and sleep had eluded her the previous night. The closing stages of a murder investigation, her mind going through the evidence so far, the people they had interviewed, what was true and what was not.

'Beth Madison's affair with Ralph Davidson did not end with the publication of his book,' Victoria said.

Natalie was not shocked. A cynicism she had acquired in her time with Homicide. It was not something she liked, but it was inevitable.

'Proof?'

'Online. Australian Government, Independent Parliamentary Expenses Authority. As a former prime minister, the public purse picks up the tab for him, transportation, hotels, stationery, an office, and sundries. He's required to submit detailed information with invoices. Amazing what you can find with a little digging.'

'Recent?' Natalie asked.

'One week after Sasha Cornell's body was found, a flight to Tasmania, a rental car, a house on the west coast.'

'Can you prove that Beth Madison flew there with him?'

'He didn't fly with her, too obvious,' she said. 'He went on his own and drove a rental to a former colleague's house, even though he would have been entitled to a government vehicle.'

'Proof that Beth was there?'

I've got the dates when he flew. Qantas, business class. He's on the passenger list going and coming, five days in Tasmania.'

'And Beth?'

'She was out of town, checked on her movements. Not so easy, but she left one day later, flew via Adelaide, and purchased a ticket from there to Tasmania. Used her mother's maiden name, but I found it. She took a bus from Launceston to Strahan on the west coast of Tasmania, and Davidson picked her up there. Four days later, he left, and she flew back two days later.'

Natalie had noticed it before. Victoria Adderley, Legal Department, State Crime Command, had the makings of a good investigative police officer.

'Suspicious,' Natalie replied.

'Definitely. Comparing notes in the wilds of Tasmania?'

'Lovers reunited, or was it platonic?'

'You can draw your own conclusions. Whatever it was, they would have discussed Sasha Cornell.'

'Davidson's behaviour has been out of character, a disaster of a confrontation with a reporter. The man was flawless in leadership, losing his way in retirement. Early dementia? It's been spoken about with Bernie, but I don't hold with that. The man was astute when we met him, but the former prime minister was less than impressive.'

'And his bedtime companion has been less than honest.'

'And due for another summons to Parramatta,' Natalie said. 'As an adjunct, anything you need to tell me?' Aware that Victoria and Payne had seemed pally, but were they sharing a bed, or was it flirtation?

'Nothing. Why the interest?'

'No reason to condemn or comment, but one day, if the proverbial hits the fan, ethics committee, that sort of thing, I need to know what to say, how to defend or deflect. I'm on your side, you know that.'

'I do,' Victoria said. 'Thanks for asking, but nothing, not yet. Just harmless teasing, a bit of fun.'

The red-faced fair-skinned lawyer was a better investigator than a liar. Natalie suspected the truth and would protect her friend at any cost if that day came. In the meantime, a woman sat in her home in the Eastern Suburbs, and a former lover sat in his, no more than a ten-minute walk from her.

Chapter 27

Natalie realised that advising Beth Madison to present herself
early the next day would be counterproductive, as it was known
she and Davidson had met on the west coast of Tasmania to
coordinate their story and for sex, sun, and sand, although there
would not have been much sun and sand. She had been there
with her parents in her early teens, dragged from pillar to post,
the last holiday she had with them, and Tasmania, an island state
to the south of the continent, the wind blowing from Antarctica,
was more reminiscent of an English climate than Australia's.
When she had visited, December had been cold and rainy, even
sleeting snow on Mount Wellington at the back of Hobart, the
capital city.

Beth Madison reclined in a chair at the back of her house,
close to the pool, sitting up with a start when Natalie appeared
alongside her. It was not Strahan weather, but warm and balmy,
with a gentle breeze from the north.

'Caught you unawares,' Victoria said as she sat beside the
woman.

'I've no more to say. Aren't you exceeding your authority,
entering my house uninvited?'

'The side gate was open. Telling lies, sparing with the
truth, and having it off in Tasmania with Ralph Davidson is not
how to enamour yourself to the police. Does your husband
know? He seems a decent man, given you a good life, and there
you are, shacked up in Strahan with your former lover.'

'How? How do you know?'

'You better level with me, Beth, or it's Parramatta, bright
lights and the third degree.'

'You could have phoned and asked me to meet you there.'

'I could, but you would have made a phone call, got a
former prime minister to advise you, the Official Secrets Act
thrust under our noses. We're not concerned if Davidson is the

greatest villain alive or if he cheated the Australian taxpayer out of millions. Too long ago to concern us. We're interested in two murders, one not far from here. I can't see you killing Josh Costello, and Davidson's not going to get his hands dirty, not unless Costello knew something, figured out that blackmail wasn't a bad idea, out on his ear since Howarth took over Bernie's empire. What's it to be? Will you start telling the truth?'

'You have the truth. And yes, we did meet in Tasmania, not for what you think. We needed to talk to ensure our stories tally after Sasha's body had been found. Sydney's too hot for us currently, people prying, reporters staking out Ralph's house, suspicious of him from the press conference. They are looking for dirt, but it's not sticking, and he's vague.

'His wife's hassling, only staying for the perks. I'm his crutch. He realises I can be trusted. I was angry when I spoke to Sasha, but time and wisdom have mellowed me. He's a great man, did a lot for this country, and okay, he was sleeping with me and lining his back pocket, but you can't blame him. Everyone is doing it; why not him?'

Natalie felt she should offer an opinion. She was of country stock, a handshake as good as a signed contract, business conducted differently, and she did not believe that Davidson had been honourable, but under his prime ministership, the economy had boomed, good fiscal management on his part. Unlike the current custodians in Canberra, the capital of Australia, who were making a hash of the upcoming downturn with no plans other than to keep plodding on, talking up the economy and accentuating the positive, deflecting the negative, hopeful that it would blow over. But her father saw through the platitudes and realised that times were not good, and her mother was constant in that it was time for their daughter to find a good man and settle down. Ever practical, Natalie loved her mother but appreciated the practicality of her father, who called a spade a spade, not a shovel or a digging implement.

'Tasmania? Did you sleep with him?'

'My husband knew where I was, and so did his wife. We realised that we might be found out, tongues would wag, and assumptions would be made. However, it wasn't that. Ralph made a fool of himself with the daughter of a former colleague and allowed himself to be baited.'

'And you had supplied the ammunition. Did he know?'

'He does now, thought I was a bloody fool, but he forgave me, as I forgave him when he dumped me. There's history between us; I can't deny it.'

'Love?'

'Yes, genuine, but history was against us. I was younger than him, but I wasn't a foolish schoolgirl. Sure, I was taken in by the man's importance, but it was love for both of us. But he couldn't afford to divorce his wife, who knew too much. She's a vindictive woman, a harridan. Give her a broomstick, and she could have a starring part in The Wizard of Oz, the wicked witch of the West.'

'That bad?'

'She's the daughter of a bishop, had a harsh upbringing, and believes in propriety. No doubt cold showers in her youth, but she's stood by Ralph and turned a blind eye when he was with me. She is not a person to like, but she had the contacts when Ralph was after preselection to a safe parliamentary seat in the Eastern Suburbs. He'll not divorce her, and she'll stay with him through thick and thin. Besides, most of the assets are in her name, break him to divorce her, and I won't leave my husband.'

'You and Ralph, Tasmania, a shared room?'

'Another time, we would have made love, but not in Tasmania. That belongs in the past, but Ralph knows that you and Haddock won't stop fishing, and Howarth will destroy anyone, shift the blame if he can. He's the villain, or haven't you figured that out?'

'We have, but can't prove it.'

'I will coordinate with Ralph, preserve his legacy, and not inflict further pain on him. He did not kill Sasha or Josh Costello. You must believe that.'

'Are you sure? Are you certain Ralph Davidson is not stringing you along?'

'I am.'

Natalie did not have the confidence that Beth Madison had, although she thought she was probably right in her estimation of the man. For now, the investigation would focus on adult movies, Duncan Howarth, and a sullen person named Gazza Blake. As for the statement that the former lovers had not slept together in Tasmania, that was baloney. She had phoned the cleaner at the house, a long chat about the previous occupants, the state of the bed, had it been slept in, had there been congress, a polite term for sexual intercourse. The cleaner had given the truth and confirmed what Natalie believed, but whether Davidson's wife and Beth Madison's husband knew it was unknown. Regardless, Natalie would keep the secret she thought irrelevant in the murder investigations.

***

Approachable, affable, and ready to give an autograph. The relentless campaign to enhance the hero status of Duncan Howarth continued unabated. Invites to sporting events, the opportunity to present medals, to kiss on both cheeks the female winners, to shake the hands of the men. Haddock watched the man's ascendancy in popularity, bemused that people could be fooled by an insidious man who was shamelessly flaunting himself.

It was, to the two police officers, an exercise in futility. The man, if guilty of a crime, would be arrested on the merits of the evidence, not on whether he would win a popularity contest. His trial would be adjudicated by a judge, two barristers arguing his guilt or innocence, and a jury of twelve deciding the man's fate.

Why Howarth needed to conduct such a campaign when he, as an intelligent man, knew the police were focussing on him made little sense, but Ralph Davidson, his ego intact even if his political cunning had waned, had fallen for the trap of over self-belief.

Two streets away from Beth, her recent roommate sat at his walnut desk, a view of Sydney Harbour through the balcony window in front of him. He was a troubled man who reacted calmly when Haddock knocked on his door. Natalie had left her car outside Beth's and strolled the short distance, marvelling at the opulence of the houses as she walked. She knew leaving her vehicle outside one house and walking down the street would have caused Beth to phone Ralph. It had been Haddock who had wised her up to the subtle tactic, knowing that two persons, in two houses, would be on the phone to each other, comparing notes, attempting to come up with a response, especially after one had spoken to Natalie, said very little outright, but inferred more by her body language and her denials.

'Welcome in,' a woman in her early seventies said. Natalie knew this was the harridan, the woman that Beth despised, the wife of Ralph Davidson, a person who had stood by her husband through thick and thin. The house was magnificent, a sweeping staircase in front of Haddock and Natalie as they entered, oil paintings on the walls, marble on the floor. Opulence in the extreme, not like the place that Davidson and Beth had occupied in Tasmania.

'Your husband?' Haddock said.

'Inside, in his office. Always pleased to meet members of the police,' Agnes Davidson said.

Natalie wasn't fooled. She looked at the woman's eyes, unblinking, dark as sin. She judged the wife to be as Beth had described, polite and ingratiating to those she needed to be, malevolent and dismissive of those she did not. And for now, she needed a pliable police force, good public relations, and a sweet tone to her voice.

Upstairs, on the landing, a man's voice. 'Sergeant Campbell, Inspector Haddock, please come up.'

An invite into the lair. Were they Hansel and Gretel, invited into the gingerbread house, ready to be gobbled up? Would they be able to repulse the charm offensive? Natalie had experienced the treatment with a Supreme Court judge and believed she could recognise the signals. Duncan Howarth had tried it, working with a gullible populace, and Davidson had been a master of manipulation in his day. Natalie was prepared, but she knew Haddock wasn't. He could not read the signals, not as well as her, as she had been trained in psychology and reading body language, but thought it also more a woman's instinct that saw people for what they were.

In the brief interaction with Davidson's wife, she had formed the opinion that the woman was a hater who used people to advantage and discarded them when no longer required, and that Beth Madison, a flawed character, was a loving woman and that Davidson might well have been fond of her, even loved her.

'Walked into a trap with that interview?' Natalie said in the confines of Davidson's office. The formalities had been dealt with: hands shaken, cups of coffee given to Natalie and Haddock, a look at the view, chit-chat about this and that, the weather, state of the economy, even the current prime minister, who Davidson freely admitted he didn't think much of.

'I did. The daughter of a former colleague threw me off kilter,' Davidson replied. 'You've met with Beth?'

'I have. On the phone to you?'

'Yes, but you expected that, the reason you left your car outside her house. Sergeant, don't make a mountain out of a molehill. We have an unusual relationship, but it is founded on a fondness for each other.'

'Not when she was about to spill the beans to Sasha Cornell,' Haddock reminded the man.

'No beans to spill, Inspector. Politics is about compromise, working with people you might not like, and making agreements that benefit some and disadvantage others. Regarding the mining lease in Queensland, there were anomalies and multiple reasons why it shouldn't have gone ahead, but I made a decision. How can any major infrastructure be without contention? The environment and the Barrier Reef are paramount, but progress must continue. Without any, this country wouldn't be what we have today. I don't want to lecture, but you understand I'm right. Maybe I shouldn't have taken Beth on a few trips, take criticism for that, a rap over the knuckles for errors I might have made as a politician. We're all guilty of some sin, a missed clue in a police investigation, an incorrect political decision, or an inappropriate relationship. I don't include my relationship with Beth in that.'

'Your wife? Does she understand about her?'

'She does not approve, but that is only natural. I am a political animal, fuelled by ego and the need to feed it. My relationship with Beth was the result of it. As for her, I believe she has been honest in that she was young, enamoured of an older, powerful man, and has not suffered due to it.'

'Your wife?' Haddock asked again.

'She knew, realised I would not break it off with her, and the book wasn't the catalyst. The relationship with Beth had run its course, and she knew it. Only she did not have a focus, no direction in her life. Lost, she looked for a friend, found it in Sasha, and made a story about dirty dealings, money changing hands, political intrigue, and corruption in high office. These days, our relationship is cordial, as you well know, and my wife is civil with Beth.'

Natalie thought, in essence, the man was telling the truth. There was one question that needed to be asked. 'Tasmania?'

'My wife knew; her husband does. Face to face with Beth, just the two of us, no prying eyes. A phone call wouldn't suffice. You're aiming to make arrests, and you're under pressure. Howarth's making a nuisance of himself, capable of deflecting blame from him, pushing it onto someone else.'

'You don't trust him?'

'Not at all. The man's the devil incarnate. He's without a conscience, amoral, and psychopathic. I'm not saying he killed Sasha or Costello, but if he had, he wouldn't have a conscience about it.'

'Do you admire him?'

'As a skilful operator, yes. As a person, no.'

'Tasmania,' Natalie reiterated. She wasn't sure if it was relevant, but she needed the truth.

'What did Beth say?'

'Nothing untoward happened.'

'Then stick with that,' Davidson said. 'It is not relevant.'

Natalie thought it might be after the denial. If the relationship was still emotional, what would each do for the other? But for now, Davidson was talking about Howarth, and he was more important than two lovers shacked up in Tasmania.

'You're aware that our investigation is focused in another direction and that Duncan Howarth's involvement, not fully defined, might be relevant.'

'I am. Not officially, but on the grapevine. Due to my former position as prime minister, I am privy to more information than the man in the street. Sasha was intrigued with movie making, not the plot but the visuals. And that, due to her encouragement and her father's financial input, it expanded into a large-scale operation, threatened by overseas interests.'

'Which evolved into the importation of drugs into this country.'

'And you believe that Duncan Howarth is involved?'

'He's always been there, and Bernie Cornell placed great faith in him. Bernie was shrewd, would have known what the man was, used him to advantage, even encouraged Sasha to spend time with him.'

'The son he never had?' Natalie asked.

'Not the son he wanted. I knew Bernie in the early days; he was ruthless and determined and would not take no for an answer but an underlying decency about him. Sasha was the same, a worthy successor to his legacy. Those who didn't know the man formed their opinion based on the media's portrayal of him. He bent the rules, used his wealth to get things done, and to grease the wheels.'

'Bribes?' Haddock interjected.

'Does that surprise you? You're a police officer; seen the reality. But even so, an inherent decency. Howarth doesn't have any decency. Bernie did, and Howarth always shows it, even if it's not there. The reason he's making himself visible nowadays, although he doesn't understand or care that the law is impartial.'

'He doesn't understand the crimes he might have committed?' Natalie asked.

'You must have psychologists who will tell you this. The man cannot believe that whether it's adult movies, drug importation, or murder, he has committed a crime. The most dangerous of individuals.'

'Proof?'

'He was considered as viable for political office, a safe electorate. I sponsored him, and background checks were made. Not the normal process, but a few persons had suspicions about him.'

'Which persons?'

'Political, sporting, influential.'

'Bernie Cornell?'

'He had expressed an opinion when I asked him. Howarth was inveigling himself into Bernie's confidence, always ensuring a good result in whatever Bernie charged him with. Bernie was sharp before Sasha disappeared, but he started to wither after she didn't return. Not that you'd notice it, but it was clear her disappearance affected him, understandable as you would agree.'

'He was sharp with us.'

'That was the appearance, but Howarth was there before Sasha disappeared. Bernie used him and encouraged Sasha to transfer her affections from Costello to the man. Maybe she saw through him. I wouldn't know. But Costello, not the sharpest tool in the shed, an occasional philanderer, wouldn't do her wrong, not in the long-term, not while Bernie was alive.

'Howarth continued with Bernie; the man's fading, doesn't see as clearly what Howarth is, and then, on his death, Duncan Howarth rises to the top, master of all he can survey. He would have made a great politician, only his focus would have been on himself, not those who voted for him. An exceptional individual, dangerous as hell. He's your man, must be.'

'No evidence,' Haddock said. 'We know he organised Sasha's body to be found, but apart from that, where's the proof.?'

'Senator Wimbush, that bastard, have you spoken to him?'

'No way to get to him. Is he as bad as he's portrayed?'

'Worse. I've met the man on several occasions. He charmed Sasha into his bed. And you're right, you'll probably not get to him, too tight with the political process in America, a future president. He's got the credentials, the political and financial backing, untouchable.'

'And in Australia, doesn't Howarth?'

'Tough nut to crack. Arresting him will take solid evidence, and he'll have the sharpest legal minds behind him. I wouldn't want to be in your shoes, eat you both for breakfast. Superintendent Payne, up to the task?'

'You're remarkably well-informed,' Natalie said.

'I am. I care about what happens in this country and am conscious of what Howarth is. He could be the man you want, capable of it, but don't assume he is.'

'You're a charming man, a skilled politician, a wordsmith. How do we know you're not spinning us a line, taking advantage of your obvious attributes to treat us as fools?'

'Well said, Sergeant, Natalie. I could be. Don't trust me totally; maintain a healthy degree of scepticism; investigate me further if you want. Victoria Adderley, still working on the mining lease, trying to find out if I took a bribe?'

'Not at present.'

'Good. Tell her to meet with me, and I'll go through what I've got, explain the reality, and calm her concerns.'

'She's not Beth, and you're not the lothario you were back then. Victoria Adderley's a skilled lawyer, not easily taken in by sweet words, flights overseas, and romantic hideaways in Tasmania.'

Natalie knew she had baited him. She wanted to know if there was another side to the man hiding behind the charming exterior, the eloquent speech, and if there were psychopathic tendencies. After all, Davidson had not risen to the top political position in Australia without ruthless actions and skullduggery.

Instead, the man laughed, a belly-aching laugh. 'Good on you, Sergeant. You thought you would have one last attempt to make me show my true colours. You'll go far. The reason Payne wants to promote you.'

'All persons are still suspect, even you, Sir,' Haddock said.

'As it should be. One favour, if possible.' Davidson said.

'If we can.'

'Go easy on Beth. She's innocent of any crime, and yes, I'm fond of her, always have been. I treated her shabbily once, political expediency, but I'll not do it again.'

Chapter 28

Behind Ralph Davidson's carefully-crafted veneer, there appeared to be a beating heart, and he had felt a fondness for Beth. Natalie and Haddock knew that dealing with politicians, judges, and Duncan Howarth was fraught with risks due to their skills in the manipulation of the truth and glib tongues. And that Davidson was a master of the art, as was Duncan Howarth, who had been in the limelight since his youth.

The problem for Natalie and Haddock was that Duncan Howarth was the obvious choice as the murderer and that more than one person had pointed the finger at him. But was the pointing based on facts they might have known, or was there personal or professional malice? Josh Costello had been evicted from his secure, well-salaried position in New York within days of Bernie Cornell's death, but had he complained to the person responsible? And if he had, what had resulted, apart from his death? It seemed important to focus on that angle, barring any others, as they were painfully thin. Aspersions, innuendo, and pointing the bone, to use an Australian Aboriginal means of dispensing justice, meant nothing without proof.

Davidson believed Howarth was the villain, and so did Uxbridge, but what was he? A sleazy peddler of sex and now drug trafficker, arrested after the Drug Squad had raided his premises, two sniffer dogs rifling through the stock, revealing at the back, hidden under other boxes, a carton of sex toys with heroin inside.

The man had avoided criminal charges throughout his long career, even though he had sold sex toys, had a bar at the back of his shops, girls gyrating, some for hire, but now, in his seventy-eighth year, arrested and led away in handcuffs, two weeks in the cells, before his release on compassionate grounds. Medical evaluation from two doctors confirmed what the man had said at the police station. 'Advanced cancer, no point having a trial for me, won't be around to answer the charge, might not make it till the end of next month.'

Natalie and Haddock visited the man at his house, a sprawling edifice, neat and tidy inside, with a wife who fretted over him and a dog that lolled close to an open fire. Two personas to the man: one, that of a peddler of sex, catering to those who were titillated by the products on sale in the shops, packaged in a paper bag after purchase, and those who enjoyed the shows and the women; the other persona, family man, pillar of society, a loving wife, a close group of friends who probably knew where his money came from, but did not concern themselves.

'All those years, and what's your legacy? Not good,' Haddock said.

Uxbridge picked up the mug of coffee his wife had left for him, kissing him on the cheek before she left the room.

'Salt of the earth,' Uxbridge said.

'Does she know where the money comes from?' Natalie asked. Regardless of the man's condition, she could feel sympathy, no reason to harbour anger or hatred as he prepared for death.

'Always. Not the details, never asked, thankful for the life I've given her.'

Ralph Davidson's wife might have been thankful, but Natalie was sure she never gave her husband a kiss or hot drink, one of the reasons he had strayed. But Uxbridge's wife, who knew of her husband's business interests, had never asked about them, never complained, although whether she knew about his venture into drug manufacture and distribution was unclear. She would now, yet she still loved the man.

'You pointed us towards Howarth,' Haddock reminded the man.

'I did.'

'Why?' Natalie asked. 'Ralph Davidson believes he could have killed Sasha, but we've no proof. We regard him as a thoroughly bad person, but that does not make him a murderer, and Blake seems involved wherever we turn.'

'Why are you talking to Davidson?' Uxbridge said. 'What's he got to do with it?'

'Another angle we were investigating, but it doesn't hold up. He knows Howarth and knew Bernie Cornell when he was starting out. The man has good insight; not sure if we trust him or you.'

'Drugs was a more recent venture.'

It wasn't, Natalie knew. It went back to when Sasha disappeared, but it wasn't important, as the man was dying. Speculation was good, but the proof was all-important.

'Blake? Was he involved with the drugs?' Natalie asked. The dog had moved and come over close to her and was lying at her feet.

'Blake's handy to have around. He didn't know about the drugs, not from me, might have suspected, probably did, the man doesn't miss much.'

'No conscience with what you were doing?'

'I catered to the market. It's not for me to be an arbiter of what they should or should not buy or use, supply and demand. I'm not the only person in Australia dealing in drugs. There are others, much bigger than me.'

'Howarth?'

'I don't know, and that's the truth. He wouldn't get his hands dirty, nor would Bernie Cornell. Cornell was the money man who could set up the major contracts and strike the deals. You will not get anything to stick to Howarth.'

Natalie wasn't so sure. People make mistakes when under pressure, and Howarth was feeling the heat. The public relations campaign had soured after various persons came forward on social media to say that Duncan Howarth wasn't all he was portrayed to be and that there was a dark side to the man.

Competitors of Bernie, now competitors of Howarth, used the anonymity of social media to criticise, to make up outrageous stories, most not true, but social media didn't look for proof; the person targeted would be condemned in the telling.

***

The case had wound on for too long, and Superintendent Payne was becoming concerned. He had given Natalie and Haddock a free rein, counselled them when needed, and given them a swift kick in the rear when required, but his patience had worn thin. Costello's death was recent, and those responsible were visible, only unknown. Whether two murderers or one murderer was unclear. The first murder required more forethought in the disposal of the body, and the second had only needed the expanse of Sydney Harbour, but why allow the body to be found? It was one possibility, but it didn't make sense. A warning to whom?

Haddock believed the body's discovery was unintended, as if there had been an outgoing tide, it would have drifted away, out through the entrance to Sydney Harbour, no more than a few kilometres away, and into the Tasman Sea. Natalie had to agree, but regardless, leaving the body to the whim of the tide was to leave it to chance. Either a body is disposed of in such a way as to never be found, or it is not. Blake had been professional in the concealment of Sasha's and it was unlikely he would have made an error with Costello.

'Who do we have?' Natalie said. It was the two of them, eight in the evening, at a Chinese restaurant close to State Crime Command. Haddock was dealing with family issues again. This time, his daughter, whose attendance at school was infrequent, and he knew, although his wife preferred not to, that their daughter and her boyfriend were visiting his home when his parents were at work. He realised that a lecture would not suffice, not with two rampant teenagers, and that a hefty clip around the boyfriend's ear would be appropriate. It was the twenty-first century, two decades in, and the right of the individual, regardless of age, prevailed, and teenagers in love could do what they wanted, whenever they wanted, and with whoever.

Approaching the boyfriend, grabbing him by the collar, giving him a good shake and threatening him would open him, a police inspector, to censure, but Haddock knew he couldn't leave the situation alone.

'Talking to her might help, but she's looking to others for advice, to her peers,' Natalie said. But she had grown up in the country, and her father had spoken to her sternly on one occasion about her promiscuous manner, short skirts and displaying the goods, and whether she was careful, which she was. He had advised, and she had listened, and within six months, the initial surge of adolescent hormones and experimentation had lessened. But Haddock's daughter was just sixteen, another three or four years before she wised up and realised that young men profess love but don't know what the word means, other than a way to get the female to loosen up, and that the young woman, in this instance his daughter, believed in love eternal.

'Who are equally as confused as her,' Haddock replied.

'You need to spend more time with her, not berating her, but try and see her side, to be a father figure, not an absent parent.'

'Easy to say, hard to do. I've tried, but opening up with her is not so easy for me to do. Too long a police officer, cynical, hardened, dismissive most of the time, and you advise me to be emotional and loving with her, not sure I can do it.'

Discussing Haddock's daughter was not the reason they were in the Chinese restaurant, and Haddock knew that it would take time to resolve the concerns about his daughter, probably when she realised that the current boyfriend would not last long and that he would be after another female, notches on his belt, one more for the count, comparison with his friends vis-à-vis how many females they had seduced.

'Costello?' Natalie said, getting the conversation back on track.

'Why allow the body to be found?'

'And how could they be certain it would be? Watson's Bay, a lot of people during the day. Was the place important? Did it

240

have significance, as Pinchgut did? And if it did, for whom? Forget the approach that the body could have drifted out to sea because someone erred. Adopt the idea it was planned and that certain facts are relevant. Why Watson's Bay? The body had been in the water for several hours, and Costello had been murdered.'

'The body would have had to be dumped near where it was found. Tied to the side of a boat, released not more than a few yards from the shore on an incoming tide. Or planted on the beach. We must assume a vessel near Watson's Bay. There has been no evidence that a water-sodden body had been transported on land.

'Blake had been smart with Sasha, continues to maintain his innocence, and he could have orchestrated Costello's murder. But that requires a motive.'

'Assume Blake murdered Sasha, hiding in Palm Beach for whatever reason. The Wimbush angle might be a red herring, even if the man's corrupt. Think homegrown. Sasha is troubled on her return to Australia. She has had a brief romance with Wimbush, slept with Howarth, lived with Costello, and realised that the only man who truly loves her is a heavily-tattooed runt from the Western Suburbs. She's a woman, moved by unrequited love, even if she has the character of her father, ambitious, ruthless, and determined.

'She's of an age to marry, settle down, and have children. She can have the child, but not the devoted attention of the father. Could she have slept with Blake at Palm Beach, attempting to sort her life out, unsure which direction to turn? Not with Blake, not long-term, and below her financial and social status. Wimbush has passed her over, Howarth's a bastard, and Costello's playing the field.'

'Are you saying that Blake committed both murders?' Haddock said, aware, once again, that he, the master when she had been foisted on him as a partner, was now the student.

'I'm saying that Blake killed Sasha and that Howarth knew. Whether that was at the time or later is unknown. Although I believe he knew soon after, as Howarth was making his move on Bernie's empire, a shoulder to lean on in the man's hour of grief. Sasha's death would have been advantageous to the man, as if she had lived, he would not have control of Bernie's empire. Blake had a relationship with Howarth back then but wouldn't tell us, whatever happened.'

It was a hypothesis. It was what they would run with, unsure of a resolution, but determined, regarding it as their last crack at solving the two murders, conscious that soon they would be usurped as the primary investigating officers and the investigations given to another group of police officers. That had been made clear later that night when Natalie and Haddock met with Superintendent Payne.

***

Gazza Blake sat in the interview room at State Crime Command. He had been brought to the station in a marked police car and shown the necessary courtesy, but no more. He had dressed for the occasion, a navy-coloured suit. He sat quietly in the room while the hypothesis crafted by Natalie was outlined. She delivered it, Haddock attentive, Blake increasingly disturbed, fidgeting in his seat and biting his nails.

Haddock was pleased, aware that once again, the young female sergeant he had tutored was now at the peak of her investigating skill, a brain that was both logical and intuitive, a mind that could see through the fog to the other side, weighing up what was relevant and what was not. He knew it would not be long before she was promoted, although he hoped they would remain a team; he, the titular head, but equals united in a common cause, the solving of homicides. If only his home life was as homogenous, he would be a happy man, but he realised that would not be easy.

'Gareth Blake,' Natalie said, 'I've outlined the facts, and of all those we've interviewed, you are predominant in our thought processes. Further investigations will continue at the house in Palm Beach and at Watson's Bay, an attempt to find the boat where the body was before it floated ashore and was held there as the tide receded. What say you? Today is not the time for procrastination or pointing us in another direction. Duncan Howarth has serious clout, plenty of money, and lawyers to protect him, passing the blame to others. And you are the one he will pass it to.'

'But…' Blake attempted to say, but Natalie wasn't finished yet. She had more to say and could see the man opposite visibly shrinking in his seat, undoing the top button of his shirt, and loosening his tie.

'You killed Sasha, who had spurned you, the one person that truly loved her. Wimbush, who may be the greatest villain, is protected by the American political system and the elites. Duncan Howarth has his reputation, money, and legal expertise. Even if he's guilty, proving it will take more than your word. And Warren Uxbridge will soon pass on, and he'll take any secrets he has to his grave. You're the bunny in the middle, defenceless, at the mercy of others who will do whatever is necessary to protect themselves and throw you to the wolves. It's happened before, will happen again, and Howarth's psychopathic. He doesn't regard any action, including you spending a long time in prison, as wrong. Your association with the man is to your detriment.'

'I didn't kill her,' Blake blurted, his voice quivering, his nails bitten to the quick.

'You found her,' Haddock said.

'I did, but I didn't kill her. I was angry, every right to be.'

'In your anger, you held her under the water. There she was, trying to figure out her future, rejected by Wimbush, discarded by Howarth, other than an occasional lay, and living with Costello, who she didn't love, but would have married. What could you give her? A nobody in the shadows. No social cred, no wealth, a minimal education. She's there by the pool, wearing a bikini, possibly topless. You can feel your emotions and the need to have her, and even though she professes friendship, she rejects you.

'In her anger, she says words she shouldn't have, calls you a mongrel, insults your manhood or lack of achievement. This is the daughter of Bernie Cornell. She knew how to put a person down and did it to you. In anger, am I right? You grab her, throw her into the pool, a leaf catcher nearby, and then, her head is under the water, and she's dead.

'You're confused, full of remorse, unsure what to do. You can't contact the police, knowing you would be charged and convicted. But there's one person, Mr Clean, Mr Successful, and you've got the dirt on him. You phone him, tell him there's been an accident, and ask for his advice. You use what you've got on him as a lever, but Howarth's psychopathic. He doesn't care about you or Sasha, only if an advantage can be gained. He knows Bernie's reaction, but he's not got the man under his control yet; he needs time for that. He comes to Palm Beach, or you meet in a neutral location. He might have called you a bloody fool, or maybe he was conciliatory, knows he's got you over a barrel, and makes you do work for him of an increasingly nefarious nature. Any more bodies we don't know about?'

'I'm not a murderer. It was an accident.'

'Manslaughter, we'll go for that,' Haddock said. 'A signed confession?'

'Yes. Your sergeant is correct. She was a lovely woman, better than those she went with. She had grown up around them, emulated them, but there was an underlying softness. I would have done anything for her, but I killed her. And yes, she was taking time out at Palm Beach, having fallen for Wimbush, similar to Howarth, but someone she thought would do right by her, a strong religious background, but the man was Howarth personified, the anti-Christ, and he had used her and then discarded her.

'I visited her often at Palm Beach, and we spent hours together, by the pool and in the house, and no, we were not lovers. Her choice, not mine. To her, I was the friend, no more than a lap dog. I enjoyed my time with her, but then, you know what happened.'

'Howarth?'

'He suggested Pinchgut and Leo Hannan's father hadn't been involved. I knew how to get to Pinchgut, and Howarth

244

ensured I would not be disturbed. I didn't understand why he wanted her there, but I did what I was told, told Leo that his father had been involved.'

'Proof?'

'The poem was Howarth's idea. I realised that my hold on him, his hold on me, was over. Or I thought it was.'

'You contacted Costello?'

'Who else to turn to? I needed someone on my side, as, given time, I would be charged with Sasha's murder. But it backfired. Instead of Costello going to the police, which would have implicated me, or keeping quiet, he told Howarth. Supposedly, the hatred between the two ran deep, not surprising given Sasha's predilection for musical beds. I was out of my depth, and then Costello was dead. Howarth knows it was me who had spoken to Costello.

'A boat near Watson's Bay. The two men met there to iron out their differences. Costello is desperate to get his old job back in America. I can give you the name, take you there. Howarth calls me, and I hotfoot it out to the boat. Costello's dead, a nylon cord around his neck, in the water for hours, tied to the boat. Howarth's got me over a barrel and knows I'll do whatever he tells me. I release the body, but I don't know about boats and the tide and thought the body would drift out to sea. I had placed weights on it, but they slipped off, and then the body was on the shore, and people were walking by. Impossible to risk being seen.'

'You were there?'

'I was, but not when the man died. I've got the goods on him; he's got the goods on me. Touché, both cornered. I'm expendable, but I've wised up, made sure I have the dirt. An iPhone, on audio record, in my back pocket, and on that boat, the man's arrogant, and he starts talking, tells me that he had killed Costello, a violent argument. I knew he had killed him, but it's on record, but he doesn't know it. He was enjoying himself on that boat, thought I was a nobody, which I am, but I'm street smart, learned my lessons the hard way.'

'Does it clear you of Sasha's murder?'

'He spoke about it, recounted what had happened that day, and why he had thought of Pinchgut, the room, and the wall where she would be sealed. It wasn't difficult for me to seal her there. The room was deemed unsafe, and I had the key, and the door had been bricked over. Undisturbed for seventeen years until Leo Hannan made the discovery. He was glad of the money, sickened by what he discovered, but I was thankful. I knew there would be complications, the reason I am handing you a hard drive with the download from my iPhone.'

Blake put his hand into the right pocket of his suit jacket, withdrew the hard drive and passed it across the desk. 'Exhibit one,' he said. 'Proof that Sasha's death was accidental and that Howarth murdered Costello.'

It was not the primary exhibit, Sasha Cornell's body was, but as Natalie and Haddock listened to it, a team of crime scene investigators were alongside the boat identified by Blake.

Two hours later, one of the crime scene investigators phoned Haddock. 'We've found Blake's and Howarth's fingerprints and a nylon cord similar to that used to strangle Costello.'

That afternoon, at three thirty-four, Duncan Howarth, in handcuffs, was led out of his office and out onto the street, to a marked police car waiting to transport him to State Crime Command in Parramatta, where he would be formally charged with a multitude of crimes, the most significant, the murder of Josh Costello. Natalie would charge him, as it had been her who had seen through the contradictory statements and had given the impetus and the final focus to the investigation.

A press statement from Howarth's legal team emphasised the man's innocence and that a vigorous defence would be mounted, although the public and the media did not need to wait for the trial. Duncan Howarth had become persona non grata, public enemy number one. His fall from grace had been fast and dramatic; devolving Bernie Cornell's empire would take much longer.

The End

ALSO BY THE AUTHOR

DI Tremayne Thriller Series

Death Unholy – A DI Tremayne Thriller – Book 1

All that remained were the man's two legs and a chair full of greasy and fetid ash. Little did DI Keith Tremayne know that it was the beginning of a journey into the murky world of paganism and its ancient rituals. And it was going to get very dangerous.

'Do you believe in spontaneous human combustion?' Detective Inspector Keith Tremayne asked.

'Not me. I've read about it. Who hasn't?' Sergeant Clare Yarwood answered.

'I haven't,' Tremayne replied, which did not surprise his young sergeant. In the months they had been working together, she had come to realise that he was a man who had little interest in the world. When he had a cigarette in his mouth, a beer in his hand, and a murder to solve he was about the happiest she ever saw him, but even then, he was not one of life's most sociable people. And as for reading? The occasional police report, an early-morning newspaper, turned first to the racing results.

Death and the Assassin's Blade – A DI Tremayne Thriller – Book 2

It was meant to be high drama, not murder, but someone's switched the daggers. The man's death took place in plain view of two serving police officers.

He was not meant to die; the daggers were only theatrical props, plastic and harmless. A summer's night, a production of Julius Caesar amongst the ruins of an Anglo-Saxon fort. Detective Inspector Tremayne is there with his sergeant, Clare Yarwood. In the assassination scene, Caesar collapses to the ground. Brutus defends his actions; Mark Antony rebukes him.

They're a disparate group, the amateur actors. One's an estate agent, another an accountant. And then there is the teenage school student, the gay man, the funeral director. And what about the women? They could be involved.

They've each got a secret, but which of those on the stage wanted Gordon Mason, the actor who had portrayed Caesar, dead?

Death and the Lucky Man – A DI Tremayne Thriller – Book 3

Sixty-eight million pounds and dead. Hardly the outcome expected for the luckiest man in England the day his lottery ticket was drawn out of the barrel. But then, Alan Winters' rags-to-riches story had never been conventional, and some had benefited, but others hadn't.

Death at Coombe Farm – A DI Tremayne Thriller – Book 4

A warring family. A disputed inheritance. A recipe for death.

If it hadn't been for the circumstances, Detective Inspector Keith Tremayne would have said the view was outstanding. Up high, overlooking the farmhouse in the valley below, the panoramic vista of Salisbury Plain stretching out beyond. The only problem was a body near where he stood with his sergeant, Clare Yarwood, and it wasn't a pleasant sight.

Death by a Dead Man's Hand – A DI Tremayne Thriller – Book 5

A flawed heist of forty gold bars from a security van late at night. One of the perpetrators is killed by his brother as they argue over what they have stolen.

Eighteen years later, the murderer, released after serving his sentence for his brother's murder, waits in a church for a man purporting to be the brother he killed. And then he is killed.

The threads stretch back a long way, and now more people are dying in the search for the missing gold bars.

Detective Inspector Tremayne, his health causing him concern, and Sergeant Clare Yarwood, still seeking romance, are pushed to the limit solving the murder, attempting to prevent more.

Death in the Village – A DI Tremayne Thriller – Book 6

Nobody liked Gloria Wiggins, a woman who regarded anyone who did not acquiesce to her jaundiced view of the world with disdain. James Baxter, the previous vicar, had been one of those, and her scurrilous outburst in the church one Sunday had hastened his death.

And now, years later, the woman was dead, hanging from a beam in her garage. Detective Inspector Tremayne and Sergeant Clare Yarwood had seen the body, interviewed the woman's acquaintances, and those who had hated her.

Burial Mound – A DI Tremayne Thriller – Book 7

A Bronze-Age burial mound close to Stonehenge. An archaeological excavation. What they were looking for was an ancient body and historical artefacts. They found the ancient body, but then they found another that's only been there for years, not centuries. And then the police became interested.

It's another case for Detective Inspector Tremayne and Sergeant Yarwood. The more recent body was the brother of the mayor of Salisbury.

Everything seems to point to the victim's brother, the mayor, the upright and serious-minded Clive Grantley. Tremayne's sure that it's him, but Clare Yarwood's not so sure.

But is her belief based on evidence or personal hope?

The Body in the Ditch – A DI Tremayne Thriller – Book 8

A group of children play. Not far away, in the ditch on the other side of the farmyard, lies the body of a troubled young woman.

The nearby village hides as many secrets as the community at the farm, a disparate group of people looking for an alternative to their previous torturous lives. Their leader, idealistic and benevolent, espouses love and kindness, and clearly, somebody's not following his dictate.

An old woman's death seems unrelated to the first, but is it? Is it part of the tangled web that connects the farm to the village?

Detective Inspector Tremayne and Sergeant Clare Yarwood soon discover that the village is anything but charming and picturesque. It's an incestuous hotbed of intrigue and wrongdoing. And what of the farm and those who live there. None of them can be ruled out, not yet.

The Horse's Mouth – A DI Tremayne Thriller – Book 9

A day at the races for Detective Inspector Tremayne, idyllic at the outset, soon changes. A horse is dead, the owner's daughter is found murdered, and Tremayne's there when the body is discovered.

The question is, was Tremayne set up, in the wrong place at the right time? He's the cast-iron alibi for one of the suspects, and he knows that one murder can lead to two, and more often than not to three.

The dead woman had a chequered history, though not as much as her father, and then a man commits suicide. Is he the murderer, or was his death the unfortunate consequence of a tragic love affair? And who was in the stable with the woman just before she died? More than one person could have killed her, and all of them have secrets they would rather not be known.

Tremayne's health is troubling him. Is what they are saying correct, that it is time for him to retire, to take it easy and put his feet up? But that's not his style, and he'll not give up on solving the murder.

Montfield's Madness – A DI Tremayne Thriller – Book 10

A day at the races for Detective Inspector Tremayne, idyllic at the Jacob Montfield, regarded by the majority as a homeless eccentric, a nuisance by a few, had pushed a supermarket trolley around the city for years.

However, one person regards him as a liability.

Eccentric was correct, a nuisance, for sure, mad, plenty thought that, but few knew the truth, that Montfield is a brilliant man, once a research scientist. And even less knew that detailed within a notebook hidden deep in the trolley, there is a new approach to the guidance of weapons and satellites—a radical improvement on the previous and it's worth a lot to some, power to others, accolades to another.

And for that, one cold night, he died at the hand of another. Inspector Tremayne and Sergeant Clare Yarwood are on the case, but so are others, and soon they're warned off. Only Tremayne doesn't listen, not when he's got his teeth into the investigation, and his sergeant, equally resolute, won't either. It's not only their careers on the line, but their lives.

DCI Isaac Cook Thriller Series

Murder is a Tricky Business – A DCI Cook Thriller – Book 1

A television actress is missing, and DCI Isaac Cook, the Senior Investigation Officer of the Murder Investigation Team at Challis Street Police Station in London, is searching for her.

Why has he been taken away from more important crimes to search for the woman? It's not the first time she's gone missing, so why does everyone assume she's been murdered?

There's a secret; that much is certain, but who knows it? The missing woman? The executive producer? His eavesdropping assistant? Or the actor who portrayed her fictional brother in the TV soap opera?

Murder House – A DCI Cook Thriller – Book 2

A corpse in the fireplace of an old house. It's been there for thirty years, but who is it?

It's murder, but who is the victim and what connection does the body have to the house's previous owners. What is the motive?

And why is the body in a fireplace? It was bound to be discovered eventually but was that what the murderer wanted? The main suspects are all old and dying or already dead.

Isaac Cook and his team have their work cut out, trying to put the pieces together. Those who know are not talking because of an old-fashioned belief that a family's dirty laundry should not be aired in public and never to a policeman – even if that means the murderer is never brought to justice!

Murder is Only a Number – A DCI Cook Thriller – Book 3

Before she left, she carved a number in blood on his chest. But why the number 2 if this was her first murder?

The woman prowls the streets of London. Her targets are men who have wronged her. Or have they? And why is she keeping count?

DCI Cook and his team finally know who she is, but not before she's murdered four men. The whole team are looking for her, but the woman keeps disappearing in plain sight. The pressure's on to stop her, but she's always one step ahead.

And this time, DCS Goddard can't protect his protégé, Isaac Cook, from the wrath of the new commissioner at the Met.

Murder in Little Venice – A DCI Cook Thriller – Book 4

A dismembered corpse floats in the canal in Little Venice, an upmarket tourist haven in London. Its identity is unknown, but what is its significance?

DCI Isaac Cook is baffled about why it's there. Is it gang-related, or is it something more?

Whatever the reason, it's clearly a warning, and Isaac and his team are sure it's not the last body that they'll have to deal with.

Murder is the Only Option – A DCI Cook Thriller – Book 5

A man thought to be long dead returns to exact revenge against those who had blighted his life. His only concern is to protect his wife and daughter. He will stop at nothing to achieve his aim.

'Big Greg, I never expected to see you around here at this time of night.'

'I've told you enough times.'

'I've no idea what you're talking about,' Robertson replied. He looked up at the man, only to see a metal pole coming down at him. Robertson fell down, cracking his head against a concrete kerb.

Two vagrants, no more than twenty feet away, did not stir and did not even look in the direction of the noise. If they had, they would have seen a dead body, another man walking away.

Murder in Notting Hill – A DCI Cook Thriller – Book 6

One murderer, two bodies, two locations, and the murders have been committed within an hour of each other.

They're separated by a couple of miles, and neither woman has anything in common with the other. One is young and wealthy, the daughter of a famous man; the other is poor, hardworking and unknown.

Isaac Cook and his team at Challis Street Police Station are baffled about why they've been killed. There must be a connection, but what is it?

Murder in Room 346 – A DCI Cook Thriller – Book 7

'Coitus interruptus, that's what it is,' Detective Chief Inspector Isaac Cook said. In a downmarket hotel in Bayswater, on the bed lay the naked bodies of a man and a woman.

'Bullet in the head's not the way to go,' Larry Hill, Isaac Cook's detective inspector, said. He had not expected such a flippant comment from his senior, not when they were standing near to two people who had, apparently in the final throes of passion, succumbed to what appeared to be a professional assassination.

'You know this will be all over the media within the hour,' Isaac said.

'James Holden, moral crusader, a proponent of the sanctity of the marital bed, man and wife. It's bound to be.'

Murder of a Silent Man – A DCI Cook Thriller – Book 8

A murdered recluse. A property empire. A disinherited family. All the ingredients for murder.

No one gave much credence to the man when he was alive. In fact, most people never knew who he was, although those who had lived in the area for many years recognised the tired-looking and shabbily-dressed man as he shuffled along, regular as clockwork on a Thursday afternoon at seven in the evening to the local off-licence.

It was always the same: a bottle of whisky, premium brand, and a packet of cigarettes. He paid his money over the counter, took hold of his plastic bag containing his purchases, and then walked back down the road with the same rhythmic shuffle.

Murder has no Guilt – A DCI Cook Thriller – Book 9

No one knows who the target was or why, but there are eight dead. The men seem the most likely perpetrators, or could have it been one of the two women, the attractive Gillian Dickenson, or even the celebrity-obsessed Sal Maynard?

There's a gang war brewing, and if there are deaths, it doesn't matter to them as long as it's not their death. But to Detective Chief Inspector Isaac Cook, it's his area of London, and it does matter.

It's dirty and unpredictable. Initially, the West Indian gangs held sway, but a more vicious Romanian gangster had usurped them. And now he's being marginalised by the Russians. And the leader of the most vicious Russian mafia organisation is in London, and he's got money and influence, the ear of those in power.

Murder in Hyde Park – A DCI Cook Thriller – Book 10

An early-morning jogger is murdered in Hyde Park. It's in the centre of London, but no one saw him enter the park, no one saw him die.

He carries no identification, only a water-logged phone. As the pieces unravel, it's clear that the dead man had a history of deception.

Is the murderer one of those that loved him? Or was it someone with a vengeance?

It's proving difficult for DCI Isaac Cook and his team at Challis Street Homicide to find the guilty person – not that they'll cease to search for the truth, not even after one suspect confesses.

Six Years Too Late – A DCI Cook Thriller – Book 11

Always the same questions for Detective Chief Inspector Isaac Cook — Why was Marcus Matthews in that room? And why did he share a bottle of wine with his killer?

It wasn't as if Matthews had amounted to much, apart from the fact that he was the son-in-law of a notorious gangster, the father of the man's grandchildren.

Yet the one thing Hamish McIntyre, feared in London for his violence, rated above anything else, was his family, especially Samantha, his daughter. However, he had never cared for Marcus, her husband.

And then Marcus disappeared, only for his body to be found six years later by a couple of young boys who decide that exploring an abandoned house is preferable to school.

Grave Passion – A DCI Cook Thriller – Book 12

Two young lovers out for a night of romance. A shortcut through the cemetery. They witnessed a murder, but there was no struggle, only a knife through the heart.

It has all the hallmarks of an assassination, but who is the woman? And why was she beside a grave at night? Did she know the person who killed her?

Soon after, other deaths, seemingly unconnected, but tied to the family of one of the young lovers.

It's a case for Detective Chief Inspector Cook and his team, and they're baffled on this one.

The Slaying of Joe Foster – A DCI Cook Thriller – Book 13

No one challenged Joe Foster in life, not if they valued theirs. And then, the gangster is slain and his criminal empire up for grabs.

A power vacuum; the Foster family is fighting for control, the other gangs in the area aiming to poach the trade in illegal drugs, to carve up the empire that the father had created.

It has all the makings of a war on the streets, something nobody wants, not even the other gangs.

Terry Foster, the eldest son of Joe, the man who should take control, doesn't have his father's temperament or wisdom. His solution is slash and burn, and it's not going to work. People are going to get hurt, and some of them will die.

The Hero's Fall – A DCI Cook Thriller – Book 14

Angus Simmons had it made. A successful television program, a beautiful girlfriend, admired by many for his mountaineering exploits.

And then he fell while climbing a skyscraper in London. Initially, it was thought he had lost his grip, but that wasn't the man: a meticulous planner, his risks measured, and it wasn't a difficult climb, not for him.

It was only afterwards on examination that they found the mark of a bullet on his body. It then became a murder, and that was when Detective Chief Inspector Isaac Cook and his Homicide team at Challis Street Police Station became interested.

The Vicar's Confession – A DCI Cook Thriller – Book 15

The Reverend Charles Hepworth, good Samaritan, a friend of the downtrodden, almost a saint to those who know him, up until the day he walks into the police station, straight up to Detective

Chief Inspector Isaac Cook's desk in Homicide. 'I killed the man,' he says as he places a blood-soaked knife on the desk.

The dead man, Andreas Maybury, was not a man to mourn, but why would a self-professed pacifist commit such a heinous crime. The reasons aren't clear, and then Hepworth's killed in a prison cell, and everyone's ducking for cover.

Guilty Until Proven Innocent – A DCI Cook Thriller – Book 16

Gary Harders' conviction two years previously should have been the end of the investigation. A clear-cut case of murder, and he had confessed to the crime and accepted his sentence without complaint. But now, the man's conviction was about to be overthrown, but why? And why is Harders not saying that his confession was police coercion? His prints are on the murder weapon, but Forensics has found another set.

Not only is there proof of either the Forensics department's error, incompetency or conspiracy, but Commissioner Alwyn Davies is getting tough on crime, draconian tough.

Detective Chief Inspector Isaac Cook and Chief Superintendent Richard Goddard are under pressure to take sides, aware that a positive return ensures promotion, but at the cost of their respective souls.

Davies has powerful backers, persons willing to make a deal with the devil. To allow violent putdown of those who disrupt the streets and removal of those who cause unsolicited and anti-social crime.

The plan has merits, a return to the safe society of decades past, but where will it stop. Who will say it's time to ease off, and then, what's the Russian mafia got to do with it? Too much from what DCI Cook can see, but he's powerless.

Murder Without Reason – A DCI Cook Thriller – Book 17

DCI Cook faces his greatest challenge. The Islamic State is waging war in England, and they are winning.

Not only does Isaac Cook have to contend with finding the perpetrators, but he is also being forced to commit actions contrary to his mandate as a police officer.

And then there is Anne Argento, the prime minister's deputy. The prime minister has shown himself to be a pacifist and is not up to the task. She needs to take his job if the country is to fight back against the Islamists.

Vane and Martin have provided the solution. Will DCI Cook and Anne Argento be willing to follow it through? Are they able to act for the good of England, knowing that a criminal and murderous action is about to take place? Do they have an option?

Sergeant Natalie Campbell Thriller Series

Dark Streets – Book 1

A homeless man, Old Joe's death was not unexpected. Not until it was found to be murder.

This was Darlinghurst Road, Kings Cross, once a hub of inequity, of strip joints and gentleman's clubs, of licensed premises and restaurants. But now, the area is changing, going upmarket, another enclave for those that can afford it, not a place for the homeless, nor is it a place of murder, but then there is another murder in Point Piper, upmarket and exclusive; a woman, her throat cut.

Detective Gary Haddock's a seasoned hand in Homicide, but he's baffled by the murders that continue. Statistically, Sydney's Eastern Suburbs doesn't have murder, but after four, are they serial or random, and if they are serial, why?

Sergeant Natalie Campbell from Kings Cross Police Station is wet behind the ears when she pairs with Haddock but soon learns she is more astute than he is, although she's a risk taker. He has to protect her, but she will take the investigations forward.

Steve Case Thriller Series

The Haberman Virus – Book 1

A remote and isolated village in the Hindu Kush Mountain range in North Eastern Afghanistan is wiped out by a virus unlike any seen before.

A mysterious visitor clad in a spacesuit checks his handiwork, a female American doctor succumbs to the disease, and the woman sent to trap the person responsible falls in love with him – the man who would cause the deaths of millions.

Hostage of Islam – Book 2

Three are to die at the Mission in Nigeria: the pastor and his wife in a blazing chapel; another gunned down while trying to defend them from the Islamist fighters.

Kate McDonald, an American, grieving over her boyfriend's death and Helen Campbell, whose life had been troubled by drugs and prostitution, are taken by the attackers.

Kate is sold to a slave trader who intends to sell her virginity to an Arab Prince. Helen, to ensure their survival, gives herself to the murderer of her friends.

Prelude to War – Book 3

Russia and America face each other across the northern border of Afghanistan. World War 3 is about to break out and no one is backing off.

And all because a team of academics in New York postulated how to extract the vast untapped mineral wealth of Afghanistan.

Steve Case is in the middle of it, and his position is looking very precarious. Will the Taliban find him before the Americans get him out? Or is he doomed, as is the rest of the world?

Standalone Novels

Malika's Revenge

Malika, a drug-addicted prostitute, waits in a smugglers' village for the next Afghan tribesman or Tajik gangster to pay her price, a few scraps of heroin.

Yusup Baroyev, a drug lord, enjoys a lifestyle many would envy. An Afghan warlord sees the resurgence of the Taliban. A Russian white-collar criminal portrays himself as a good and honest citizen in Moscow.

All of them are linked to an audacious plan to increase the quantity of heroin shipped out of Afghanistan and into Russia and ultimately the West.

Some will succeed, some will die, some will be rescued from their plight and others will rue the day they became involved.

Verrall's Nightmare

Historians may reflect on what happened, psychoanalysts may debate endlessly, and although scientists would attempt to explain, none would conclusively get the measure of all that had occurred.

Others, less knowledgeable, aficionados of social media, would say that Benedict Verrall was mad, or else the events in a small hamlet in the south of England never occurred and that it was a government conspiracy. That Samuel Whittingham was a figment of Verrall's imagination and the storms and their devastation, unprecedented in their scope and deaths, were freaks of nature, not of evil.

The truth, however, was more obscure, and that Verrall was neither mad nor was he malicious. Although he was responsible for instigating what was to happen, that hadn't been his intention.

He did not believe in the paranormal or the metaphysical, but then, he had not considered the brain tumour pressing down on his brain.

Or was it Verrall's madness, either the dream or the nightmare? That will be for the reader to decide.

ABOUT THE AUTHOR

Phillip Strang was born in the late forties, the post-war baby boom in England; his childhood years, a comfortable middle-class upbringing in a small town, a two hours' drive to the west of London.

His childhood and the formative years were a time of innocence. Relatively few rules, and as a teenager, complete mobility due to a bicycle – a three-speed Raleigh – and a more trusting community. It was the days before mobile phones, the internet, terrorism and wanton violence. An avid reader of Science Fiction in his teenage years: Isaac Asimov, and Frank Herbert, the masters of the genre. Still an avid reader, the author now mainly reads thrillers.

In his early twenties, the author, with a degree in electronics engineering and an unabated wanderlust to see the world left England's cold and damp climes for Sydney, Australia – the first semi-circulation of the globe, complete. Now, forty years later, he still resides in Australia, although many intervening years spent in a myriad of countries, some calm and safe – others, no more than war zones.